COIN HEIST

Visit us on the web at
www.adaptivestudios.com

Library of Congress Cataloging-in-Publication Data
Ludwig, Elisa.
Coin Heist / by Elisa Ludwig.

ISBN 978-0-996-06660-0 (hardcover)
ISBN 978-1-632-95016-1 (ebook)
1. Juvenile Fiction. 2. Juvenile Fiction - Law & Crime. 3. Fiction - Coming of Age. 4. Juvenile Fiction - Social Issues - Friendship. 5. Juvenile Fiction - Action Adventure - General.

Typography by Torborg Davern

ELISA LUDWIG

COIN HEIST

ADAPTIVE BOOKS

An Imprint of Adaptive Studios
Culver City, CA
www.adaptivestudios.com

 @coin_heist

 www.facebook.com/coinheist

ONE

ALICE

ART CLASS WAS PRETTY MUCH MY DOWNFALL. SO FAR I was barely hanging on to a C minus, which meant I really had to focus on what Mr. Rankin was saying as he rocked in his Campers and pointed at the digital projection of falling coins lighting up the wall of the Philadelphia Mint lobby. Something about art and language? Culture and power? Art being currency? Currency being power?

"The Design of Everything" had a reputation as one of the better electives for juniors at Haverford Friends. With his hipster cardigans and blondish goatee scruff, Rankin looked like he lived and breathed art, and his lectures proved it. He was a great teacher. And I was an otherwise excellent student. But here we were, on a field trip on a snowy February day, and try as I might, I couldn't tune in. It was all so . . . abstract. So fuzzy. Give me a bunch of numbers any day.

Also distracting was the fact that Jason Hodges was standing uncomfortably close to me, the navy blue of his parka lodged in my peripheral vision.

"Consider yourselves lucky—not many people get this opportunity," Rankin was saying as a Mint employee appeared to his left, a guy with a thick flap of black hair and a too-tight pinstripe shirt. "Ah, here he is now. My man."

"Sorry I'm late, Tom," he said, clapping him on the shoulder. Then, to us, "I'm Brad Garcia, your guide for today."

"No problem," Rankin said. "We're ready when you are."

The guest pass had gotten us through the security lines (longer than an airport but minus the pat-downs), where we'd signed in and were scanned for suspiciousness, and now Garcia, who said he was the operations manager, was giving us a spiel about the house rules, turning off our phones, not taking photos, and using our inside voices. This place, a hulking mass of concrete taking up a city block, was clearly no joke.

I felt Jason shift impatiently beside me. His dad was the headmaster of HF, and I'd known Jason since eighth grade. Well, "know" is a relative term. We all knew each other at HF—there were only a hundred or so kids in the junior class, and most of us had been going to school together since kindergarten. It's not like he ever talked to me, though.

It was only just recently that I'd noticed him toting his guitar around between classes and goofing around in the dining hall with his bandmates. He'd suddenly become sort of *hot*: shaggy brown hair, soulful hazel eyes, a lanky frame with just enough muscle.

The mere thought was embarrassing, though. Me? Alice Drake? Crushing on Jason? No. At a place like HF, you stuck to your own territory. And Jason Hodges was from another continent.

You could use the set theory in mathematics to explain most social realities: if O (Jason) was a member of A (his subset, a.k.a. Zack Pickering and his band friends), which was in turn a member of B (the HF junior class), he was technically included in B as a subset member. On the other hand, I wasn't part of A or even B because I wasn't a set and I had no members—though I *could be* a member of a set, if people, like, acknowledged me. (If you want to get technical, that made me a *null set*. Which wasn't even plain old nothing. It was *immeasurable* nothing.)

"Here at the Mint, we have our own special police to guard our facility, and we move our goods in armored trucks," Garcia said. "You'll recognize our force by their badges with the eagle perched on top."

"Do they pack heat?" Jason asked.

"Yes, they're armed," Garcia replied politely. "They're real police, just like you see on the streets of Philadelphia."

Jason raised his hand, but not before blurting out his next question. "Can we see their weapons?"

"Well—"

Rankin broke in. "I don't think that's going to happen,

Hodges. You're lucky Mr. Garcia has been kind enough to agree to take us on a behind-the-scenes tour," Rankin said. "Let's not make him regret that, okay? You were saying, Brad?"

"Real lucky," Jason whispered in my ear as Garcia moved on. "That's his cousin, you know."

I fumbled for a remotely intelligent response.

"Rankin's cousin?" I asked. *Fail.*

"Yeah. That's why we're here. My dad said—"

"Hodges," Rankin cut in. "You with us?"

Jason mumbled some apology, and I made a mental note to ignore his presence. Rankin was notoriously tough, and talking to Jason wasn't going to help my cause.

"Okay then. FYI, there are others who might actually like to see the Mint."

"Oh yeah. Right," Jason said. Another tour had come in behind us, and the rest of the group had scooched to the side. Jason moved, but in an exaggeratedly slow way, hound-dogging his head, which had everyone laughing.

Everyone, that is, except Rankin, who shook his head and closed his eyes, like he was trying to teleport himself to another location. "Herding cats," he muttered.

Also not laughing was Dakota Cunningham, who, in set theory terms, was a member of the powerset, and as such was part of everything HF. She was pretty much a living year-book: president of, like, twelve clubs, in many of my honors classes, invited to every prep-school kegger in the five-county area, and, most nauseatingly of all, very pretty in a blonde,

Swiss, muesli-eating sort of way.

"Well," Garcia continued. "Here at the Philadelphia Mint, we print a million new coins every half-hour—that's sixteen million during our operational day."

Garcia led us past the Mint's bald eagle mascot and over to some displays of money from colonial times. "Before 1792, people used a variety of foreign and colonial currency to purchase goods. Then Congress passed the Coinage Act, enacting a single currency and creating the Philadelphia Mint. Today, the Philadelphia Mint and the Denver Mint are responsible for all of the coins circulating in the United States. You'll know the coins that come from our facility because they have a P on them. We also design limited-edition, medals, bullion, and commemorative coins."

We slipped into a theater area where three screens told us the history of the place. In the dark, I snuck another look at Jason.

I knew I wasn't the only one who found him attractive. He'd actually gone out with Dakota in middle school and plenty of others since then, including Ella Shonfield and Chloe Benezet.

I did enjoy watching all this stuff from a distance, the getting-togethers and breaking-aparts, the crushes and heartbreaks—almost like I was a scientist observing rats in a maze. At least I didn't have to be caught up in the maze myself. The truth, embarrassing to admit, was that I was as much of a romantic as anyone else. *Your time just hasn't come yet*, my mom always said. I was getting a little tired of waiting.

But unless something seismic happened at HF, I might have to wait a while longer. Or become someone entirely different than me.

Garcia lined us up at a special door marked EMPLOYEES ONLY and rubbed his hands in anticipation. "Now we'll proceed to the design studio. You guys are getting to see a part of the Mint up close that hardly anybody gets to see. Right this way, if you please."

"I don't please," Benny Yizar muttered, his hands shoved deep into the pocket of his hoodie, shoulders slumped. I caught his eye. He simply stared back, dark eyes glinting.

Benny was new to school this year on a football scholarship. You weren't supposed to know who had funding, but you always did. Benny kept to himself mostly, even after he helped bring our usually pathetic team to the IntraFriends league championship last fall. Not that it was saying much. All the Philly prep schools had sucky teams, and lacrosse had always been considered the sport of choice.

Maybe Benny had figured that out, because he usually looked like he would rather be anywhere else but here. The only time I saw him genuinely psyched was when he was driving around in his souped-up muscle car.

"I have a question," Dakota announced loudly. "Who decides which president gets to be on the quarter?"

Garcia smiled broadly, revealing pink gums. "I'm glad you asked that. Elected officials, artists, and occasionally members of the public submit ideas for new coin designs." He waved his arms to show us the people at work at computer stations all around us. "We hire our own sculptors and engravers to model new designs."

Rankin hit the wall like he was giving it a high-five. "There you go! Just what I was saying. You don't think art is relevant in today's world? Think about this: You can make a very nice living as a mint sculptor."

Dakota side-twisted her long, naturally golden hair and everyone watched, transfixed, as she asked about how people got picked to be put on stamps. Garcia, of course, did not know the answer. Why? Because, newsflash, the Mint did not produce stamps. Dakota and me were both good students, but she had to really work for it.

We stopped in front of an empty station. "While in the past, coins were modeled with clay, we currently rely on 3-D modeling software, the same kind that Hollywood uses for movies such as *Frozen*," Garcia said.

I felt my phone buzz in the front pocket of my jeans. Probably Greg, wondering when we would meet for Math Team.

Garcia invited us to huddle closer to the computer, so we could see the software he was describing. I was stuck at the back so I had to stretch up on my tiptoes. Being five feet (on a good day) was no picnic, and I had been mistaken for a lower-school boy on more than one occasion in the quad. Draw your own conclusions about my chest size.

With a few clicks Garcia logged into the application. On the screen, a 3-D coin design flipped and spun, as though someone was about to make a bet. And then he was in. I wondered how much of this info was stored on the server—it seemed insecure for such a serious operation. Just out of curiosity, I picked up my phone and looked at the network settings.

"I don't believe it," I murmured, shocked by what I was seeing. A hacker's field day.

"What?" Jason asked. I startled a bit—I hadn't realized I was speaking out loud. He was so close, I could actually smell him—a little hint of pot smoke mixed with laundry detergent.

"The network," I whispered, because Garcia was still talking. "I mean, really, guys? That's the best you can do?" It was WEP-encrypted, which was a joke. It was basically the same thing as a home wi-fi network. I would have expected way more from any federal building, let alone the one in charge of most of our nation's currency.

"What about it?"

"It's just old-school, *super* crackable. If someone wanted to break in and start counterfeiting coins, it wouldn't be hard." The whole process unfurled in my mind. It was like when I was on the Math Team, sitting in front of my computer—I could always see six steps ahead to how everything would eventually play out.

He angled his head in disbelief. "Really."

"Really," I insisted, maybe overstating the case a teensy bit. "A breeze."

My cheeks were hot. Ridiculous, I told myself. It wasn't even like he had a great personality. This was strictly hormonal.

Garcia showed us how the computers calculated tool paths to manufacture the design precisely. "We now have the precision of a laser. Specially designed cutters reproduce every detail of the image, and the final product needs very little hand-cleaning."

He led us into the die shop, where the tools that make the coins were created and maintained. A wall of windows close to the ceiling allowed the official tour groups above us to look down at the action. I saw some young kids, maybe third-graders, jockeying for the best view. Jason was waving to them and pretending to crank a gigantic metal press. I had to laugh. He was like a mime on steroids.

"We start with a steel blank on which the design is imprinted as the master hub. The hub creates the die. The die blanks are put through the assembly line to create a stamp. And then robot arms give them a polish."

"I heard about those online—they're big in Japan," Jason said.

More laughs all around us. "Dude," Dylan Sanders said, giving him a high five.

Dylan Sanders, lax goalie, was the son of a state senator and current man-piece of Dakota. He spoke strictly in monosyllabic words. *Dude.*

"What about mistakes?" Dakota asked, rolling her eyes at the two snickering guys. "Are there ever coins with mistakes?"

"Yes, occasionally we find errors in the design. The digital model might be missing lettering or design elements." Garcia said, running a hand along the back of his neck in a way that made me think it was a sore subject. "We try to catch them early. A machine called a waffle will scrap the coins before they go into circulation, and then we recycle the metal. But on rare occasions, an error coin does slip through the cracks, and it can be very lucrative for coin collectors, some selling for millions of dollars. Bad news for us, though."

The plant floor was divided into two sections—one for coins and a smaller area for the special medals and commemoratives. Garcia stopped us at the coin area, where we saw the waffle in action, high-pressure rollers pressing together to reduce coins into a mutilated, distorted mess. Any remainders were tossed into a scrap heap on the floor below.

"I wonder why no one's tried it," Jason said loudly, so I could hear him over the deafening sound. He'd been standing next to me, by my count, for at least twenty-five minutes. Only on a field trip would this even be possible. "Hacking in, I mean."

"Who knows?" I yelled back. I wasn't a big-time hacker, but I knew enough to get information when I needed it. "But it's not just getting into the system. You'd have to come back for the goods. That would be the hard part."

As we crossed to a quieter area of the floor, I heard the rumbling buzz of another phone in another pocket. Then, closer by, someone else's Droid sounded, a tone like a whirring spaceship. A third phone rang out with a few bars of a Rihanna song. Strange.

A thought distantly registered: *It's Friday. Everyone must be making plans.* My plan was already made. The usual: after

Math Team practice, we usually played D&D.

"I thought we asked you not to leave your phones on," Rankin interjected. "Come on, people. How hard is it to part with your precious devices for an hour or two?"

Garcia was unfazed as he continued with the tour. We were strictly Rankin's problem, even if we broke the rules at the Mint. "Later, the coins are drawn here through the washing machine, which removes any tarnish or contamination, and then the upsetting mill, which raises their edges."

What was upsetting was the fact that my phone was buzzing in my pocket again.

Can you wait a minute, Greg? Ravenloft is a pocket dimension. It's not going anywhere.

Cupping the phone closely, lest Jason bear witness to my lameness, I saw that it was in fact a text from Greg, but it wasn't what I was expecting.

Did you hear? About Hodges?

Huh? I guess I had Jason on the brain, because at first that's who I thought he meant. Then I heard Dakota's husky gasp. "No way," she said. "Not Mr. Hodges."

"What?" Dylan asked.

Dakota held up her phone. "Cops came in today and took Mr. Hodges away in handcuffs!" Her voice held a hint of delight at the edges, the news entirely too juicy for her to suppress it. Then, realizing that Jason was among our group, her face fell back into its usual nice-girl mask and she gave him a sympathetic, closed-lip smile.

"What?" Jason said, butting his face over Dakota's arm. "Let me see that. Who said?"

"Junibel Simmons just texted me," Dakota said. "They let school out early. She said it's utter chaos."

Jason's dad, led away in handcuffs? Mr. Hodges was as uptight as they came, the kind of guy whose bowtie held up his pants.

What the what?

Jason was still looking at Dakota's phone, his face slack. It was the first time I'd ever seen him without a joke or a goofy expression. Whatever had happened was a surprise to him too.

It kind of reminded me of the day I'd caught that email from Sheryl on my dad's computer. It blew me away. I mean, my dad and I had our problems, but he discovered cancer treatments for a living. He and my mom had been together forever. The information just wouldn't register.

So I could imagine what Jason must have been feeling. More than anything, I wanted to reach out and give him a hug. But he would've thought I was a weirdo. He probably already did think I was a weirdo.

There was no time for hugging or anything else though, because Rankin was trying to regroup us. "People. I need you to focus." He clapped. "Hello? We still have more stuff to see."

"Did you know about this, Mr. Rankin?" Dakota asked.

"No," he said, his eyebrows knitting together. "But let's not allow locker room conjecture to ruin our visit . . ."

"Junibel is a very reliable source," Dakota insisted. "It's not just rumors."

"Fine, Dakota, but Mr. Garcia here has other things he needs to tell us."

Not like it mattered, though. Our "exclusive" tour was nowhere near as interesting as the scandalous gossip hovering around us. Nobody was going to pay attention for the rest of the trip. Design might have been a lot of things, but it couldn't compete with real life.

Figures. The first time a guy I find cute actually talks to me is the day his dad gets arrested. Maybe I'd even jinxed him. Maybe some people, like art, were better appreciated at a distance.

TWO

JASON

AS I CROSSED OVER THE ICY PATH FROM OUR BACKYARD to the official school campus on Monday morning, I felt it—all the eyes on me. Like I was walking into some sort of surprise party. A surprise party of doom.

Everyone had already heard the story, and school hadn't even started yet.

If you want to get your secret shared with a thousand people in five minutes, tell a Friendian. The kid will tell their mom, who will tell all the people at her golf club, and then it will trickle down through the parents' association, the alumni network, the board, and finally back down to the rest of the kids. And don't even mention the staff. The janitors and cafeteria workers know *everything* about *everything*.

So yeah. Grab a megaphone. Text everyone you know. My dad was arrested. For embezzling the school's endowment.

It was so weird. My dad? The guy who did warrior poses before he took his blood pressure meds with grapefruit juice every morning? The guy who'd instituted a stricter dress code (no cleavage, despite my complaints) and tougher rules about parking on HF's campus? The guy who, my whole life, had told me that anything could be achieved with discipline?

I still couldn't really wrap my brain around it, other than the fact that he'd been in jail all weekend, and my mom had spent most of that time in her bedroom. There is seriously nothing worse than hearing your mom cry.

I just felt . . . shocked. Sure, I'd seen my dad at the computer, moping around and whatnot when some stock went down. But I always thought he was day-trading with our family's money.

I thought he had it under control.

"I told him it was glorified gambling," my mom said on Friday night after it all went down, as we sat staring at his empty kitchen chair. "I told him we had your college to pay for. I had no idea it had gone this far, that the debts were so big."

Now she was stuck on two-hour phone calls with his lawyer, trying to figure out how we'd post the $1 million bail. Think that sounds like a lot? My dad pissed away $50 mil, apparently. Of the school's money.

Looking back, maybe I should have questioned it when he bought me stuff like a bike, a brand-new Jetta, and a sick amp for my guitar, with me barely asking. I guess I was so excited, I just didn't think twice. We'd never had a lot of money before. I thought headmaster was just a cushy job.

Which was the only good thing about it, really. I mean, I realized early on that I could never live up to Jim Hodges' insane expectations. So I became the anti-Jim: class skipper, homework ignorer, and assembly sleeper, not to mention dress code violator (jeans were only comfortable with holes!). It was easier to not do anything than to constantly field his critiques of what I could be doing *better*.

He thought it was my own little phase I'd grow out of, that it had nothing to do with him, of course. The morning he was caught, he'd said, "You're in your own world, Jason. But some day you're going to have to grow up and join the rest of us. And maybe then you'll stop embarrassing me."

Who knows? Maybe the great Jim Hodges had seen the end coming. Because right now it seemed like my own world was officially done with. This was purgatory. Hell was next.

They were *staring*.

Everyone knew. I caught sight of Chloe Benezet whispering to Dylan Sanders. Chloe used to be cool, shaving the side of her head and writing poetry, but since we broke up, she'd become just another preppy in riding boots. Dylan laughed at whatever she was saying. They looked like a couple of hyenas circling a carcass.

More stares from the rest of them, hanging out by their lockers. People who would call out my name and fist bump me just last week were now keeping a creepy distance, like I was diseased.

I knew if I could be funny, then no one would feel sorry for me.

"I guess you guys found me out!" I called out. "Yes, I got a nose job. Now can I have some privacy, please?"

That did it. Only a few people laughed, but at least most of them stopped staring. I sauntered down the hall as if it were all a big hilarious joke.

Mondays generally sucked, but this one went down in the books. It was almost like being the new kid all over again. Those days in middle school. Torture.

Jessica Katz snorted when I passed her desk in Algebra. In French, I could swear Monsieur Rydel was extra evil, curling his tongue over the "*s'il vous plaît*" when he asked me to read out loud from *The Count of Monte Cristo*. Even Dianne the lunch lady gave me a pitying grin when she plopped a carton of fries on my tray. "Rough times, huh, Jason?"

"Very rough," I said. She'd always been nice to me, even when I was the new kid. She used to save me the end slices of the Sicilian pizza, because she knew I liked the pieces with the crust. And then it occurred to me that what my dad did could affect her, too. If the school was in trouble, she could get . . . I didn't even want to think about it.

"I hope everything is okay." *With you*, I meant.

"It'll be fine," she said, scraping the tray for strays. "HF isn't going anywhere."

I took my tray and sat down at my usual table at the back of the dining hall, next to the guys in my band. Zack was there, chowing down on some unidentifiable foil-wrapped object he'd smuggled in from home. He raised it in greeting.

Zack was basically the reason I'd survived middle school or HF at all—we'd met at an afterschool music program, and we'd started what later became our band Mixed Metaphors, with him as the lead singer and me writing most of the songs and playing guitar.

Zack called teachers by their first names, and they never bothered to call on him in class. He had a hot new girlfriend every semester, and he barely had to talk to them. His older brother got us into parties at UPenn, and even the dudes in his brother's fraternity didn't mind having him around. I had to give him props—he was untouchable. And I was too, just by virtue of sitting with him at lunch.

"What's up, sucker?" I said.

"Not much," he replied. "Hey, listen, as your friend, I should warn you that The People are talking."

"Who's talking?" Then I thought better of it. "No, forget it. I don't want to know."

I was pretty sure The People involved at least one of my exes, and including Chloe, there were enough of them to start an official Anti-Jason squad. Hey, it wasn't my fault that girls always seemed to get mad at me.

The contents of Zack's sandwich lodged in his cheeks. "It's bad, dude. I heard that some kids think you were in on it."

WTF? "So I'm an accomplice now?" I laughed, probably too

loudly, over the lump in my throat. "I guess I broke into every-one's lockers too, then hacked into their library accounts."

He gulped his Gatorade, his dark hair hanging over the bot-tle. "I'm being serious, man."

"I know, I know. But you told them it wasn't true, right? I mean, he's innocent."

"Of course, bro. I tried. But I'm only one man. I can't slow the tide of misinformation. It flows where it will."

"Like shit?" I asked. I looked up and saw a few cute fresh-man girls staring at me, and not in a good way. Why was *I* on trial now? This was crazy.

"*Exactement.*" He was back to his lunch tube. "You know how it is. These people love drama. Don't sweat it."

Right. Easy for him to say. I got up to leave, wrapping up my uneaten food. I couldn't keep the smile going, and I defi-nitely didn't want to break down in front of Zack, who had a black belt in apathy.

"Where are you going? I thought we were going to discuss band business. You're cool, right?"

"Yeah, yeah. I forgot my phone. Tell the other guys I'll see them at practice." I needed to get out of the fish bowl. I needed to be alone.

In Rankin's art class I could almost pretend things were nor-mal. It was the last period of the day, and in art, at least, I didn't have to answer questions. I didn't have to speak at all. Which was good, because my brain was spiraling into a blur of dark thoughts, like that night Zack and I got some bad pot from his brother, and I ended up lying on the floor of his room, my heart racing, thinking I was going to die. None of which I'd mentioned to Zack as he went on about how it was totally kind bud and how he felt like butter melting over a plate of pancakes.

Rankin went around the room asking everyone what we were going to do for our Mint follow-up projects, due the following week. We were supposed to come up with a proposal for a piece for the Mint that would demonstrate "design at work" or some BS like that. I'd been too busy trying to calm my mom down and figure out if I had any savings from my summer jobs that we could cash out.

I stared out the window at the arts quad. In the center was the sculpture my dad had commissioned from Simon Lamberton, the guy who pioneered land art in the 1960s. It was supposed to look like flowing water, "the fountain of knowledge," but right now it was just a gigantic hunk of metal. Lamberton's assistants were constructing it right here, forging iron in our workshop in the arts center. My dad thought it would be a "wonderful learning opportunity" to install it where we could watch the progress, and some of the arts classes were even invited to help Lamberton's assistants. (The great artist himself had never been on campus, to my knowledge. They were communicating with him via Skype.) He wanted me to help out too. "Come on, Jase," he'd said to me. "This doesn't happen every day. Take advantage. Use your talents." What did he think, that I could be Picasso or some shit? Didn't he realize that almost *everyone* got a C in Rankin's class? Rankin was a hardass. My supposed art skills definitely wouldn't help me here.

For the moment, though, no one was working on the sculpture. Since the ground froze over in December, it had been closed up with a padlocked chain-link fence.

I thought the statue was kind of cool, but it was controversial. Some of the parents were pissed that my dad was replacing the flagpole that had been there for the entire 150-year history of the school. My dad said it was a symbol of HF moving into modern times, part of the bigger capital plan for campus expansion, when the school was going to build five new facilities and branch out over another ten acres. This was just the beginning. In the meantime, original art would give us an edge, he said. How many schools could boast a museum-quality sculpture on their grounds? Of course, now I had to wonder where the money for that thing had come from, and I probably wasn't the only one.

How many schools could boast a thief in the headmaster's office?

Suddenly, Rankin was standing in front of me, his blond beard level with the top of my head. "Hodges? You with me?"

So much for not having to speak. I was not with him. I had nothing.

"Your idea? Yes no maybe?"

I shrugged and gave him the smile I usually gave teacher's when I knew I was about to blow smoke up their ass. "Still thinking, sir. The wheels are turning and whatnot."

"You only have two weeks to complete the project from start to finish, so I suggest you come up with something quickly." He tapped my desk with two fingers, a warning signal. "Don't blow it off, Hodges. You're better than that."

Was I, though? Of all the teachers in school, Rankin was the only one who pushed me. But I kind of liked Rankin, even if he clearly hated me. Yeah, psychoanalyze that.

Thankfully, we were on to the brainstorming part of class—free time. Drawing always helped calm my brain. It was something I was good at without having to try. And at least it would look like I was working.

I walked over to the paper drawer, where Dakota Cunningham was already standing with one of her clones, Junibel Simmons. The real Dakota was bad enough, but here was a weak imitation—skinnier, shorter, with frizzy hair and a nervous twitching mouth. Junibel just had that aura of desperation about her.

"'Scuse me," I said, trying to push past them.

"Jason! Do you seriously not have a follow-up idea?" Dakota asked me, pretending to be all concerned. She'd been my middle-school girlfriend, but it wasn't like we were still friends or anything. It didn't matter. Everyone's business was Dakota's business. She turned everything into her own personal task force.

I shrugged.

"He'll give you an incomplete. Why don't you just sculpt

something, one of the famous medals? I can give you one of my ideas."

"I've got it covered."

I'd done very well up until now never doing my homework. Why should I change a winning formula? My dad's voice came into my head: *Because you can do better.* Then my voice back to him: *Oh yeah? Like embezzlement?*

"You could at least make an effort for once," she said. "I mean seriously."

Had my dad put her up to this? "This isn't a group project," I said. Back when we were 'going out' in sixth grade, we'd spent two weekends working on a papier-mâché manatee, but I'd bailed the day before it was due, because my friends were going to a rock-climbing gym. Our manatee ended up being flipperless, basically just a gray blob. By lunchtime, Dakota had publicly dumped me in the hallway, saying that she'd only liked me because I was new and now she realized I was a loser. Only she could get away with dumping someone for as nerdy a reason as a grade and still come away as the cool one.

"She's just trying to help, Jason," Junibel said.

"I don't need help," I finally snapped. Only after the words were out of my mouth did I realize that Dakota was, yet again, getting a rise out of me. All these years and she still made me feel like crap. I quickly smiled and tried to make a joke. "Unless you want to coordinate outfits. Then you can definitely help."

Dakota sighed. "Fine. Keep playing dumb. You can flake on

class, but you'd better not do this on prom night. We're counting on you, and you'd better play covers."

"Yeah," Junibel said. "You need to learn 'Don't Stop Believing' and 'Apache'."

Whatever. Mixed Metaphors would never play anything that involved a g-synth. We were strictly dance pop, inspired by '90s Manchester bands. Dakota knew that. In our brief relationship, I'd introduced her to all of my favorite bands, like the Stone Roses. And I think she actually got into my music, too, though these days she probably listened to whatever everyone else listened to.

Dakota walked away and so did her clone, and all there was left was the scent of their flowery perfumes hanging in the air. That and Alice Drake, standing where Dakota had been, shaking her beanie-covered head.

"Wow," Alice said with a smirk. "That's some help we can all do without."

She was nice enough, but I didn't want anyone pitying me, especially not a girl who wore a beanie over a bowl cut. What was she going to do, beat them up? Alice was pretty much the last person who could improve this situation.

"It's nothing," I said, repeating the mantra of the day. "It's cool."

She shrugged and grabbed some paper. At least she knew when to give up.

I was almost safely back to my seat, paper in hand, when I ran into the folded arms of Arno Shepherd, a smirk slashed across his scrawny face. "How does your dad like jail?"

"My dad's actually in Aspen," I said very slowly and loudly, aware that everyone was listening. "Skiing. The conditions are great right now." They all knew I was joking, but what was I supposed to say? I didn't want to have to make excuses for the guy, because the truth was that I couldn't. I had no goddamn idea why he'd done what he'd done.

The bell rang and I stepped out into the quad. The school day was over. I could finally walk home and lock myself in my room with my guitar. No one would bug me there. Not my dad, who was obviously in a jail cell. Not my mom, who would be on the phone for a zillion hours.

My feet crunched over the frozen grass. As I got closer to the sculpture, I heard a splat. And then another. I turned to see Dylan Sanders and Gus Flaherty pegging eggs at the hulking iron monster.

"Your dad's a thief," Dylan said. "Can we return this thing and get our parents' money back?"

All the feelings I'd been bottling up boiled over into rage. Burning, bubbling rage. Screw this kid with his sweater vest and his three-generation Haverford Friends family. He didn't know what the hell he was talking about. He and Dakota were perfect for each other. My fists balled up so tight, I felt blood swelling in my fingers. I imagined slamming Dylan against the fence so hard that the chain-link would brand his back.

But wait. I couldn't let them get under my skin. I had to let this roll off me. It wasn't really Dylan Sanders I was angry with.

Or Dakota, either. It wasn't their fault my life had been ruined. And if it had been up to me, I'd get rid of the sculpture, too.

So I shrugged. "Can I have one of those?"

He handed me an egg. It was cold in my hand, solid. I fired away and it exploded, leaving trails of gloppy goo on the $500,000 piece of crap that was my dad's crowning achievement. And for the first time all day, I actually felt better.

THREE

DAKOTA

YOU KNOW WHAT WAS THE SADDEST? THE MOMENT WHEN it became clear that the student government was a sham. I'd been brought up to think I could do anything, fix anything, but here was a problem that affected the whole student body, and we were powerless to fix it. I was beginning to wonder if I should throw in the gavel. Except our president Simone Gyo was already clutching it tight, banging it against the assembly lectern.

"Could everyone please settle down, please?" Simone waved her arms like a demented bird.

As vice president, I stood to her left and tried to look official. Even though Simone was a senior and I was a junior, and typically juniors never got picked for student council, we'd managed to convince the students of Haverford Friends that we were a worthy team during the fall election. We'd run a good campaign. A great campaign, really. We promised to get more funding for the coffee bar so they could upgrade to a real cappuccino machine, to extend the school gym hours, and to widen the dress code policy to include sleeveless shirts again, which wasn't going to be easy with hardnosed Hodges. The free iPhone covers my dad ordered didn't hurt, either. They were black with silver printing: GYO GIVES / CUNNINGHAM CARES.

I cared. I cared way too much, probably.

Which was why the fact that I was standing in front of the entire school at our weekly Tuesday morning assembly, about to drop a bomb that would ruin all of their lives, was extra painful. With Mr. Hodges out, the assistant headmaster Ms. Coyle had called Simone and me into her office that morning to tell us she had to slash the student budget for extra-curriculars.

"We simply don't have the resources," she said. "We'll leave the prom in place, of course, though you'll probably have to change the location. And the newspaper and yearbook will stay. Other than that, you'll need to tell the students to hold off. On pretty much everything."

We broke the news to our council members via text just minutes before the meeting was supposed to begin. There wasn't time for debate or anything else. The show had to go on.

Turns out, as much as Simone loved the power of the gavel, she was a complete mess when it came to doing anything trickier than scheduling a car wash. She'd broken down in tears just before we stepped on stage and begged me to speak at the assembly in her place. I thought, well, this is my duty—this is what a vice president does, fill in for the president in a crisis situation. Now was my chance to step up, to save the day, to at least try to make things better for all of us.

Now, looking at the crowd of students, I wished like anything I hadn't agreed to do Simone's dirty work. They looked so unsuspecting, sipping from their reusable water bottles and coffee cups. HF kids were nothing if not an enviro-friendly bunch. How would they react when I told them that plans for the green roof were being scrapped? It was a disaster.

I cleared my throat. Usually I rehearsed my speeches in the mirror, but of course there hadn't been time for that. Campaigns and promises and winning votes were one thing. This— this was something else.

Smile, I told myself. *Smile and maybe they won't realize how bad it is. You're Dakota Cunningham, and they think you have it all under control.*

"So. We have a bit of bad news. We're going to have to suspend some student activities, due to compromised funding." Here I turned to my printed list. "That includes the following: Aikido, Asian Students in America, Beatles Appreciation, Birding, Black Student Alliance, Bollywood Club, Chess, Chinese, Community Service, Creative Writing, Ethics, Film Views, Good Greens, Inkwell, Math Team, Mock Trial, Quaker Ambassadors, Queer Straight Alliance, Robotics, Spanish Language Immersion, Stock

Market Watchers, Young Democrats, and Young Republicans. Oh, and SCUBA."

Silence. I glanced at Simone, who seemed to be inching farther and farther away from the lectern.

And all I could do was keep smiling. A big, painful, recently-whitened smile.

At least, until the silence broke.

"Are you kidding me?" Darius Fitzsimmons, president of both the Queer Straight Alliance and the Young Republicans was on his feet. "They can't do this! We have our big demonstration project coming up!"

I didn't know which of his clubs he was referring to, or which project, but it didn't matter.

"You'll just have to hold off for now," I said, repeating Ms. Coyle's line.

That led to a room-wide eruption of blurted questions. Everyone wanted to know what was going to happen to *their* club or group. Our school was known for its extra-curriculars, that was a selling point, and it was something that kept us all engaged in HF life and primed for college. I loved HF. It was old and beautiful, and being here made me feel part of something bigger, a long tradition of students who went on to do great things. I loved it, and I couldn't believe this was happening.

"Are we still taking our class trip to Colonial Williamsburg?" Rav Patel wanted to know.

"No," I replied. "The trip is off."

"What about Diversity Fest?" asked Sienna Grimes, co-chair

of the Black Student Alliance. "We ordered all our t-shirts. We can't cancel it. Not if you guys still get to do your wonton thing." Here she pointed at Simone.

"The 'wonton thing' is called the Chinese Culinary Celebration," Simone explained from behind my shoulder, her voice timid. "And that's canceled, too."

"All events are going to be canceled, except for prom, *The Oracle*, and yearbook," I confirmed.

This affected me, too, I wanted to tell them. I was an editor of *The Inkwell*, the school literary journal; a founding member of the Spanish Language Immersion club; a co-chair of Film Views. I would have had a starring role in *Titanic*, too, if my parents had let me audition.

"They're not going to let us work in the soup kitchen anymore? What are we supposed to tell the people at St. Alban's Shelter?" Daphne Gibbons, a student council wannabe, cried out. 'Sorry, we can't afford your lunch anymore?' 'You have to starve?'

"This is outrageous!" someone yelled.

"Insane!" someone else said.

From then on, individual words got lost in the buzz of chatter. Simone tapped the gavel, trying to maintain order. All the individual faces turned into slashes of angry, bitter confusion. They were mad at me. *Me*, when none of this was my fault. I mean, believe me, if I could have done something, I would have.

"I'm sorry," I said. "I'm sorry."

Only then did I remember what my dad, David Cunningham of Cunningham, Schwartz, and Kieffer, always liked to say: "Never apologize, and never explain." Maybe it was good advice for a corporate lawyer, but it hardly came in handy when you were facing down a room of pissed-off overachievers. HF students loved their activities. Activities were good for transcripts, and transcripts were good for college acceptance, and none of us needed to be reminded that the whole point of going to a school like HF and having your parents shell out $45,000 a year was so you could get into a good college and have a good life. I mean, I'd never even wanted to be on the student council. It was my parents who said I should run, that it would help get me into Harvard, *their* Harvard. Never mind that only one person of each class at HF got into Harvard every year, and that brainiac Alice Drake was a total shoo-in.

Everyone thought I had it all together. If only they knew how much work it took to pull off this DAKOTA CUNNINGHAM sham. Every afternoon spent at school on some extracurricular, hours of late-night cramming, Saturdays with SAT tutors. But that wasn't enough—there were the free periods spent studying *Teen Vogue* and *Allure* to stay ahead of all the trends, morning jogs followed by 200 crunches, a ten-part skin and hair care regime, literally. I was naturally pretty, sure, but it took *work* to get to the next level. Lunchtime was devoted to normalness: sitting with my parent-approved boyfriend, gossiping with my parent-approved popular friends, and trying to shut off my constantly churning brain. No wonder I'd spent a good part of last summer in a fancy version of a nuthouse—my parents covered it up, of course, by telling everyone, including my boyfriend, that I was at a pre-college Japanese immersion program. Anything to keep up the illusion of my perfection.

If anyone ever found out, I'd be so dead. I might as well jump out of the HF belfry.

And now they were all looking at me like I was to blame for this crisis.

Too bad *Titanic* was canceled. It would've been an appropriate production for a school going bust.

"Sorry?" Sienna stood up and yelled. "You're *sorry*? This whole place is sorry!"

I wanted to run. I wanted to hide. I wanted to puke. God, if only I could escape into the bathroom right now.

But I couldn't. All I could do was look out at the sea of kids, feel their disappointment, and curse that stupid moron Mr. Hodges for screwing us all over. Because what he did? It was costing us *everything*.

I felt faint. *Get it together, Cunningham. They're watching you.*

I tried one of Dr. Pollard's Valium breaths. In for three, pause for one, out for six, pause for one. Ever since my stay at the Eastlake Center, I'd found myself using his technique for relaxation more and more.

Another smile. "We're going to try our best to work this out and get our funding restored. In the meantime, does anyone have any more questions?"

The bell rang.

Thank god. Before I could take any more comments or questions, the assembly was finally over. I exited the stage through the back, walking out toward the dressing room. No one would be in there now.

I wouldn't throw up, I decided. I would show some restraint. I could just do a few more breaths, gather my thoughts together. A few moments alone was all I needed to regain my composure.

Except Jason Hodges happened to be standing in my way. Typical. His whole shaggy, unkempt, too-cool-to-care thing was really getting old. Hadn't anyone told him that he needed to use a comb once in a while if he didn't want birds to start camping out on his head?

"What are you doing back here?" I asked coldly. What kind of person would just joke around like nothing had happened? If that were my dad, I'd be hiding in my bedroom with my Frette sheets pulled over my head, possibly lining up plastic surgery appointments so I could live in disguise the rest of my life.

"I needed a music stand for my band practice," he said, eyeing me up. "Or are you going to cancel that, too?"

His tone was teasing, but still. How dare he put this on me? I was annoyed at him from the other day in Design, when he'd blown me and Junibel off when we were only trying to help. Like his "cool" music taste made him better than us. "Ask your dad," I snapped. "He's the reason for all of this."

That did it. The clueless smile slipped away, and I felt a little bad for hurting his feelings.

That is, until he snapped right back. "Sucks about all your clubs. There go your college applications, huh? Now all those admissions people will think you're just mediocre like the rest of us."

He was insulting *me*? The slacker who'd used his dad's job as an excuse to do nothing but mess around all these years? The guy who'd taken class clown–dom to a new level? Well, now his dad was out, and he couldn't get away with being a clown anymore. Nobody had to kiss his ass, because he was just a regular student like the rest of us. No, he didn't deserve my sympathy.

"The sad thing is, you have no idea what it's like to work hard or participate in anything. You've never even joined a club."

"Well, seeing as how everything has been axed, it's a good thing, right?"

"Your dad basically ruined our school, Jason. Do you even care about that?"

"This isn't a council speech here, Cunningham, so you don't have to speak on behalf of the student body. He didn't 'ruin the school', okay? It was a misunderstanding." His voice sounded confident, but I could see that he didn't believe what he was saying. And was I imagining it, or was he the tiniest bit shaken up?

"So the police *misunderstood* when they found pages of evidence showing how he cooked the books?" This part I'd heard from my dad, who knew someone familiar with the case.

He said he would never represent Hodges, because what the police had was so damning that criminal charges were definitely going to be brought. The jury would see the paper trail, and there would be no way he'd get off. My dad said Hodges would probably serve time. Hard time.

"I don't know what they found. It was a mistake. Whatever."

"And he's still in Aspen, right?"

Now he was really flustered. "I don't have to explain anything to anyone." When I didn't respond, he added, "And even if I did, you'd never understand, because you've never made a mistake before, have you, Cunningham?"

I'd made plenty of mistakes. Who hadn't? Obviously, he thought I was some goody-goody priss. Well, this wasn't about me. If we were a community, like HF was supposed to be—I mean, that was our motto, wasn't it, *discamus ut serviamus*, 'We learn so that we might serve'—then we should all be working together to make things better.

Something else bothered me: the fact that Jason actually bought into DAKOTA CUNNINGHAM, just like everyone else. He of all people should know better—he should know that there was more to me, because he knew me way back when, before my life became all caps, when I was still allowed to be in school plays and do things just for fun, when I still had control over who I was or who I thought I'd be. I wasn't perfect. I was human just like he was. Well, it was one more reason that Jason Hodges deserved what was coming to him. He didn't just act like an idiot. He *was* an idiot.

"Say what you want, but what he did affects all of us." I sniffed. "It was selfish, and it was wrong."

"I get it, okay? Message received, loud and clear." Jason shouted, kicking the music stand so it fell down in a noisy clatter. "Do you think I'm enjoying any of this?"

Then he stalked down the hallway and left me in the quiet that I'd hoped for.

Had eternally chill Jason Hodges really just cracked, right in front of me?

My hands were shaking. There was no way I could get through this day now, not without a little relief.

Damn him.

I turned on my heel and headed for the dressing room to do what I had to do.

Jason Hodges was wrong. I was a walking mistake. I just hid it better than anyone else.

FOUR

BENNY

THE GLOWING NUMBERS ON MY PHONE STARED AT ME, all ugly-like. Twenty minutes until American History started, and I had to call my grandmom and move my car out of the senior parking lot. I'd been running behind this morning—lots of traffic on 76 headed out of the city—and it was the only spot I could find. But I'd learned the hard way that you got a "ticket" for taking one of the precious senior spaces. This school was too much. No way was I gonna let some security guy tow my Mustang. My Mustang was my one true love.

All the kids in the Upper School were squeezing through a tiny little door out of assembly. If I went that way, I'd be late for class. I couldn't afford to have any teachers giving me detentions. I was one of exactly six kids "of color"—we were all lumped together—at this place. I couldn't afford anything bad on my record. It had to be perfect if I was going to get into college.

I backed up, remembering there was another exit down by the front row of seats that led out to the Arts Center classrooms and the Drama Studio. That was the way to go if I wanted to get out quick.

Nobody noticed me as I wove back through the rows of seats. That pretty much summed up my life at Haverford Friends: nobody ever noticed me. Even on the football team, where I was the best wide receiver they'd probably ever have, the guys mostly grunted at me. They were clueless.

To be fair, they did invite me to their keggers once in a while. Well, really only once, but I couldn't go. They were always being held in some park where all the prep school kids got together, but it was an hour from my house. Not to mention my grandmom would go bananas if I was arrested for underage drinking or got a DUI. Maybe if I did stuff like that, I wouldn't be so invisible. Then again, I could be just as invisible at a party, a red Solo cup floating around.

The first kegger was in September, after we won our first game in, like, one trillion years, and I guess I blew my chance because no one had really asked me to anything since. No biggie. Not like I had anything in common with these rich dudes with their overpriced cars and blonde girlfriends and dads with pink pants. My car was a 1993 model someone had abandoned at my uncle's garage, where I worked nights and weekends. It took me awhile to get it back into order, but I'd tricked it out myself, slowly adding new parts whenever I could afford them. I always gave my grandparents most of my paycheck when I got it, so there usually wasn't much left for me. My uncle and my buddy, 'LT,' had helped me with the labor—lots of Sunday afternoons working on that thing. It was nothing like the Range Rovers or Beemers people drove to HF, but none of those kids had any idea how satisfying it was to mend a brake line, replace an oxygen sensor, or fix a Pitman arm.

As for my dad, he was back in the Dominican Republic. I hadn't seen him since I was four. We talked on the phone, but he wasn't coming back to the States any time soon—wasn't allowed to. And the only girlfriend I had was in my head: Jennifer Lawrence. My buddies at my uncle's garage made fun of me that I picked the *Hunger Games* chica over the bikini calendar girls that hung on the walls at the garage, but I didn't care. She was hot. If I ever got to meet her, it'd all be over. She'd forget all about those Hollywood dudes.

The Arts Center was quiet like a funeral. I'd never really hung out here much except for Design class. That was another crazy thing. Design class. Who needs a design class? I'd taken it 'cause my advisor said it was the way to go, since I wasn't into photography or video. The metalworking class I wanted to take (easy A for me for sure, and those kids got to help build a sculpture in the quad) was all filled up. Mr. Rankin was always trying to get us to think about stuff like the little heads on quarters. That dude was all right, but as far as I was concerned, coins were just money.

And money was what I needed to help my grandparents

out. They'd done so much for me already. They were the ones who found out I could get a football scholarship to Haverford Friends—that was after my boy Diego got arrested for boosting cars. They said I had to think of myself and my *opportunities.*

I didn't want to leave my boys in North Philly, but even I had to admit that I didn't have much of a future if I stayed at Thomas Janson High. The kids there carried guns, and we didn't even get books unless the teachers paid for them. The budget for Philly schools like Janson was getting cut every year, and every year they took something else away. There were no nurses, no gym class, no milk. At Haverford Friends I had a computer, a college counselor, crazy shit like philosophy classes, squash courts, and couscous for lunch. I mean, HF students actually got on vans to give out soup to guys that lived in my neighborhood. I was lucky to be here, I guess, but if anyone ever thought I'd get used to a place like this, they were crazy. I just had to survive it.

And I almost didn't. Just as I passed, the door to the dressing room opened, clocking me in the face.

"Oh. Sorry." I covered my forehead and nose where the wood made contact, and I could feel it getting red. Don't know why *I* apologized.

Maybe because it was Dakota Cunningham behind the door. Yeah, I knew her name. All the girls at HF looked alike to me, but Dakota had a little Jennifer Lawrence in her—at least in the eyes and butt. Sometimes in Design class I would squint and pretend. She had it going on and she knew it. Everyone did. I'd heard some guys on the team talking about her. She had a boyfriend, Dylan Sanders, who she'd been with since freshman year, and they still hadn't had sex, according to Dylan. *The hottest prude in school,* one dude on my team said. *Maybe's she just not feeling it,* I wanted to say, but didn't. *Maybe whale-belt-wearing golf club dudes ain't her thing.*

"That's okay," she said quickly. She reached up and pulled on her hair, twisting it to the side. I'd seen her do that a lot in class. Then she wiped around her mouth.

I noticed her face looked kinda flushed and she seemed a little embarrassed or something. Or maybe it was me that was embarrassed.

"That was a good assembly," I said. Even though it hadn't been. All the kids were going bananas because they were getting their activities cut. Welcome to my world. No money, no fun.

"Um, thanks?" Then she gave me the side-eye, all suspicious. "Are you being sarcastic?"

"No, no," I stuttered. Had I pissed her off? "I just meant, you handled it well."

She paused, looking me up and down like I was making fun of her.

"I really didn't. But I didn't have a choice. Those people? They have no idea what it's like, to be up there, trying to put a happy face on terrible news, trying to make everyone feel better about everything when really there's no way—oh, never mind. I could go on forever."

Clearly. She was babbling. But she seemed upset, and I was tired of feeling invisible. If she wanted to talk, I was happy to listen. "So you think it'll stay this way?"

"I really don't know," she said. "I mean, I'm not the one to ask."

"It's bad, huh?"

"Yeah." She sighed and then looked at me as if seeing it was me, Benny, for the first time. Then she whipped her bag over her shoulder. "I better get back to class."

"Okay," I said, feeling like an idiot. She'd looked right at me—that was more than she'd ever done—but I guess she didn't like what she was seeing 'cause she was rushing off. *Good job, Yizar.*

As she was walking away, it hit me—why she was acting so freaky. She'd just thrown up. My cousin Luisa had done the same thing when I'd caught her puking once. The nervous eyes, flicking side to side, not meeting mine. Wiping her mouth. Keeping her distance. Pretending like everything was normal. People say poor kids don't get anorexia, but that's not true. They also say rich kids don't act ghetto, and I'd seen plenty of kids at HF walking around with their pants low, throwing gang signs in the halls, using the n-word like it was going out of style.

I stood there for a moment, watching Dakota walk away. She was hot and all, but the girl clearly had some issues. If she was just gonna ignore me like everyone else, then I wouldn't waste my time talking to her again.

Then I remembered: time. I was going to be late to History. Shit.

FIVE

ALICE

"SO WHAT WERE YOU SAYING THE OTHER DAY, ABOUT THE Mint?" Jason asked. He was sitting next to me in Design class, for the first time ever.

I frowned. "The Mint?"

"About the security. The network?"

Of course. The day when he'd talked to me. It was about hacking. "Just that for a place so important, they're practically inviting a zero-day."

"A what?"

"An attack that takes advantage of vulnerabilities or weak spots," I explained. My stomach was doing weird things that felt like hunger, despite the fact that I'd just eaten a corn muffin during morning break. He was *right there*—inches away—my body knew it even if my brain wasn't admitting it.

Come on, Alice. Get a grip.

"Huh."

Well, it was obvious he was there because he had nowhere else to sit. Within days of the news about his dad, Jason had become *persona non grata* at Haverford Friends. No one wanted to be associated with a crook, or in this case, a crook's son. It was sad, really. He was still making snarky jokes whenever anyone mentioned his dad, but everyone had stopped laughing at them. Social math: In set theory, there's a hierarchy, organized by how deeply the sets are nested into one another. Every day, Jason was slipping down the hierarchy a little more.

So I couldn't get too excited. In fact, there was nothing to do but focus on my Mint project, which was a rendering of a new commemorative coin. My plan was to scan the design I was drawing by hand into the computer once it was approved and turn it into some kind of three-dimensional rendering. Given a choice, I generally preferred to do everything auto-magically, since computers were my language, my art.

I had some questions for Mr. Rankin about my plan, but he'd already retreated into his office. He'd been acting off lately—he never showed us any funny videos or asked us about our weekends anymore. It was like everything that went down with Mr. Hodges had cast this big shadow over the whole school. I mean, I got why people were bummed out about their activities and stuff, but it was all going to blow over, wasn't it? A place like HF, which had been around forever, would have to bounce back. I'd heard they were going to do a search for a new headmaster. By next year, there would be a whole batch of new students, and they'd raise more money and everything would be forgotten. Our evil headmaster would be reduced to a little eraser smudge on the school's history.

Speaking of smudges, I snuck a glance over at Jason's paper. It looked like he was drawing a coin, too.

"What do you have there?"

"I don't know," he mumbled. "It's just in the early stages."

"I hope you're not making a commemorative."

"Why? Do you think I'm stealing your idea? Because I'm not."

"I didn't say that," I said quickly. Jeez. I'd never heard him sound so down.

I knew Jason had it worse than anyone, but the rest of us were stressed out, too. I was taking the PSATs again over the weekend, and I had at least twenty hours of homework. I should've been thankful that Math Team was suspended because of budget cuts, but I wasn't. It was my only chance to blow off steam, for me anyway. Greg and I had even tried doing something else, something normal after school—we'd gone to the mall yesterday—but it felt all wrong. We couldn't really relate to each other unless we were role-playing or running equations.

Also adding to the stress was the fact that now I had to spend more time at home, which meant seeing my mom doing things like make my dad's favorite pork chops for dinner even though he was late and obviously with Sheryl the skanky secretary. She still had no idea. How could she be so stupid? Even though she'd invited Greg to stay for dinner, he'd insisted on getting home to study for his Chemistry test, so it was just me and her across from each other at the table, with me trying to avoid her eyes.

Now that Jason had mentioned it, though, I did feel a little suspicious. Maybe he *was* copying my assignment. I couldn't be sure. I mean, people tried to copy my stuff all the time.

Then again, why would anyone try to copy me in art class? Reality check: I was an art idiot.

Jason hovered guardedly over his work, digging his pencil into the page, making hatch marks. He was making them more aggressively now, I noticed. "Yeah. No. Mine is different. I'm doing something historical. And it's a medal."

"Okay," I said, my voice coming out weirdly high-pitched. *Forget I mentioned it. Forget I'm even sitting here.* The more I thought about it, the more annoyed I felt. I mean, I was the only person in school still willing to talk to Jason—against my better judgment. Shouldn't he be grateful?

We were both quiet for a while, letting the sound of our markings take over. Then he spoke again. "Well, so, if someone wanted to hack in, how would they go about it?"

I lazily dragged my pencil around the paper, giving the coin a three-dimensional edge. "Hypothetically, you mean?"

"Hypothetically." He looked up. The goofy smile was back and his hazel eyes—they actually lit up. Why was he always trying to hide them with that hair?

I couldn't help but feel flattered that he wanted to hear about this stuff. It was my specialty, after all, and I knew I could impress him. "Well, first, you'd use a Fire Pwn unit. Do you know what that is?"

He shook his head, wide-eyed.

"It's a little device you can get that's loaded with wi-fi, Bluetooth, cellular, and ethernet, so basically you can communicate with it from anywhere at any time. The cool thing is that you just plug it into an outlet. It looks like an ordinary power strip, so no one would even notice it."

"Where do you get it?"

"Online," I said, like duh.

"And how does it help?"

"It's like a stealth operator. It bypasses all the network controls and gets into the system without being detected. So from there all you'd have to do is figure out the weaknesses. Like, the places where someone could get in." I'd never personally used one myself—I'd just read about them on message boards.

"How does it find them?"

"Sniffing."

"Sniffing?"

"You know, sorting through the traffic."

"And then?"

I shrugged. "And then it would probably take a couple weeks but you could crack the password. Once you got on the system, you could see where the administrator computer was. From there it depends on how the internal network works and what you want it to do. But there's a lot less security on an internal network, so once you're on, you could get in there and maybe change things."

"Like, change the number of coins they're making?"

"Maybe."

"Huh," he said. "That's pretty smart."

"Thanks," I said, feeling myself blush a bit. I *was* smart. It was just nice to have someone like Jason recognize it.

"Cool stuff. Very cool." He looked like he was thinking something over.

"Are you planning on hitting up the Mint?" I was joking.

"What?" He looked offended. "I was just curious. I'm not a thief, you know."

Ohhh. "I really didn't mean . . . I wasn't . . ."

"I know. But everyone's acting like I personally did something wrong, like I was in on my dad's little secret, when I didn't have any more of a clue than you guys did."

Gone was the smile, the tilt of his head. My insides rippled. This was a real conversation we were having. Maybe there was more to Jason than I'd thought. Maybe hiding underneath all the shaggy hair and pothead jokes was a smart and interesting person?

"Parents do stuff we can't control," I said. "My dad—he's done some really dumb things lately. Like very clichéd mid-life crisis things. I want to tell him to stop, but it's not like he'd listen to me anyway. He thinks I'm just a dumb kid. The man thinks I still collect stuffed animals."

He looked at me with interest. "So what did he do?"

I paused and looked at him. He was staring back at me intently, still with those hazel eyes shining. Why not tell him? It wasn't as bad as what *his* dad had done—or was it?

"He's bonking his assistant. I stumbled on an email." This was the first time I'd ever said it out loud, and the words sounded just as tacky as the reality. To be perfectly honest, it wasn't exactly "stumbling" so much as "snooping"—I'd reconfigured my dad's spyware so that I could monitor his network activity instead of vice-versa. I mean, he didn't trust me, so why should I trust him? But I was only looking to find out what they knew about my online activities. I was mortified. Disgusted. In all these months, though, I hadn't told anyone. Not even Greg.

"Ouch," he said. "Really?"

Did Jason pity me? That wasn't the same as being genuinely nice. It occurred to me that he might think I was a complete nerd. Not getting that I was actually *choosing* not to be like Dakota and all the rest of them. Being like them was easy—all you had to do was dye your hair and buy the regulation outfits and basically just follow the crowd. But who was I fooling? My "thinking cap" was a choice, maybe, but my negative bra size was not.

Jason was still looking at me, so I kept talking. "It isn't fair, you know? They're supposed to be the ones figuring stuff out. They're supposed to be the ones who have their shit together."

"Even when they ruin schools," he said. "I'm supposed to go on acting like it's normal, even though everyone hates me by association."

"But Jason, everyone knows you had nothing to do with this thing."

"Do they?"

"They'll forget about it. Just give them time." I wanted to cheer him up, even though I wasn't entirely sure that last part was so true.

"I hope so." His face relaxed into a smile again, and I felt better. "Do you—"

His eyes broke away from mine in mid-sentence, and I turned to see where he was looking. Dakota Cunningham had just walked into the room.

"Do I what?" I asked, trying to snap him out of it. Dakota was now standing in front of the glass display case where Rankin put the "Design of the Week," one of her slim legs twisted around the other as she peered through it, probably wondering when her design would be there. Because it wasn't enough for her to be on every page of the yearbook, was it? She wanted to be an art superstar, too.

"Never mind," he said.

Whatever. Jason wasn't deep or interesting. He was just a dude, staring at a typical hot girl. The surface, the goofy stuff, was all there was.

The bell rang, and I gathered up my stuff and headed for the door. *Let him be an outcast*, I thought. *I have better things to do.*

"See you," he called out after me, but I was already walking down the Arts Center hallway, feeling ridiculous, as usual.

SIX

JASON

"THIS BLOWS," CHADDIE GALLOWAY ANNOUNCED AS WE set up in a walk-in closet in our drummer Max's basement. "There's barely room to hold my guitar."

When my mom and I were forced to move out of the headmaster's house, the band had lost the old stone carriage house out back that we'd been using as the Mixed Metaphors practice space. We had a lot of work to do to get ready for prom, so Max volunteered his game room for our Tuesday jamming sessions. Except his mom had already booked that space for her mahjongg group. She didn't want us to disturb her with our "racket," so basically our only choice was to try and squeeze four dudes, all their gear, and their rock star dreams into the basement storage closet. It was a pretty nice storage closet, but still, we looked ridiculous all crammed together in there. Also? We couldn't smoke up before practice now, so everyone was weirdly anxious and high-strung. Or maybe that was just me.

"I'm sorry. We could look for a rental if this doesn't work," Max said. He was the shortest of us, the smallest and the most timid, with a screechy little voice. But he had some sweet equipment, and therefore, he got to be our drummer.

"It'll work," I said. The last thing I wanted to do was rent a space. It was too much effort. And too much money.

"I don't see how we're supposed to do it here," Chaddie said. "What could it cost? A few hundred bucks a month?"

A few hundred I didn't have. "We'll figure it out," I said.

"Figure out a new space? Or this one?" Chaddie pressed me. "The only way this one would work is if we get rid of some of the stuff down here." He pointed to the shelves of boxes holding who knew what.

"Which we can't," Max said. "Not allowed."

I couldn't deal with Chaddie. Was this seriously what he was worried about? When the whole school was falling apart? I'd seen Dianne in the cafeteria that morning, and she'd informed me that the school had cut back the budget for the lunch program. "I think it just means we need to stop serving salmon," she said, trying to smile. "So enjoy it while you can."

I could see the worry in her eyes, though. And it wasn't just her. One of the security guys, Jed, told me they'd cut back his weekend hours.

It sucked for us, sure, but all these people who worked at

HF, this was their *life*. This was how they supported their families. And I'd heard that rumors more cuts were coming.

Where was Zack when I needed him? I needed someone on my side—or at least to get Chaddie off my back. I checked my phone and saw Zack had texted to say he was on his way.

Late as usual. That was Zack. He always did things on his own time, and it usually included a stop-off at Wawa for a hot dog stuffed into a bagel. It annoyed me, yeah, but I usually just let it slide. Why make a big deal? Of course, right now I was eyeing up the door like a neglected puppy, waiting for him to come through.

My dad was still in jail. In the meantime, Ms. Coyle had come by to very politely explain that the school was taking back the house, since it was only supposed to be inhabited by the acting headmaster, which my dad no longer was. We had three days' notice to *vamanos*.

My mom and I had packed up what we could and moved into a little one-bedroom apartment down the road in a complex called Sagebrush, which sounded a lot nicer than it was. The walls of the building looked like cork and our unit smelled like rancid cooking oil, but it was okay. I mean, it was nothing like the headmaster's house, where there was a living room *and* a family room *and* offices for both my parents, not to mention a big fireplace and three bathrooms. The kitchen in our new apartment was what the realtor called a "galley," I was sleeping on a pullout couch with zero privacy, and my mom and I were sharing a bathroom now, which was just . . . gross. "It's an adjustment," my mom said. Understatement of the century.

Losing your dad, your house, and the life you'd always taken for granted? Yeah, I'd say that's an adjustment, all right.

I had to find a way to turn this around, for her and for everyone else. Dakota was right. It wasn't just us. This thing affected so many innocent people. *Maybe I could rob the Mint,* I thought idly.

Finally, Zack appeared in the doorway, guitar case slung over his shoulder, a white waxy Wawa bag crumpled in his hand.

"What's up, sucker?" I said, barely able to contain my relief.

"Sorry guys, I was hungry. I couldn't rehearse on an empty stomach."

"Thank God," Chaddie said. "Now we can actually start."

We couldn't do anything without Zack. I mean, technically we were co-leaders, with Zack doing more of the management and me doing more of the creative vision stuff. We'd come up with the band together, but even though Zack was the lead singer, the name was my idea, and I'd written all the songs. I was also the one who'd come up with the idea of wearing clashing plaids at our shows. Granted, we'd only had one so far, but it had gotten us the prom. The prom was two months away, but now I was wondering if we'd even be ready by then. We'd already missed a couple weeks of rehearsal as we figured out the new practice space situation.

Zack wanted us to start with our best song, "First-World Problems," which had a tight bass line and a jangly chord progression.

Chaddie counted off, but when Max came in off-tempo, he threw his arms down again in frustration. "This is really lame. I can't even hear myself."

Maybe just my opinion, but a guy whose first name was Chadwick wasn't the best judge of lameness.

"Stop being a pussy," I said.

"I'm not a pussy. This room is claustrophobic."

"It's totally fine," I said. I strummed a few notes and scraped my knuckles on the wall. Jesus, it hurt. But I didn't want to admit he was right, so I stifled my yelp of pain.

It *was* ridiculous, but as the person related to the person who'd caused all of this trouble for us, I didn't want them to know I was stressing out. Make adjustments, like my mom said. This band was the best thing I had going. The only thing, really.

I mean, it was important for all of us—I got that.

As we fumbled through the first few bars, I had to wonder. Maybe all this time I'd thought we were good because I'd been high. Because right now, hearing what I was hearing, I was pretty sure we sucked.

Max hit a few beats out on his snare and then pumped the pedal onto the bass drum. Zack cupped his hands over his ears. "Aagh. It's too loud."

"I'm not even mic'd," Max said.

"You're killing me. I can't hear my own voice."

"What do you want me to do?" Max asked. "I'm trying my best over here."

"Okay," I relented. "Max, do you think we could try in your garage or something?"

"I guess my dad can move one of his cars when he gets home. But that's in a couple hours."

We didn't have a couple of hours. We had *an* hour. Less than that, as we'd already wasted twenty minutes. "What are we playing at prom?" Zack asked.

"Dakota requested a bunch of covers. I have the list at home," I said.

"Covers? I thought we were going straight original," Chaddie said. "Covers are lame."

"It's prom." I shrugged. "People want to hear music they already know. And I promised Dakota we'd have some."

"Then she should get a DJ," Chaddie said. "I thought you of all people would want to play our own stuff, Jason. You're always saying we should do our own thing and not sell out."

"I do want us to play our stuff," I said quickly, not wanting this to turn into a thing. But even I had the good sense to know that high-school girls wanted something they could dance to. "Just not if it's gonna cause riots or flaming corsages and whatnot."

"Flaming corsages," Max said. "Maybe that's a song title."

Chaddie put down his guitar. "What's the point of us doing it if we're just gonna flake out? Are we a real band or not?"

I laughed. "Of course we're a real band."

He jutted his chin upward, defiant. "Yeah? Where are all the gigs you promised us we'd have by now? The all-ages shows in Philly and your friend's club in New York? How come we still don't have anything else lined up?"

Okay, so maybe I'd overpromised a bit—and maybe he'd picked up on that. It wasn't exactly a friend but an acquaintance of a guy I'd known at music camp three summers ago, who was now an intern at Mercury Lounge in NYC. And yeah, I had said I was going to go pound the pavement on weekends and get us some gigs downtown. It hadn't happened yet. I fully intended to—I'd just been busy. And then lately . . .

"We'll get them," I said. "And we have a gig already, playing in front of the entire junior and senior classes. That's like two hundred and fifty people. You never know what that could lead to—"

"You're lying," Chaddie cut in. "He's lying about the friend in New York."

"I'm not *lying*," I sputtered. Where was all this pressure coming from all of a sudden? "I just need to text the guy. Can we just focus here? I'm working on it . . . Zack, tell them."

"Yeah," Zack said unconvincingly. "You've said you're working on it."

The truth was it hadn't turned out like I thought. I thought if I started writing great songs, the rest of it would fall into place—we'd have people begging us to play shows. We'd be legendary. But writing good songs was hard work.

"You always say this band is the most important thing ever, and you want to be famous and blah blah blah, but the truth is you haven't done crap," Chaddie said.

What? Was he serious? "That's not true! I'm carrying all the weight here, all the responsibility. I'm doing things behind the scenes, spreading the word, trying to get us on college radio . . ." I struggled to think of other things I could/should be doing, but I was coming up short.

Zack tried to turn around to face me, only there wasn't quite enough room to fully rotate. "Look, dude, no offense, but maybe this whole thing isn't working out anymore."

No no no, I thought. *My partner can't crap out.* "It's working out fine," I said. "I don't know what the big deal is."

"The big deal is we can't play in a closet," Chaddie said. "Right, Zack?"

Zack shrugged to back him up. "It's pretty uncomfortable."

"But we can't quit before our big prom gig," Max said.

"How can we have a gig if we can't practice?" Chaddie asked. It was a chicken-and-egg dilemma. "It's your fault we're in this mess, Jason. So I think you need to take care of it."

I knew what he was getting at. But if no one was going to mention my dad outright, I certainly wasn't going to.

"Okay. I'll find us a new space," I said, finally. What else could I do? I had to just go with the flow, even if the flow was more shit. "Let me look around."

"I've gotta go write my history paper." Chaddie was already halfway up the stairs. Max followed him, saying he was going to get a soda.

Ugh. The doubt had already spread around like some green toxic gas in a cartoon. I could feel it hanging in the room, as everyone packed up the instruments they hadn't even used.

I wanted to be in a band. I wanted to be in a great band. The problem was, deep down, or maybe not even so deep down, I knew they were right about me. I couldn't be counted on to make it happen. It was just like my dad always said, that I stopped short of delivering the goods. No wonder he was embarrassed of me.

"Thanks," I said to Zack once it was just the two of us.

"What? I had to air my doubts." Zack chomped down on his sandwich, whatever it was. I wanted to grab it from him and chuck it across the room. And then what? We'd fistfight or something? We were best friends who hung out and debated the merits of Jarvis Cocker's vocal style. So instead I just packed up my gear and told him I'd call him later.

When I pulled the Jetta up to one of the spots outside the apartment, I found my mom waiting on the front step. She was all bundled up in her winter jacket and scarf, which made her look even tinier than usual.

"Where've you been?" she asked, standing up. "We have to go. Visiting hours are almost over."

"I don't want to see Dad. I'm sorry, but I'm not going." I had barely talked to him since he was put in the slammer. "I have homework to do."

"Well, he wants to see you," she said, all annoyed. "And really, right now? You're going to start doing homework, today of all days? Let's go."

"It's cold out here," I said. "You could have called."

"I didn't want to use up our minutes. Let's take your car. You get better mileage."

The Montgomery County Correctional Facility was a good half hour away in Norristown, a long way off from the Main Line. My mom sped the whole way, making me fear for the safety of my car.

She parked in the lot in back of the jail after a guard waved us in. I noticed two very large dogs barking and tussling around in the SUV next to us when we pulled up. It had an HF sticker on the back windshield.

"I guess Harold Smerconish is here," my mom said.

"The trustee guy?" I asked. That was good news. Maybe he was here to tell my dad how they were going to rescue the school. "You can go in without me. I'll watch the car."

"The guard will watch the car. This is a prison. No one's going to steal it."

"What about escaped convicts?"

"I'm not going in without you, Jason. You're coming."

My voice was hoarse, like something was caught in my throat. "I don't want to. Mom, please."

"Look, Jason. This isn't easy for any of us. But you sitting out here pouting is just going to make my life more complicated, okay? Because then I'll have to explain to your father why his son is abandoning him. Don't make me do that." She put her cold hand on my arm, and I noticed her diamond engagement band was missing. She was only wearing the slim gold wedding band, and there was a pale spot where the other one used to be.

I looked up into her face, her sad, shiny eyes. For a terrible moment, I realized what it must be like to be her right now, and it wasn't pretty. My mom deserved way better than this, and I wished, suddenly, that I could help her out.

"Okay," I agreed. "I'll come in, but I'm not gonna talk to him."

"Suit yourself." She clutched a plastic bag full of items she was dropping off for my dad—a pair of slippers, a couple pairs of socks, some underwear, and a paperback novel. Tom Clancy? My dad never read that crap. Maybe he was worried he'd get beaten up in jail if he was seen reading Proust.

I followed her into the lobby where a guard behind a desk made us sign in. Then we were led down a long squeaky-floored hallway to a room. My dad was in there, wearing an orange jumpsuit, and he already had a visitor sitting across the table from him. As we got closer, I saw that it was indeed Harold Smerconish. I recognized him from the annual headmaster's brunch they held at our house. Well, our old house. There was some other man next to him in a suit. A lawyer? All six of their hands were resting on the table between them.

When he saw us, my dad stood up and waved to us from across the room. The eager smile on his unshaven face—well, it was pathetic. Seeing that, I wished like anything I'd stayed in the car.

The guard directed us to a row of gray bucket seats along the wall. "Wait here."

"Can't we see him now?" my mom asked.

"Not until his first two visitors leave," the guard said.

"But there's only a few minutes left," she pleaded.

"Rules," he responded, glowering at us.

My mom muttered some curses under her breath. I sank down into the plastic chair. From where we were sitting, I could hear most of my dad's conversation.

"We don't have a choice," Smerconish was saying. ". . . enough for the end of the fiscal year. And then we'll need to make arrangements."

"I never meant to do this," my dad said, shaking his head, and for the first time I could ever remember, I thought I actually heard a sob in his voice. *Oh god.* "You know that, right, Harold?"

"I'm sorry, Jim, but we're not here to talk about that," Smerconish said.

The lawyer spoke up. "The board's decided to strip you of your title, effective immediately."

"And what's going to happen to the school?" my dad asked.

"The best action would be to close after May," the lawyer said. "Sell off the assets. Pay creditors. Pay employees."

The school was *closing*? Jesus. It was worse than the rumors.

My dad would be responsible for shutting down Haverford Friends, founded 1886. Some legacy. Forget his stupid sculpture, his plans for expansion. They were going to bury him in the quad. And I was going to have to move to Atlantic City, become a blackjack dealer and change my name. All these years I'd been the one to disappoint him, not the other way around.

"Oh God," my dad was saying. "Payroll . . . ?"

"Is very, very tight. We're trying our hardest, but short of some unexpected windfall . . ." Smerconish said. "We have no good options."

They were going to stiff employees, that's how bad it was. My dad was worse than scum.

Then the two men stood up. "We'd better go," Smerconish said. "Good luck, Jim."

He pumped my dad's hand in his gigantic one, then buttoned up his barn jacket—no HF alum was complete without one. It was the official uniform of preppy older guys everywhere. I noticed deep worry lines carved into his forehead. The wrinkles of someone who constantly made big decisions.

Smerconish had sent all five of his kids to HF, back in the day. They were in college or older now. He was supposedly some big real estate guy who owned a bunch of stuff. But he mostly seemed like all the other HF trustees—old, wealthy, and worried about keeping the school going for future generations of old wealthy people.

"Cold one out there, huh, Sarah?" he said to my mom as he passed us.

It sure as shit was cold in here. Arctic, by my thermometer.

My mom only nodded, and then the guard waved us over

so we could sit down with my father, the prisoner. I felt sick to my stomach.

"Jason! I've missed you."

He reached out to hug me, but I just sat down in the seat, ignoring his outstretched arms and his sad little forced smile. He wasn't who I thought he was. Mr. Discipline? What a joke.

The great Jim Hodges had ruined so many lives, including his own. And now he was pretending everything was dandy? I wanted no part of it. Though, of course, we'd always be linked. People would always think of me as the headmaster's son, even when the headmaster was demoted to a jailhouse toilet cleaner.

He looked hurt, but I ignored it. I was here strictly as a favor to my mom, not because I cared about him. I was pissed. I was so pissed, I couldn't hide it.

Looking at him, sitting there in his orange jumpsuit, underweight and tired and ashamed and pitiful, I swore then and there that I'd never again let anyone down, not like my dad had done to the entire HF community, with his half-finished statue and his half-baked schemes and his lies—so many stinking lies. No matter how much DNA we shared, I'd never be like him. I was going to fix his mistakes and make it right, for everyone at HF. Somehow, and I wasn't sure how, I'd have to do it. I would have to keep the school open.

I thought of Alice, all that stuff she'd said. *The Mint.*

It was crazy, but maybe we could make it work. I had to try *something*.

My dad settled back into his seat, realizing that I wasn't

going to return that hug. "So where've you been, man?"

"Nowhere," I said. "Home."

"I'll be there soon. Soon as I can."

What I said next was maybe a little cruel. But he deserved it, didn't he?

"No rush," I told him. "We're doing fine without you."

SEVEN

DAKOTA

"DAKOTA, WE NEED TO TALK." MY DAD, DRESSED UP IN HIS lawyer uniform—blue suit, burgundy tie, white shirt with extra extra starch—leaned up against the Calacatta marble countertop in our kitchen.

A typical morning in my house: My parents were up at 5 a.m. to go to their krav maga class, and I did my jogging thing. We were all showered in our respective bathrooms by 6:30, and now we sat, as we always did, with our green smoothies (antioxidants! iron! calcium!) and espressos from my dad's imported Italian machine—he liked to remind us that it was *the absolute best, engineered by the company that makes Alfa Romeos.* (He had one of those, too, in the antique car collection that took up an entire climate-controlled building next to our house.)

Sometimes I think my dad wished I'd been engineered by Alfa Romeo, too—it would have made his job easier.

I mean, it wasn't like that for my older sister Hansen. Everything she did was automatically okay—even though she didn't always strictly follow their plans. She'd been home from Brown over the weekend, so there was a big flurry of activity before she arrived, getting her room ready, making dinner reservations at her favorite Japanese place downtown, and then she showed up and said she was in the mood for tapas so we went to Amada instead, everyone going along and ordering patatas bravas like it was nothing, when I was really craving toro, but of course nobody asked me. Everyone worshipped Hansen, even though she chose Brown over Harvard, a Development Studies program over Econ, a new boyfriend with earrings the size of dinner plates over her rugby-playing high school boyfriend Chase. It used to drive me nuts, a little, how it was so effortless for her, but the way things were going lately? I was kind of glad that she was around to help balance the crazy of my parents.

"You just have to tell them to back off," she'd said to me. "You need to set some boundaries."

Easier said than done.

Now that she was back at school, the full laser beams of their attention were focused squarely on me and what was going on at Haverford Friends. I could see it glinting in my dad's steel gray eyes.

"I know what you're going to say, Dad," I countered. "I've

thought this through, and I don't think suing the school is a good idea."

My mom laughed, a loud chirp that shook her shoulders, though it barely moved her tightly sprayed scoop of hair. "Sue the school? Hardly. That coconut has been tapped. No no no."

"What then?" I asked.

"What your father is trying to say is that Haverford Friends can't possibly deliver the goods with no money in the budget. And you shouldn't have to compromise your dreams because of someone else's criminal activity, Dakota." She rubbed her forehead, where there were still natural furrows. She was not one for Botox or Restylane—and so far, a macrobiotic diet and exercise six days a week had kept her looking youthful.

My dreams? All I knew was that I was supposed to go to Harvard, and I hadn't really thought beyond that. Well, that's not entirely true. When I was a little kid, I'd had that silly dream, to act and sing on Broadway. But my parents said it was a dead end professionally, so they told me to grow up and set that fantasy aside.

"So you're going to help? You'll work with the rest of the parents' committee to raise the money?"

My dad shook his head. "No. We had a conference call last week, and it's not going to work. No one wants to contribute to a school going through a federal investigation. And frankly, it's a bad investment because chances are it won't be here in another year." That's when he pulled a brochure out of his inner suit jacket pocket and handed it to me.

"Bertrand Academy?" I said, reading the cover. "New Hampshire. What is this? A boarding school?"

"Eleven percent of graduates go to Harvard. Eleven percent." He paused, like a lawyer addressing a jury, to let that sink in.

I didn't have the heart to tell them that I wasn't smart enough for Harvard, and no amount of extracurriculars or special tutors or gifts to the school could change that.

"We spoke to the admissions director there, and she said she couldn't make any promises, and it's probably too late for this term, but if we got her your test scores and transcripts this week, she could schedule you in for an interview." My dad winked at me, proudly, like he'd already won his case. "Mom and I looked at your schedule, and it seems like the eighteenth would be a good day for you. Mom can take off that day, too, so we can book the flight today."

Of course they'd looked at my phone. And you know what? That wasn't the thing I was most freaked out about. "I don't want to go to boarding school."

My mom held up a manicured hand. "Honey, this isn't just any boarding school. It's the boarding school that delivered five presidents and just about every CEO of every important Fortune 500 company. It's the best foundation you could possibly have."

I'd always thought HF was the best foundation. At least that's what I'd been told. "I don't want to switch schools. I'm in the middle of everything."

"That's why you'd start in the fall. If you're worried about Dylan breaking up with you, I wouldn't. He knows he's got a good thing going. I can talk to his father if you want . . ."

"No!" I practically shouted. I hated when my dad tried to meddle in my love life. If I could even call Dylan a love life. At one time, I'd had a crush on him, definitely. But these days I could barely hold a conversation with him. All he ever wanted to talk about was lacrosse and video games. I wasn't even sure I was attracted to him anymore, not like I'd say that in front of my parents, who would freak out—they loved me dating a state senator's son. We were HF's resident power couple, and my parents, themselves popular in high school, wouldn't accept me dating someone beneath my social station. "It's not about Dylan. It's about school work . . ."

"Well, you shouldn't worry about that. If need be, you could repeat eleventh grade, just to make sure you had everything in place," my dad said.

"I can't repeat eleventh grade." The idea was hideous. Hansen had said it herself: *The sooner you get to college, the sooner you can be your own person.*

"There's no stigma. It's very common when people transfer to Bertrand," my dad explained, patiently, like he was talking to an elderly client. "The curriculum is so sophisticated that some students need a catch-up."

"I can't. I won't. Besides, the eighteenth is in two weeks and I have exams, I have papers. We have the prom to plan, and the yearbook . . ."

My mom raised her eyebrow at my dad and nodded subtly, like *Let me do this.* "Don't you see that you're holding on to a sinking ship, Dakota? Haverford Friends might not be around next fall, and even if it is, there will be cuts. There will be fewer teachers, no activities, no *SAT prep.*"

"I'm already taking private SAT prep," I pointed out.

"But you might want to avail yourself of the school's SAT prep as well next year. You never know. You want to have options. The point is this: You've worked way too hard to give up everything now. Also, Bertrand is not too far from Brown, and Hansen said she could come visit you on the weekends. Or you could visit her when you don't have to study."

"You talked to Hansen about this before mentioning it to me?" That was the ultimate.

"I wanted her input," my mom said.

"How about *my* input? This is my life!"

"You're getting all worked up," my dad said, setting down his espresso glass with a tiny little clink. "I told you we should wait on this, Monica. At least until after the school day. Now she's going to be distracted."

"You're right. I *will* be distracted." I nervously ran both my hands through my hair, messing up the twenty minutes I'd spent arranging it. "You guys don't understand. I have enough to worry about right now. I don't want to think about switching, and even if I did, I can't handle applying to some other school. It's too much work."

"We can take care of it for you," my dad said.

"That would be cheating." Was he losing his mind? "Besides, I'm responsible for too many things. People are depending on me, and it would be selfish for me to just bail out. I'm the council vice president. Ms. Coyle said I'm supposed to help keep up the spirits of the students."

"She said that?" My mom shook her head in disgust. "That's *her* job. Your job is, simply, to be the best. And you're doing that, sweetie. Which is why I don't want you to throw it all away out of some misplaced loyalty."

"It's not misplaced. I've been at HF since pre-kindergarten. You always told me that I had to wear my colors proudly. And I'm doing that." They were the ones who'd encouraged me to care so much. They were the ones who'd told me to get so involved and devote myself to the school's motto. And now they wanted me to throw all that away and think only of myself?

My dad looked at his watch. "We need to get going, Monica. Dakota, we'll talk about this later. I suspect you'll be home earlier than usual?"

Of course they were leaving mid-conversation. Of course they were going to waltz off and leave me here while the anger crept up my throat and choked me. The simple truth of it was, they owned DAKOTA CUNNINGHAM. They'd get it trademarked if they could.

"I might stay to work on the prom," I said. There were no plans for council to meet, but with my other activities canceled, I was in no hurry to come back here. Especially not now with this new kick they were on. Boarding school? Really?

And yet I knew, no matter how hard I tried or what arguments I made, that I'd never convince my parents. They were professional debaters. They would always, always win. I might as well start packing my bags.

"Right. Prom! I can't wait. You have to make the most of these memories while you can." My mom looped the strap of her leather briefcase over her shoulder and leaned down to kiss my forehead at the same time. "It's going to be chilly today. Don't forget an extra layer. And make sure you send that thank-you note to Aunt Lisa. There's some kale and quinoa loaf in the fridge for dinner you can heat up when you get home."

"Okay," I said.

When they were gone and the garage doors had rumbled shut and the house was quiet, I couldn't help myself. I didn't really have time, but the urge was stronger than reason.

Up in my bathroom, I shut the door out of habit and undid my hair, then pulled it back extra tight. I stared at myself in the mirror. The parts were all there, the face everyone else saw. But what they didn't see was the rage boiling underneath. It was ugly and there was no makeup to cover it, no cream to make it burn less. If I didn't do something, it was going to kill me.

And then? I did what I always do. I leaned over the toilet and made myself gag. My hands were shaking, my skin was clammy, and the taste was putrid. I felt small and helpless against the reflexes of my body. Throwing up was weak. It was something that girls with no discipline did. But when it was all over I felt a sense of calm settle over me. I lay back on the bathroom floor, the tiles cool and smooth on my skin. I forgot, for a moment, about Bertrand, and Dylan, and my parents, and school, and student council,.

Maybe I liked having a secret from my parents. Maybe I liked knowing I was just as flawed as everyone else. Either way, this, right here, was the only thing that was mine. The only time I could be myself. Dakota Cunningham without the caps.

EIGHT

BENNY

MY ADVISOR MRS. DIAMOND RUSHED INTO HOMEROOM
like a white-lady tornado, right in the middle of video announcements. She was usually just there, waiting for all of us to file in,
like it was her house or something, and we were her guests.
Now she brushed past our desks, her jacket swishing.

"Sorry, everyone. Sorry I'm late."

Grumbles. It was too early for more than a grumble.

Meanwhile, on the smart board screen, two kids in ties
who were way more awake than the rest of us talked about the
weather.

*Thirty-one degrees today with a chance of snow . . . kinda
mediocre. Davis? Back to you.*

It's like that now, Cody, so get used to it.

It *was* like that now. Mediocre all over. The video announcements used to be a full half hour and now it took about five minutes. No more sports announcements, 'cause no teams were playing. No plays. No pep rallies or meetings or events. Not even the nerdy guy talking about Science Club. I hadn't realized how much I liked watching that little dude until now.

Mrs. Diamond set her bags down on her desk and went about taking attendance, mumbling names to herself as she went. When she got to mine, which was the last one, of course (*Y*s represent!), she looked up. "There you are. Benny, I need to talk to you. Do you have a moment?"

"Sure," I said, a little worried but glad to have a reason to get out of my seat. Now that the announcements were over, the rest of homeroom was usually just sitting around alone listening to everyone else gossip. Talking about their weekends and how much beer they drank and who hooked up with who. Stuff I didn't need to know, because I didn't know any of these people.

Mrs. Diamond was pushing sixty and had dyed blond hair cut real short. I slouched up to her desk and waited to see what kind of trouble I was in, but then she looked up at me with a smile that made me even more nervous. The last time an old lady smiled at me like that was when my grandmom took me shopping at the end of the summer and told the salesperson at Kohls that I needed nice school clothes.

"Benny, I just had a meeting with the bursar's office, and I'm afraid I have some . . . uhh . . . unfortunate news. They said that with everything that's happened, they're having trouble making ends meet for the financial aid program next year."

"But I'm—I'm on scholarship," I blurted out. It was meant to be a secret. The teachers knew, but supposedly no one else did.

Now her smile faded some. "The future of the D.M. Jamison athletic scholarship is unclear, actually. We lost that money in the, um, situation."

Situation? Sounded more like a big hustle to me. "What about the other scholarship I got, from the state?"

"That was only five percent of your funding. You can keep it, but it's not going to be enough."

Goddamn. Was she for real? They were getting rid of *my* money now? They could do that to me, basically the only poor kid here? "Is there another scholarship I can apply for?"

"You should talk about it with the bursar. It's too late for next year. The state deadlines were in January."

"What the hell?" I didn't mean to curse in front of a teacher, but I was freaking out. How would I break the news to my grandmom, after everything we did to get me here? She'd start crying, talking about my poor mom, her terrible story. How they came over from Mexico when she was a teenager, how she started working as a mushroom picker to help make ends meet. How she met my dad around the way, and they had me when she was too young. How she got an injury on the job and started popping pills because they wouldn't send her to the doctor. How she OD'ed three months later. How my dad was deported back to the D.R., leaving me with my grandparents. I was four years old then, and I'd lived with them ever since. *Corazoncito, my job is to protect you*, my grandmom would say. *And your job is to make us proud.*

No, this would crush her into pieces. I had to graduate from HF, be the first in my family to go to college, actually have a *career* instead of a *job*. They were depending on me. "What am I supposed to do? I've been busting my butt trying to keep up my GPA. I had a great season."

"I honestly don't know, Benny. I'm trying to get more information. You're not the only one in this situation."

"I'm the only kid bussed in from North Philly."

"There are plenty of others, from other neighborhoods, kids who needed a little help to be here. They'll be in the same boat."

I knew who she was talking about. Secret or no, all you had to do was look closely. A Chinese kid whose parents owned a restaurant in East Falls. A girl with a single mom from Conshohocken. Another guy whose parents lost some money in the stock market. He was from the mean streets of Ardmore. *Ardmore.* They had a Porsche dealership in that town. All of those people were rich compared to me, and they all lived in clean, safe neighborhoods. Besides, even if they weren't, pretty much, we were all screwed.

"I'll let you know what I find out, okay?" She gave me a wink and my head spun with rage. *Don't get cutesy with me. This is my life we're talking about. My one break.*

If there was no money, I'd be back at Jansen. I'd be back with my homies, yeah, but I'd have no future. Might as well shoot me, because my life would be over anyway.

Later, as we filed into art class, Rankin handed back our Mint projects. I'd made a blueprint of the production floor we'd seen on our field trip, with all the machines and everything. I was pretty proud of it—we had only spent an hour there, but I'd been able to recreate the entire place from memory. On my paper was a pink Post-It note—Rankin didn't like writing on our "work"—with a red C. A stinking C? Under it he'd written, *This is a great rendering, Benny, but next time, try to use your imagination.*

It was the first C I'd gotten at HF, and it was one more slap in the face.

I didn't need my imagination, I wanted to tell him. I was a mechanic, and I could fix a car in my sleep. Nothing imaginary about that. And by the way? All of this art stuff was bullshit.

But what did it matter now? I was leaving. I'd never see any of these people again. Maybe that was for the best.

Instead of relief, though, I was just worried. I still had no idea how I was going to tell my grandparents. Maybe if I waited long enough, the school would call and do it for me. Even then, they'd still be devastated. This was their dream—they were getting old and they didn't have much else—and it was about to be smashed.

I sank down in the first empty seat I saw and stared into

space, thinking. If Rankin thought I was gonna pay attention to his lectures about lines and fonts now, he was crazy. I could barely even enjoy looking at Dakota, I was so low. You know times are desperate when a girl in tight jeans can't fix it.

"I don't think that would work," whispered this little girl with glasses sitting next to me. She was tiny, looked like she was twelve or something, and she always had some crazy hat on. I'd seen her around the halls, but we didn't have any other classes together. I think her name was Alicia, or Alice, or something. "You'd need at least three people. One to work remotely, and two for the haul. And, to be frank, I don't understand why you're so obsessed with this."

The guy she was huddled with was the headmaster's kid. Jason. He shrugged. "I just think it's interesting that it could be done. I think there's potential there."

"Potential for what?" she asked quietly.

"I don't know. To get some money, funds, for whatever we need."

My ears perked up.

"You're serious," she said. She was smiling this funny half-smile.

Were they talking about pulling some job? Something ille-gal? These two? That was hi-*larious*.

"It's a victimless crime," he said. "No one will lose anything, because that money wouldn't technically exist. It's not really stealing—it's more like adapting it for our needs."

"But isn't that what fundraising is for?"

"Yeah, well, it's worse than you think," he said. "What's happening here. I happen to know some stuff, and it doesn't look good."

Her voice dropped to an even lower whisper, but I could still hear her. "So you're saying you want to try it. For real. The Mint. For HF."

Time to make myself known. "So what's the scheme?"

They both whipped their heads around guiltily. The headmaster's kid grimaced, his mouth a tight little line. "No scheme. I'm kidding," he said. "It's a joke. Ha."

"You sounded pretty real to me," I said.

He looked surprised, maybe because I was Invisible Man and they hadn't even realized I was there. I probably should have just kept quiet, because now they were both freezing up.

"It's a hypothetical situation," the girl said. "We're just talking it through. Like role-playing?"

"Okay, well, if it's just hypothetical, then let me role-play, too." I'll admit I was mostly testing them, to see how far they were gonna take it. I was willing to bet this skinny kid was all talk. But the other chick, Alice, was staring at him with her big eyes. Super-serious.

"Yeah?" Jason said, checking me out. "And what can you do? You'd need to have some skills. Alice's really good at hacking. I'm good at leading and planning."

I thought about it for a moment. "I can fix cars. Or anything mechanical, really."

"Huh." He looked doubtful.

My eyes traveled around the room and locked on Dakota, who was standing nearby, wearing these sexy-ass boots. Was she listening in, too? Nah, she was probably just deep in thought about her project.

"And IDs," I added. "I can make any kind of ID." I'd been doing that for years around the neighborhood. You might think it was for buying booze, but it was actually to help kids who already had a record. The police were always coming through and stopping people, and some of these guys just wanted to avoid more trouble. A new identity would do that for you.

Alice's eyes lit up. "That could help, Jason. We could use IDs."

So maybe it was a game, like one of those things kids did with the magic cards or some shiz, but it was fun. Rankin left us alone to work on our next project, so we spent the rest of the period talking about it, the ins and outs. Who would do what, and how it would all work.

As we kept going I started to think: Maybe, if we could get enough money to save this school, they'd bring back my scholarship, and I could stay here next year and go to college like my grandparents wanted me to. Then someday I could open my own business and make enough money to pay them back for all they'd done for me. Maybe even buy them some things they needed, like a new fridge, railings on the stairs. And a new AC unit. Send my dad in the D.R. a cut.

It was the best time I ever had in any class at HF. To the point that by the time the bell rang and we grabbed our stuff for the next class, and Jason asked if we wanted to meet at lunch the next day, I actually said I would.

And then I was out in the hallway, head spinning. It *was* a game, wasn't it?

If it wasn't, what the hell had I just agreed to?

NINE

ALICE

GREG AND I WERE IN THE CAFETERIA LINE, PULLING FOIL-wrapped chicken sandwiches from under the heat lamps.

"I don't think they have the right to call these things tenders," Greg said as he peered under the bun, his acne glowing red from the light.

"Maybe toughers?" I suggested, poking mine, which had the texture of boiled rubber.

"We should start bringing our own," he said.

I agreed. With all the cutbacks, the food was getting steadily more budget every day. Where once we had organic tuna pita pockets, we now had peanut butter and jelly. The milks were half the size and the salad bar bins were filled with canned vegetables.

"Well, I better run," Greg said, gathering up the contents of his meal and heading for the cashier. "I told Mr. Jenkins I'd help him in the lab. After school?"

"Catch you later," I said, inching down the line.

When I got to the drinks cooler, I noticed Jason was talking to the red-haired lunch lady. He was leaning over the metal rail and shaking his head.

"I'm so sorry," I heard him saying, and he sounded really upset. "Look, I'll see what I can find out, okay? Don't panic. There's got to be an answer."

What was he sorry about? Even weirder was that he was talking to her like they were friends. She had to be fifty years old—she'd been working at HF since the beginning of time.

He pulled away from the rail just as I was sliding my tray along, so that we nearly collided. "Hey, Al," he said.

It always took me aback when he used that nickname. Only my dad had ever called me that.

"Hey," I said back, and we fell into step. I don't know how it happened, but suddenly we were seeing each other every day. Talking, not just in Design class, but *between* classes. Even in the coffee bar during break—in *full view* of some of his exes. Which, to be fair, included most of the girls in our grade. Social math: In set theory there's an axiom of pairing, which basically means that if A and B are sets then there's a set out there that contains both A and B. By virtue of existing, they belong together somewhere. The same could be said of Jason and the list of girls he'd hooked up with.

It was strange. He'd started to appear in my brain even when I wasn't with him. I thought about him as I showered and got dressed. And at night, when I finished my homework, I pictured him in his house, wondering what he might be doing. Which was completely crazy.

And when we talked, it wasn't just about the Mint stuff anymore. He told me all about his band and his plans to dominate iTunes someday, and I couldn't help but get caught up. I knew things about his family—his dad was still in jail, and his mom was making him go visit every week. I told him the latest about my parents, how my dad was even sneaking away on weekends now.

Now he was next to me and I felt my breath quicken. "So what was that about?" I asked, not wanting to be too nosy.

He sighed. "Dianne was just given a pink slip. Technically there's a union of service employees, and technically they shouldn't be able to just do that. But this is an extreme situation. It's so messed up."

"And you're going to help her?"

He nodded. "I'm going to get some information from my dad's office. See if there's any way I can help."

I'd never really seen this side of him before. "That's actually pretty thoughtful."

"You sound surprised," he said.

Because you act like a bimbo sometimes? "So get this. My dad called Sheryl on the way to school today. He put her on speakerphone. They were using all of these euphemisms, like 'low-hanging fruit' and 'looping each other in', but it was so obvious and disgusting. He acts like I'm five years old."

"Why don't you just talk to him?" he asked me.

"Um. Why don't you talk to your dad?" I asked back.

"Because it won't change anything."

"Bingo," I said.

When we talked like this, all the other stuff, all of his usual whatever-dude stuff fell away.

We sat down at the table and waited for Benny, for our official Mint job meeting to begin.

What started as a fantasy game, like D&D, had begun to seem more plausible. We were planning the smallest details, right down to our alibis and how we'd get rid of our prints. I didn't know what Benny thought, but the way Jason talked about it, it didn't seem like we were playing around anymore. It was like he needed to do this—to get back at his dad, or maybe to fix his dad's mistakes.

And me? Well, for starters, the idea that I could make something this big happen was intoxicating. I was in it for the thrill, for the idea that I could actually pull off a hack this size and prove that I wasn't some stupid kid. I'd show my dad and anyone else who doubted me.

There was only one problem: I still couldn't figure out how the heck we were going to manufacture as many coins as we needed without anyone noticing all the missing raw material after the job was done. I'd been poking at the holes in our plan for a few days now, but only in my head. It was time to bring all my doubts out into the open.

I pulled my iPad out of my bag and laid it down on the table between us.

"So what have you got?" Jason asked.

I opened up a document I'd been keeping with notes from our meetings and some of my own research. It was encrypted, of course, for safekeeping. "I think we have a good handle on how we'll get in, at least virtually."

"Cracking into the production system?"

"Right. I've done some research and they use Manufact-Sure. It's an off-the-shelf product they've customized for their own needs. I ran some demos of it at home, to see how it's organized—inventory, orders, accounting, that kind of thing. Should be easy to navigate. Once we get the plug into the building, it's just a matter of monitoring, really. But . . . that's not the problem," I said.

Benny emerged from the lunch line then, his tray filled with two chicken sandwiches, fries, three cookies, a yogurt, a banana, and four milks. Football players. The guy's calories in a single meal could support my whole household for a week.

"S'up," he said, fitting his broad frame into the seat across from us.

"Al was just saying that there's a problem with the plan," Jason said. Then he turned to me, his gaze intent. Those eyes. I felt something inside me flutter. "Go on."

"Well, I've been running the calculations, and I just can't see how we could get enough money out of it. Even if we punch out quarters, it will take twenty million of them to rebuild the endowment."

"So? The floor produces sixteen million coins a day," Benny said. "You're worried about time?"

I nodded. "I just don't see how we can reasonably take over production for that long without someone noticing. We need to do something in an hour or so, tops. In and out. Let alone the sheer amount of metal we'd need to use up to produce that many coins."

"Huh," Jason said, leaning back in his seat and chewing on a straw. "Well, that *is* a problem. And kind of a big one."

Blech. Like I said, I'd been reluctant to mention this, even though it had been days since I figured it out. "Anyone have any suggestions?"

Jason pressed his fingers to his temples and closed his eyes as if he was reading something internally. "What if we just went for the materials? Maybe we could get enough money if we sold the metal."

"Even if we could, you saw how huge those coils were. No way we could get them out of the building without heavy machinery." I sighed. "Benny?"

He shook his head. "I've got nothing."

Ordinarily, I could see all the angles around a problem and walk the solution through in my mind, but this time I could only see the problem.

"Let's keep thinking on it," I suggested. "There's no rush,

right? That building's not going anywhere." I'd be damned if I was going to let a little logistical issue interfere with my new-found whateveritwas with Jason.

Jason tapped his straw against the bottom of his cup. "Well, we only have until the end of the semester before the school defaults on its credit."

A semester. In the meantime, I had a physics quiz, an AP French test, three term papers, and a calculus exam.

Jason grabbed his tray and stood up. "I guess our meeting's over. Let me know if anyone comes up with anything."

Over? Don't say the word "over." "You're giving up?" I asked, my heart sinking. Maybe this had all been a fantasy after all. Maybe he never really intended to go through with it.

"No, but what's the point of sitting here if we can't figure it out? It's kind of a big problem."

"Um, because we're friends?" The words came out before I'd really thought them through. They sounded lame. Lame and desperate.

He looked at Benny and then at me. "Yeah. Sure." But in the weakness of his tone, I heard exactly what he was thinking—*yeah, right*—and my heart crumpled in five places. Just a few moments ago we were bonding, and now we were back to our old pre-Mint selves. *God.* I was so deluded to even let myself be attracted to him in any way. "I have stuff to do, though."

Benny sat up straight. "Wait. I got it. Maybe a fifty cent piece?"

For the first time I wondered if Benny was thinking it was real, too. Maybe he needed our quandary to be solved as much as I did.

"They're too rare," Jason said, still hovering over us. "We'd never be able to use them without getting caught. Unless we found a magician we could sell them to. And then he could make them disappear."

"Isn't rare a good thing in coins?" Benny said.

"Yeah, but no one uses half-dollars," I pointed out. "Except great-grandpas, and then they have caramels stuck to them."

"Shoot," Benny said. "Why doesn't the Mint print bills? We could get this thing done in a minute."

"If only we lived in D.C. or Texas . . ." Jason said wistfully. "I mean, D.C.'s not too far."

Benny shook his head. "No way, man. We're not gonna pull a job in the nation's capital."

"Shop local, steal local," I said. "Either way, we're breaking into a federal building. It's no joke."

"Good point. Good point," Jason agreed. "Oh well, like I said. I gotta go meet up with my band."

"So that's it, I guess," I said, feeling everything sink.

"I knew you guys weren't for real," Benny muttered.

Jason looked almost pissed then. "I'm completely for real," he said. "I always have been. I want this more than anyone. Otherwise I wouldn't have started this thing. I just don't see how it can work right now. Face it. We've hit a wall. And I'd rather give up before we have too much riding on it, you know?"

Maybe. We'd put in so much time and energy, though. It was like he had no confidence. This time his back was almost entirely toward us when Dakota Cunningham appeared in front of us.

"Hey guys," she said. Talk about hitting a wall. When Dakota wanted something, there was no getting around her.

"What's up?" Jason said. "Did you get lost on the way to the salad bar?"

"No. I'm here to see you." Here she looked down at me and Benny behind him. "All of you."

"What about?" Jason asked.

"You know. This thing you're doing."

"What thing?" Jason feigned surprised innocence, but he wasn't much of an actor. He still looked pretty damn guilty.

"Your meetings. Your plan. I want in."

Benny gave me a look, like, is she serious?

"What is it that you think we're planning?" I asked her, testing. There was no way she could know. Unless she'd been straight-up eavesdropping.

"The Mint, okay?" she said quietly. "Stop playing dumb. I heard you talking."

I think all of our jaws dropped simultaneously.

Silence.

"It's nothing," I said, breaking the spell. "We're not planning anything." Because now that was the honest-to-goodness truth.

"Then how come you're all huddled together? I *know* you're not studying. Look, don't try to fool me."

Jason laughed, raising his hands like he was surrendering. "Okay. You got us, Cunningham. That's what we were doing. Robbing the Mint to save HF, ha ha ha."

Her eyes narrowed. She wasn't buying his blowoff. "I can find out one way or another—you know I can, Jason. So you might as well tell me about it."

Now she had me worried. Was she going to get us into trouble? Was she going to blackmail us? I had to be careful. "If that's what we were doing, and I'm not saying it is, it would be implicating you to tell you about it," I pointed out. "You wouldn't want to risk your precious reputation, would you? And why do you even care?"

"I have my reasons," she said, biting a corner of her pink-glossed lower lip.

"It's impossible, anyway," I said. "So don't worry about it."

"What's impossible? Look, you guys, I'm pretty sure I can help out."

"Sorry, but I don't think you could," I said. "Even if we were planning something, I mean. We have enough people on our team. No available openings."

For the first time in history, I was mean-girling Dakota. It was a rare opportunity. But still she stood there, clasping her bottle of water in front of her like it was some kind of offering. "I'm serious!"

"Okay, fine. The only way you could help us," I said, knowing full well that she couldn't, "is if you can figure out how we can print enough coins in an hour to add up to fifty million dollars and use them without raising any suspicions."

"Easy. We don't make new coins," Dakota said, not skipping a beat. "Or at least not the ones in circulation now. We make an old coin."

"What? How?" Jason asked.

"Don't you remember? On the tour?" she continued. "The coins with the mistakes. Error coins. And only a few of them ever get out into the world, which is why the ones that do are worth a ton of money. So here's what we do: We take a real error coin and we mint a bunch of those, pretend like they've been lost for years but newly uncovered. And because it'd be made on the floor of the Mint, it would be legit, totally authentic. We'd need a lot fewer copies to make a lot of money and bail the school out."

She was talking like it was a bake sale or a car wash, something she could just whip up with a little can-do spirit. Then again, I realized, maybe that was exactly what we needed to get this thing going again, especially with Jason ready to jump ship at the first sign of a challenge.

"Huh," Jason said, with a frown. "What do you think, Al?"

At least he was still asking my opinion. "I think it would need an excellent design. A forgery, essentially. None of us have that kind of skill," I said. It annoyed me that Dakota was acting like it was all figured out when she'd just waltzed her way over here minutes before. It annoyed me that she'd thought of stuff I hadn't thought of. *I'm supposed to be the card-carrying nerd around here.*

"Yeah, well, Jason can make the design. He's brilliant at

drawing. Didn't you guys know that? He already got an A on his project. His medal was perfection."

"You did?" I asked him. I thought he blew off every class. I thought he'd been copying off me.

He shrugged like it was no big deal. But it was. *No one* got an A from Rankin. I was actually jealous. "Yeah. How did you know that?"

Dakota laughed. "You have to know your competition."

Yeah, okay. Whatever. So she was the all-knowing oracle of HF.

"And Alice, you're great at math and tech stuff. I'm sure you can figure out the computer part." She gave me her dazzling smile, which was only slightly less luminous than her bright blue eyes and highlighted hair. It hit me right on the flattery bone. Damn her. "So it's airtight. And of course, I'll help with the organization."

The last thing I wanted was for her to distract Jason with her boobage, but if we let her in, we could at least continue with the plan. And with her help, the plan could actually go from lunch table discussion to the big time. It was a small price to pay, wasn't it? Still, she couldn't just steamroll over the rest of us. "That's Jason's job," I pointed out.

"Really?" She laughed. "C'mon, Jason. These people must not know you very well, then."

Now she was the expert on him? *That* bugged me. And I guess Jason, too, because he was like, "What? It's my idea. I'm in charge."

"Fine. Fine. Then call me the project manager. I'll make sure we're on track. You're the boss, but I'll do the follow-through."

She still sounded like a student council speaker, but even I had to admit I was impressed. Her plan was solid. She'd clearly given this some thought. Which meant she must have been watching us for a while. Were we that obvious?

"So?" she asked. "What do you guys say?"

"Sounds like she knows what's up," Benny said. "It could work." It was the first time he'd said anything in awhile. I'd almost forgotten he was sitting with us. But it was obvious that when the silent guy actually spoke, we had our final vote.

And if we were letting her in, it was game on.

Holy crap. We were doing this thing. Actually doing it.

We all looked at each other with suspicious acknowledgment, letting the reality sink in.

"Just one question," I said. "How'd you know about us?"

"Come on now." Her eyes made a semicircle, trailing from one of us to the next. "You don't think the three of you hanging out wasn't a dead giveaway? It defies all social logic."

Darn. Maybe I'd underestimated Dakota all along. And maybe we'd have to be more careful about where we all met from now on.

"Do you think anyone else knows?" I asked.

"Would I get involved and risk my *precious reputation*?" She threw my words back at me. "No. I'm the only one who knows. Consider yourselves lucky."

Well. I wasn't about to go that far.

TEN

JASON

FREE PERIOD. IN THE LIBRARY. A BUNCH OF LIBRARY BOOKS spread out around the table in front of me. Yeah, I couldn't believe it either, but for once I was enjoying doing research.

The irony. If only my dad realized that it wasn't all his lectures but his colossal eff-up that finally inspired me to sit in the library and do research. That and Dianne. I'd looked into it and there was no case for the kitchen staff. If the school was in this kind of deep financial doo-doo, even the union couldn't help Dianne.

Thankfully there was a Plan A. Apparently there were some serious errors going on in 1983 with the Roosevelt dimes—no mint marks, two years running. Another option was the Lincoln double ear, a penny where the Lincoln head had an extra lobe due to a two-timing die strike. Pretty hot, but it was only worth $250, and that was for the very best examples. A 1950 S over D dime could fetch $500 and up. There was a Wisconsin state quarter with a misplaced leaf (it could be either high or low, according to *The Frohman's Field Guide to Coin Collecting*). Certified, perfect-condition versions went for $1,500. Not bad.

Still, we had to think bigger if we wanted to do this right. An error coin to end all error coins. Someone had to have made a mistake that brought in the megabucks.

An error coin. I had to admit, Dakota's idea was kinda brilliant. I wish I'd been smart enough to think of it myself.

Of course, now she was calling all the meetings, taking notes in code on her phone, and checking in on everyone's progress through regular texts. So far, we knew that Alice was going to go into the Mint as a tourist over the weekend to plant her hacking device in a low-visibility outlet—a utility closet or a corner somewhere. At home, she would run commands from her computer and analyze the system's weak points. Once I had the right design picked out and completed, she'd tunnel through the Mint system firewall, scan the design in, and basically trick the system into making our coins on a predetermined date. That part was well figured out, but we'd have to do some more recon to determine when and how to get into the building to pick up our stash.

And then I had to come up with a way to fence our counterfeit goods. Alice insisted that we had to slowly trickle them into the market—that selling them all at once would diminish their value. I said I would work on it, and I planned to, just as soon as I got the design squared away. I didn't have the best criminal connections—I really only knew a few weed dealers, but I figured someone would know someone who knew someone. After we fenced the coins, we'd donate the money back through an anonymous Annual Fund contribution. People made anonymous donations all the time.

Dakota had even given our mission a name: Operation EagleFly, after the Mint mascot. She said all criminal plots needed a name. Whatever. It was annoying, but I was willing to put up with Dakota in all her Dakota-ness if it meant we could really do this thing.

Still, I could tell Alice was more than a little bugged out by Dakota's presence on the team. She seemed to have some kind of beef with Dakota that I didn't get. And Benny was Benny—he never seemed to show much emotion, so his opinion on the matter was anyone's guess. He annoyed me too, sometimes. Everyone listened to him whenever he decided to open his mouth, like what he had to say was automatically going to be deep or smart. I got the feeling he thought he was better than the rest of us, like growing up in the hood made him more real or something. But we needed him to make the access IDs for us and to help us get a vehicle to make this work.

No one said we all had to be best friends. We just had to get this done.

Hands waved in front of my eyes. "You're working?"

My startle reflex had me slamming the book shut with a

bang, almost capturing a set of fingers in the process. Zack's fingers, it turned out.

"Yo. You could have amputated me there."

"Sorry," I said, all flustered. "Yeah. Just something for Design."

"Didn't you guys already have that project last week?"

He was keeping track of my assignments now? "We did," I said defensively. "But I'm doing something for extra credit."

He jumped up and jogged over to the window, then walked back with a lazy smile on his face, his dark hair flopping over his eyes.

"What was that?"

"Had to make sure the sky wasn't falling," Zack said.

"I *have* been known to do a little homework from time to time, you know." For some reason I felt myself getting worked up, even though it was defending a flat-out lie. I wasn't doing an extra credit project, and Zack knew it.

But Zack didn't know that I'd gotten that A on the coin drawing, or that it had kinda made my day. My month, really. I couldn't believe it—people liked Rankin's class because Rankin was cool, but everyone knew he never gave As. I looked at that red letter over and over, and I could almost imagine, for a minute, what it would be like to actually work hard and get good grades, like, as a regular routine. Of course, the reality was that it was never gonna happen. It was only because I needed an excuse not to visit my dad again that I'd even bothered to finish and turn in the assignment.

"Not in public, though. And not with, like, books." Zack

slumped down in a chair across from me. "Did you get the space yet?" A few days before, he'd emailed me a link to a place and asked me to drop off a deposit for $500 to reserve it, which of course I'd ignored. I still had no way of coming up with the cash, which to them was one week's allowance, but for me might as well have been $2 million. I figured if I ignored their request long enough, they'd eventually forget. That was the way things always went with Mixed Metaphors. We were dysfunctional, yeah, but it worked for us.

"Haven't had time," I said. "But we can still meet in the basement today, right?"

He drummed his fingers on the table. "Naw, dude, that's why I came. The guys said they're boycotting until you get us the new space."

"Boycotting? Come on. And by 'the guys,' you basically mean Chaddie, right?"

"Max, too. He doesn't like practicing at home. He said his mom's on his case about it. I don't know. Maybe they're right."

"Chaddie's always losing it about something. So why can't *he* figure it out?"

"Because you said you'd do it. We'll pay you back, if that's what you're worried about. It's a great space, the only one in a ten-mile radius. But if you don't get that check in by tomorrow at nine am, we'll lose it."

There was no money to front. But of course Zack, whose parents were both surgeons, wouldn't get that. He would always have someone to help him out, no matter how bad he messed up. It was easy to be laid back when you had a trust fund.

"I'm really busy. I can't do everything myself," I said, too embarrassed to admit that I had no money. "Can you do it?"

"I'm busy. Family stuff."

I didn't say anything.

"Whatever, maybe we can just get the Uh-Ums to play in our place. They'd probably be better than us anyway."

"We can't do that." There was no way in hell I was going to let the Uh-Ums take our gig. They barely knew three chords, let alone anything about real music. The only reason they were popular around school was because their singer was Allison Stadtler, and she was hot.

We needed to practice. We only had a month left until prom.

The thing was, I *was* busy. I'd promised the others I'd scope out Rankin's office tomorrow morning to try to find the temporary ID he'd used at the Mint. Benny said he could make a copy of it for us to use when we wanted to go pick up the coins. I had planned to do it before Rankin got to school, so I really didn't have time to go to the practice space.

"They're not so bad. They said I could jam with them. Chaddie, too."

"Why were they asking you? They know you're in a band," I said, narrowing my eyes. "They play *reggae*." Which was ridiculous in and of itself.

"They said they like my style. I guess they heard Chaddie complaining and they thought we were breaking up after everything, losing our space . . ."

"What?" Now he'd gone and dropped the bomb. I didn't care about Chaddie, but I couldn't lose Zack to those idiots. I felt myself scrambling. I had to stop this. "We're not breaking up. Look. The reason I haven't gotten the space is I'm broke. It wasn't just the school. My dad lost everything." I hadn't wanted to admit that to anyone, especially since all this time I'd worked so hard to seem like a real Friendian. Now Zack knew the truth, and he saw how upset I was. I almost felt like crying.

"Oh," he said.

"Hey. Don't tell anyone that, okay? It's just between you and me?"

"Right on," he said, his tone so even that he could have been responding to a Happy Mondays song or the pattern of light on the ceiling. *Right on* was his go-to motto, and he used it way too often. I wished for once he could act like something actually mattered. "Hey, you could borrow it from someone, right?"

I glanced up, hopeful. "Are you offering?"

"Me? Remember what happened the last time I lent you money? For the Florida trip? A year ago?"

Shoot. "I'm still good for that, man. Just not . . . now."

"I can ask the guys, if you want."

"Don't!" I yelped. I knew he'd have to explain it to them, and I didn't want him to do that. It occurred to me then that there was a reason they wanted me to front the money: No one trusted me with their share. "No worries. It's cool. I'll think of something. Just don't join that band, okay?"

He shrugged. "I have to consider my options, dude."

"I'll get the space." Even as I promised him, though, I knew I'd never be able to pull it off. It just wasn't doable.

We both heard some dudes laughing then, and we looked up. Arno and Dylan were in the corner mocking us, Arno playing me with a sad look on his face. "You homos having a fight?" Dylan called out when he saw us looking.

Zack shot them a middle finger. "I guess I can't be seen with you anymore—it's hurting my reputation. I'm out."

He was joking, so I forced a laugh. "See ya, sucker," I said.

I watched him go, feeling uneasy. Without Mixed Metaphors, I had nothing.

Well, maybe not nothing. There was Operation EagleFly to think about. At least with that crew, I had an important role to play. *If you have what it takes to be a leader*, I heard my dad saying.

When Zack was gone, I opened up the book again.

There it was. The answer.

The 2009 American Samoa quarter.

For one thing, the date was perfect, fitting Alice and Dakota's stipulation for a recent example, so the metals would match what the Mint uses now. Close enough that an expert wouldn't be able to tell our version from the real error coin.

The error was doable, too. A missing motto: "Samoa, God is First." They were now selling for $205,000 per. I got out my phone and did a quick calculation. That meant we'd only need two hundred and forty-three coins or so. A quick job, timewise. And that was only—I did some more figuring on my phone—six rolls of quarters, which would weigh three pounds. I could fit that shiz in my shoes if I had to.

"Ladies and gentleman, we have a winner," I murmured.

I took the page over to the photocopier and set it down on the glass top. The light of the machine flashed as it scanned the image, and I felt a wave of excitement. I'd take this home and start on the rendering right away. If it was anything like my medal drawing, it would be a piece of cake.

I carefully set the still-warm copied page inside of my history notebook and put them both in my bag. As I walked out through the library's double doors, I was almost tempted to sing out loud. For once I was going to get something done and see it through to the end. Something big. Something that really mattered.

The next morning I got to school earlier than I ever had before, which was made even harder by the fact that I had to bike the whole way. My mom had finally bitten the bullet and sold her car, so these days she was driving my Jetta.

When I got to the end of HF's winding driveway, my face was burning from the wind but I felt good—better than I'd felt since the whole thing with my dad had gone down. The school was mostly empty, and the plan was still ticking along like clockwork.

My dad was one of the few people to ever show up this early. He said it was so he could read the paper in peace and quiet, but now I had to wonder if it was so he could do more shady stuff with no one looking over his shoulder. Whatever. He was still waiting to post bail. Every time I saw my mom sitting up at the kitchen table with a mug of tea and a stack of bills, I wanted to kill him. And then there was the night I heard her yelling at him over the phone. "How am I supposed to do this on my own, Jim? How could you put us through all of this?"

Well, I was going to get the school's money back and fix his gigantic mistake.

I walked through the main halls of the Upper School and down the breezeway to the Arts Center. All of the classrooms were still dark, and the only light was the early morning sun streaming through the skylights.

Outside Rankin's classroom, I slipped my hand into my pocket and pulled out the school's master key. I'd been carrying my own copy for years, ever since I'd swiped it from my dad and made a copy at the local hardware store. It came in handy for borrowing band equipment and pulling pranks.

The master key fit so easily in the art room lock that I was almost embarrassed.

The door creaked open and the room—all of Rankin's gallery posters, our half-finished projects, and the giant Day of the Dead skeleton we'd built out of recycled soda cans last semester—was cast in shadow, all spooky-like.

The door to Rankin's office was closed, of course, but my master fit that lock too. With a slight click, the handle released.

Not wanting to turn the light on just in case, I inched tentatively forward until my eyes got used to the darkness and I could make out the shape of his desk, chair, and computer.

On the computer was a screensaver—a photo of Rankin with his wife, a pretty brunette with a pixie haircut, and his little baby daughter in a striped dress. They were all grinning at the camera looking happy and carefree. I moused the computer out of its sleep, and it opened right up to his desktop. Hadn't the guy ever heard of a security code?

He'd left his internet browser open to a job search site. So he'd been looking for a new teaching position. I felt guilt twist in my gut like a knife blade.

I did a search for Brad Garcia on his desktop finder until I came up with a bunch of emails. I thought maybe Garcia would've emailed Rankin the temp pass, but no luck. I wrote down Garcia's email address and phone number from his email signature just in case. I could always send him an email from Rankin, requesting a visitor pass—I could make up some bullshit about wanting to take a friend back for another visit. But it would have been better to come away with the real pass Rankin had around his neck the other day.

One thing was certain: The guy was a slob. I'd never really noticed the complete avalanche of papers and crap on his desk until I started rummaging through them now, feeling around for anything that felt like a plastic-covered ID card. Where would you even keep something like that? The normal rules wouldn't apply to Rankin, who clearly just threw everything onto the pile and hoped it wouldn't slide off.

Elbow deep in art projects, sketchbooks, grade reports,

and school policy books, I could only hear the sound of paper rustling all around me. Which is why I didn't notice someone entering the studio until the light turned on.

I whipped my hands away from the desk, backing away as quickly as I could. There was the sound of the studio door being shut, and then the key in the office lock. *Crap. Crap. Crap.* It was Rankin. In the flesh.

My brain raced as I quickly ran through my options. If I ducked and hid, then I would be stuck hiding until the next time he left. That could be hours. I'd made an entire school career out of BS-ing teachers; now I had to make it count. A lifetime achievement award, if you will.

I had to face it.

Act cool, I told myself as I moved to the other side of his desk, as if I had just been waiting for him. In the dark.

"Hodges?" He flipped on the light and his face looked as startled as mine felt. He was still in his ski parka and wool cap, carrying his laptop backpack. "What the hell are you doing in my office?"

Showtime. I took in a deep breath, but I was as surprised as he was when I started to cry like a two-year-old.

"What is it?" he asked, his voice softening slightly, setting down his computer bag. "What's up?"

He was in front of me then, leaning back against his desk. I was so tempted to just tell him everything. Confess and let him know how badly I felt. But I couldn't. There were other people counting on me. And no way Rankin would let us go through with what we were planning.

"I'm sorry," I sobbed. It was the fear, I told myself. That's what was making me cry like this.

Another part of me wondered, though.

"What can I do for you?" His brow was furrowed in concern. There was something about his face, so genuine and surprised, that got to me.

"It's just been hard," I said, and that at least was true.

"I know it has. I've wondered how you've been handling all of this."

"My dad's in jail. My mom's a wreck. Things here are a mess."

He nodded. "It seems bad now, but you'll get through this. If anyone can find their way out, you can. I have a lot of faith in you, Hodges. You've got a strong spirit."

He thought so? Huh. He reached out his arms to give me a fatherly bear hug. And somehow, it wasn't corny at all. It was solid and warm, and for a tiny second, I did feel better. And then I felt like a total asshole for giving him such a hard time all year. He was a good guy. Yeah, he pushed me, but it wasn't just to push me, not like my dad. It was because he seemed to really think that maybe, just maybe, I was worth the effort.

"Look, I don't like the idea of you coming into my office when I'm not here. I'm assuming you have some kind of key?"

I nodded, reluctantly.

"Hand it over."

I did, letting it drop in his palm.

"But you can talk to me any time you need to, Jason. I'm here."

"Thanks, Mr. Rankin. I appreciate it."

I wiped my face and stepped out of his office, and then out of the classroom.

I was shaking all over, still totally freaked out. Had he seen what I was doing? If so, I'd be in some major shit. I liked to think Rankin was the type of guy who would've confronted me if he had, though maybe he just didn't give a crap anymore, now that school was closing.

The sun was really pouring through the skylights now, super bright, white and pure. The bottom line was that I'd gotten out of there. I was free. I brushed off the feelings of guilt. We had a bigger goal in mind, and ultimately it would help Rankin as much as the rest of us.

It was only later that I realized that I'd handed over the last and best perk from my dad's headmaster career—my special access to the school. It was like a superhero losing his powers, and I'd done it without even thinking.

Another snag for Operation EagleFly to overcome, but I had a feeling we could handle it. With this much at stake, we had no choice.

ELEVEN

DAKOTA

"HOLD ON," ALICE SAID, RUNNING HER FINGER DOWN THE trackpad of her laptop. We were all sitting in an empty classroom on Wednesday afternoon, watching as she did her hacker thing. "I just need to . . . huh. Where did you come from, little unexpected network? We don't want you—go away."

She held up her free hand, as if to shoo the digital intruder away, and fiddled some more. Benny, Jason, and I paused, not daring to breathe. This bizarre crew, the four of us, were starting to get to know each other pretty well, so we knew enough to be silent while Alice figured this kind of stuff out. Getting together like this on a regular basis after school felt like its own kind of club—if only you could put "felony grand theft" on a college app.

I still made it to my student council meetings, but Junibel had noticed that I wasn't around as much when she wanted to go shopping or get her nails done after school like we used to.

"What have you been doing?" she asked me. "You're, like, a nonentity."

"Just studying extra hard," I said, and that was true, in a way. At one time I might have been annoyed at being called a "nonentity," but for some reason I found it kind of refreshing. Not being seen was easier than being watched all the time, you know?

And then there was Dylan. I still saw him on the weekends, and of course we were going to prom together. But he wanted to know why he couldn't drive me home from school like he used to, i.e., why wasn't he getting makeout time. Makeout time: Yet another thing on my "schedule" that I realized I didn't miss much. Honestly? He really wasn't the greatest kisser. There was no nuance, no subtlety, just mouth and tongue and heavy breathing, and then he'd always say, "You like that, baby?" like I should be grateful or something.

Alice turned around to make sure we were still watching. She seemed to enjoy the drama—maybe a little too much, as she sang out in a falsetto, "Production system . . . Production system . . . Wherefore art thou, production system?"

"Wait. That's *the* production system?" I asked. I seriously could not believe I was seeing what I was seeing, that she'd gotten in there so quickly.

Behind her glasses, her eyes were mocking. "Um, yeah.

Did you think I hacked into your locker or something? I have enough tampons, thanks."

Jason and Benny snickered.

Burn.

"Don't be ridiculous," I said nastily. "I just wasn't expecting it to happen right away."

"No time like the present, right?"

That girl had a way of making me feel so dumb. I knew when I was in the company of a hater, and when to hit back to hold my ground, but I still didn't get it. I really didn't run into this problem very often. I mean, even the girls in school who didn't like me usually kissed my ass, and then it sort of didn't matter what they really thought. But mostly everyone liked me, because even though I was popular, I wasn't actually a bitch. I wasn't a doormat or anything, but I was a decent person.

Alice was super smart, and she had already won all sorts of awards. I saw it in our AP Calculus class (that was the only one we had together—no amount of tutoring could get me into AP Physics, much to my parents' chagrin). When it came to math, she was clearly a million miles ahead of the rest of us. So there was no need to throw shade on me. Even if she was kind of prepubescent looking.

And I'd done nothing to her. Never. I'd barely even said two words to her before all this heist stuff started. And it wasn't that I was being rude—it was just practical. We didn't have much in common.

Guess she thought I was really stupid. Maybe I didn't have a genius IQ, but I did just fine, thank you very much. There were different kinds of intelligence, and you didn't need all of them to succeed in the world. So maybe I wouldn't be an astrophysicist like her. I would still do something important.

In our little meetings, she was always buddying up to Jason, which didn't help, because he wasn't exactly my biggest fan, either. It was safe to say that out of all of them, I got along best with Benny. But that's not saying much because he was mostly silent, so it didn't really count. Like getting along with the bio-room skeleton—he had that much personality.

Alice rolled her chair away from the desk. "Well, that's it. The design is in the system. MississippiState50. I just need to activate it when the time comes. I suggest we don't wait too long, though. I hid it in a little tiny corner of the database, so I don't think anyone will stumble on it, and I named the file incorrectly, so it wouldn't be discernible to the naked eye. But still, we don't want to take any chances."

"That's it then?" I asked.

"That's it." She grinned. "Done-zo."

Wow. Everyone high-fived her. She'd done it. And once again, she'd blown me away with her ability to think it all through, all the what-ifs, both technical and human.

If this thing worked, it would totally be because Alice and I rocked it, and not because of Jason's supposed leadership or whatever it was he thought he was contributing. The guy barely knew what day it was. I mean, right now, he was slumping so far down in the chair, it looked like it was going to topple over.

He was busy picking at something on his jeans—I didn't even want to know what. Pot seeds?

"And then?" I asked.

"And then we pick up our stash."

"So it's do-or-die, then. We have to go through with it, because you can't cancel the order once you put it in."

Every now and then, the reality of what we were doing hit me in a nervous surge. How on earth did we get here? Were we making the biggest mistake of our lives? I barely knew these people, and I was trusting them not to land me in juvie—or worse. That's why I had to manage things, to make sure we were doing it right. I'd given the operation a name to create some sense of collective responsibility—that was something I'd learned from the management books my dad gave me when I joined student council. You had to get *buy-in*, make people feel like *stakeholders*.

But why did I care? Why was I doing this? I guess, out of all of us, maybe I cared the most about keeping HF open? And I'd be lying if I said I didn't enjoy doing something *wrong* for once, just the teeniest, tiniest bit.

"Of course I can," she scoffed, and just like that our moment of shared awesome was gone. I was sent back to Idiotville. "Computers can move stuff around. Like email for instance. Hey, why don't you just focus on your side of things, like trying to figure out when we can pull the rest of this job off? Weren't you supposed to have that part of the plan executed by now?"

She had to go and point that out, didn't she? "I'm trying

to work around everyone's schedules," I said. I'd been thinking some time in mid-June, giving us enough time to complete
our preparations. We'd all be around over the summer—Benny
was going to be working at the garage, and I would be taking
a Mandarin immersion class. Alice was going to science camp
and Jason would be doing whatever it was that Jason did. "I
originally thought it would be a weeknight, but it seems like
most of us, including me, can't get out that late during the
week. So it has to be a weekend. Also, I want to make sure
there's no special maintenance or other events going on at the
Mint, and that will take some surveillance."

Alice rolled her eyes under their giant lenses. "That's what's
holding us up? I just hacked into a federal website, and you're
telling me we don't have our calendars synched?"

"Hey, give her a break," Benny said, his deep voice silencing
Alice's tirade. "She just said she's working on it."

I looked at him, surprised. Silent Boy in his oversize lum-
berjack shirt and hip-hop jeans was defending me? Weird. But
nice.

"Look, I'll send you guys three dates and times tonight, and
we'll pick one of them." I stared Alice down, so she'd get off my
back. "In the meantime, we'll get our surveillance operation up
and running."

Alice tugged on her earlobe. "Like I said, the sooner the
better."

Now she was just bugging me. "And like *I* said, I've got this.
What about you, Jason? Do you have the fence worked out?"

He looked startled. "I have some calls out. Should be hearing soon. I'll let you know when I do."

The meeting was over. We erased our browsing history, and Alice ran some other computer witchcraft to make sure no one could follow our tracks before we powered down her computer. By then Jason was long gone, so the three of us all made our way out to the parking lot. In the hallway, I took out my phone to text my mom to come get me.

She texted back: Sorry. In with a client. Can't get there before six. Can you do your homework or something?

"That's great," I said to the screen. The perfect end to a perfectly terrible day. "Just abandon your daughter, why don't you."

Benny, who had been walking a few paces ahead of me, turned around. "Something wrong?"

"It's nothing," I said. "My mom can't pick me up, so I'm stuck here for awhile."

"I can give you a lift," he said.

"No, no," I said. "That's okay. I wouldn't want to trouble you." The truth was I couldn't imagine riding in a car with Benny. Because that would require *conversation*, which wasn't exactly his strong suit.

He parted his lips and gave me a laser stare. "Come on, I don't have ghetto cooties or something."

Crap. Was he saying I was immature? Or, worse than that: racist? I could feel my cheeks start to burn. "Oh, it's not that—"

He laughed, breaking the tension. "Dakota. I can drive you. It's cool."

He seemed harmless enough. He had a nice face, with heavy-lidded dark eyes, extra-long eyelashes that no mascara could replicate, and milky-tea-colored skin that was surprisingly stubbly, at least for guys our age. Plus a jaw that you could chip ice on. I shrugged. "As long as it's on your way."

Before I knew it, I was sinking into the passenger seat of his immaculate black Mustang. He turned on the engine, and a Rick Ross track came blasting out, so loud I thought my eardrums might explode.

He quickly reached over to adjust the volume. "Sorry. When I'm on the highway, I can't hear that well."

"Highway? Where do you live?" I knew he wasn't from the Main Line.

"North Philly, actually."

The complete opposite direction. "Then my house is way too far out of your way."

He gave me what looked like an accidental smile, like the smile just snuck away from him and he couldn't snatch it back up. "Nah. S'cool though. You live in Bryn Mawr, right?"

Um, how did he know where I lived? Should I be creeped out by that? As if reading my mind, he said, "Sorry. I just heard you talking about it one day. Not like I followed you home or whatever."

I laughed, but it came out a little too loud. Why couldn't I act normally? At this rate, he was surely regretting offering a ride to this idiot white girl. So I reached over and turned up the stereo volume again, vowing to keep my mouth shut.

It didn't last long. "Alice was giving you a rough time today, huh?" he asked as we turned out of the school parking lot.

"That would be every day. I don't know what her problem is."

"Probably not you," he said. "It's more like what you represent."

"Which is what exactly?" I snapped. I couldn't help myself. Was he going to get on my case today, too? Benny, of all people? I mean, I had to wonder what he'd observed in his few months at a school where the rest of us had been sent since what felt like birth. What could he possibly know about me?

"The easy life," he said, pushing his palm against the steering wheel. He was a one-handed driver, as though he'd been doing this his whole life. Everyone I knew drove with their hands at the 10 and 2 o'clock spots. "You have it all together."

"If only," I blurted.

"What. That's not true?" he asked, with a sideways look and a questioning half-smile.

Well, that was what I wanted people to think. I'd worked very hard to make it seem that way, obviously, and I wasn't exactly ready to reveal my hand to this near-stranger. So I took a different tack. "She's brilliant. I have to work three times as hard as she does."

"Yeah, but it's not about school, I don't think. She's real cocky about that," he said.

"You think?" I said, and we both laughed.

"It's the other stuff. The social stuff. She's more of a loner type, like me."

Huh. Maybe he was on to something. It hadn't occurred to me that Alice would ever *want* more of a social life. She seemed perfectly content with her Math Team buddies and her *Star Trek* GIFs. "She doesn't have to be a loner. And you don't either, you know."

Now he laughed. "Yeah, I do."

"Why? You play football. You're a nice guy, and people here are cool if you give them a chance."

"Look, Dakota. I think it's pretty obvious why I don't fit in."

He didn't need to say it. I knew what he meant: Race. Class. All that fun stuff we talked about in assemblies. "Is that why you never speak in school? I mean, clearly you can talk. What you're saying right now—it's the most I've ever heard from you."

"I'm not mute, if that's what you mean. I just don't have anything to say to most of these people. And even if I did, they're not really listening. I'm just trying to graduate, go to college, get a good job. I don't have time for the other stuff."

"But if they got to know you, I'm sure . . . "

"I'm sure they'd take in a few little details to make themselves feel better. *See? He can't be too bad because he plays Xbox like me.* But it's not like they'd ever really want to get deeper than that."

I recognized the truth in what he was saying. He was so straightforward. It was refreshing.

"I get that," I said. "I feel like I talk all the time but no one knows who I really am. Go straight here."

He followed my directions. "Maybe they don't know you

because you don't let them. Maybe you keep your secrets hidden too deep."

"Maybe," I allowed, looking out the window. We were getting away from the boutiques and cafés and into the residential area of town. The houses were smaller and closer together here, but the farther away you went, the bigger and grander they got. This was one of the richest zip codes outside of Philadelphia. It made me uncomfortable—I mean, I knew Benny and I didn't have much in common, we both knew that, but looking out from the car window now, sitting next to him, it was obvious that we were from vastly different worlds. "Possibly. But isn't that why they're secrets?"

"What are you afraid of?" he asked, looking over at me. His eyes were warm and sparkly.

I felt my heart speed up. Stupid. "I don't know."

"Oh, come on. Sure you do."

"No, I—that's a good question." I pressed my lips together, thinking. "If I answer, then you have to, too."

"All right then. I'd say, maybe it's that no one would like me if they really knew me. Not having money and stuff like that, that's a good excuse. But what if it's a personality problem?"

"Bear left at the fork." I couldn't believe we were having this conversation. "I guess I could say the same thing. Like, if I wasn't the perfect person everyone expected me to be, maybe they'd realize that I'm just kind of boring."

"You're not boring," he said. "Not at all. But you're also not perfect, because nobody is. Stay on this road for awhile?"

All of a sudden, I got the strangest feeling that he knew me. Like, *actually* knew me.

We were on Evergreen Street, and for a moment I paused. I thought I would just have him drop me on the next block, at Alyson Siegel's house, which was a split-level from the 1970s with a normal-size yard. I mean, what would he think if he saw our long, pear tree–lined driveway, the stone gatehouse up front, the tennis court and pool house? My parents had named our property "Hedgerow"—there was even a little sign—and just thinking about it in the presence of Benny made me blush with shame. So freaking pretentious.

But at the same time, I realized he was sharing stuff with me, too. He wasn't ashamed of where he came from, so why should I be? It was no more his fault he was poor than it was mine that I was wealthy. We were both born into these lives by chance and, different as we were, we had that one thing in common. For the first time in a long time, I felt like I wasn't acting. I wasn't trying. I was just . . . *being*.

"No," I said. "Turn right here."

TWELVE

BENNY

IT WAS TIME TO CALL IN A FAVOR. MY BOY LT—HIS REAL name was Lautaro, but he refused to go by that—owed me bigtime for a batch of IDs I'd made for him and all of his cousins a few months ago. We needed a vehicle for Operation EagleFly, and none of us were old enough to rent one. Plus, we needed something that would be able to disappear quickly. LT was my best bet.

For some reason my mind went to Dakota, maybe because I could still smell her, like she'd left a little perfume shadow behind in the passenger seat the day before. It was cool, giving her a ride home from school. She was in my world for the first time, instead of me in hers. I'd never noticed that she was actually kind of smart and cool. The ass was that distracting.

And yeah, she was a little uptight, and a little too wrapped up in what everyone thought. But there was something else inside her, a little spark, and that made her interesting.

A drive home was a drive home, I reminded myself. A plan was a plan. We were all just working together. And I had to do my part.

I pulled off Route 1 and exited at Broad Street. Back in North Philly. At least here you didn't have to have special gate codes or drive a mile to get down a driveway. Everyone was right where you could see them. I passed by the fried seafood shops and hair supply stores, then headed east on Lehigh. Back to El Centro de Oro—the heart of gold. That's what they called our neighborhood, the area around Fifth Street. It was also the heart of the Latino community, mostly Puerto Ricans and Dominicans, but some Mexicanos like my grandparents. (Of course, other people called it the Badlands, because of the drug dealers.)

On Fifth Street, the colors of the buildings changed to light blue and yellow, the Centro music store blasted salsa, and there were big murals stretching for blocks between fake palm tree sculptures. Lately they were trying to fix up the 'hood, which was pretty cool, but it still had a ways to go. You couldn't undo decades of struggle with a few pieces of art.

I turned again onto Cambria and parked in front of LT's house. Tuesdays were his day off from work. He was older than me by about four years, and he'd dropped out of school a long time ago to start working at my uncle's shop.

We'd gotten to be friends over the past few summers, when he helped me with the Mustang and I listened to all his girl problems. He had a lot of girl problems. But LT was cool. Of all my buddies, he was the only one who didn't make fun of me for going to school in the suburbs. "Don't listen to the haters," he said to me. "You should go get yours."

He'd had a few scrapes with the law when he was my age—petty theft type things, but he'd almost gone to juvie for helping some thug with a cut-and-shut. That was before he got serious about cars and turned himself around. He was a fast learner, and when he got good enough, he left the shop to go work for a fancy joint in the suburbs, doing custom paint jobs—the big time—but he still lived at home with his parents, along with his girlfriend Carlita.

He answered the bell in a t-shirt, shorts, and flip-flops, even though it was less than fifty degrees outside. He held the door open with one hand and scratched his head lazily with the other. "Hola, Benny. What's up?"

I gave him a hug and a handshake like we always did. Then I stepped in, closing the screen door behind me, and sat down on his mom's couch. "I need your help."

"Oh no," he said. "You didn't get her pregnant, did you?"

"Who?"

"Ha ha, that's right." He pointed at me, laughing. "You don't have a girl. I forgot you're a virgin."

"You know I'm not." I was close to it, but technically I'd had sex with a girl I'd met at a party last summer. It was dark and we were drunk and she was, like, twenty and told me what to do, but it still counted. Anyway, I didn't want to get into that again. "I'm serious now, dawg."

"Okay." He smiled wide and I could see he was still making fun—he lived to annoy me.

"But you have to keep this a secret. If you want to help me you have to promise you won't tell anyone."

He bowed his head to his fingertips to show me he meant business. "You got it, man. Always."

"What if I needed a car?"

"You have a car, don't you? Did something happen to the Mustang?"

"I need a *car*," I said with emphasis.

"Oh. A *car*. Right." He sighed.

He was trying to keep his nose clean, I knew that. I wondered if this was such a good idea after all. Even telling him could get him into trouble. He was like the brother I never had, and the last thing I wanted to do was hurt him. "You know what, forget it."

He waved his hand. "No no. Tell me what you need."

"I don't want you putting yourself on the line."

"I can take care of myself, Ben. What kind of car?"

"I'm not sure yet. Something untraceable." I wasn't sure how we were getting into the Mint just yet, but I needed to know he could get me a vehicle to use when the time came. "If you can't do it, just say so."

He shrugged. "So long as it's not a Bentley."

"Naw, man. Something under the radar."

"All right. I can get you something on a temporary basis, something I can return to the shop quickly."

"A few hours is all we need," I reassured him.

"Anything else?"

"The plates?"

"I can get those too, and switch 'em up for you," he said, running a finger over his bottom teeth as he thought it over. "But Benny, this is gonna take some labor hours, hours I could be doing real jobs, plus like you said, there's the risk I'm taking here."

"I'll get you some money," I said, seeing where this was going. He was right. The IDs weren't really a fair trade. I didn't know where I'd get the cash, but I'd get it somehow. "Three thousand?"

He smiled again, his eyes gleaming but wary. "Now where are you gonna get that kind of scratch, son?" Then he held up a hand. "You know what? I don't even want to know."

"No," I said. This was a federal job, way bigger than anything he'd ever been involved with. "You don't."

If I had to, I'd hit up some of my savings, sell the Mustang. Hopefully, it wouldn't come to that, but I wouldn't leave LT hanging.

We sat for a while and watched TV until I had to go do my homework. On the way out, I clapped a hand on his shoulder. "You know how much I appreciate this."

His face was calm. "I've got your back."

128

For a short little second, I was tempted to tell him about Dakota, but then I checked myself. There was nothing to tell. It would just sound stupid.

Instead I just gave him a hug. "Later, man."

"Listen," he said as we broke apart. "I'm not going to preach to you. Just do me a favor. Whatever you're mixed up in, think about your options, okay? Maybe there's another way."

"Maybe," I said.

Then I was down the steps, back out onto the familiar streets of our neighborhood.

I could see the top of her greying hair from the doorway. My grandmom was in the kitchen like always, sitting at the round table, eating vanilla sandwich cookies as she watched the afternoon news. My granddad was out working at the hardware store. He kept saying he was too old to haul lumber, but they'd have to fire him before he'd quit.

"How was school?" she called out in Spanish. She always wanted the full rundown, and I never had much to tell.

"Good," I said. I went for the refrigerator and poured myself a glass of juice.

"You're happy there, right?"

"Sure," I said, taking a swig. "I'm happy."

I hadn't told her yet what was happening at HF. I probably should, about my scholarship and everything. But maybe we could fix it before I had to.

I looked at her little hands, which were picking up crumbs

from the tablecloth to keep it spotless. She wanted so much for me, and if I couldn't deliver it, it would break her heart. I had to save HF, because that was my only shot.

And yet, if she knew how I was planning to do it, she'd smack me with one of her magazines, so hard my teeth would rattle.

I took my glass and my backpack and started up the stairs to my room.

"Where are you going?" she asked.

"I gotta get to work," I said.

THIRTEEN

ALICE

ELEVEN P.M. ON THURSDAY. YOUR AVERAGE SCHOOL NIGHT. Except instead of working on my latest art project to salvage my grade like I was supposed to, I was sitting in my room, making mental calculations as I stared at my iCal. Dakota had finally set a date for us: June 14.

We were nine weeks away and counting. Nine weeks was a long time—almost a semester. Whole GPA points could be created and torn down in that time. Entire cliques could shatter and regroup. But it was also, relatively speaking, a blink of an eye. You'd look at the syllabus and the test that seemed so far in the future was suddenly next Monday.

So there it was. June 14. And then what? I'd prove my mastery over all things computer-related, Jason and the rest of the crew would be eternally grateful, and all of my social math theories would be cracked open. My life would finally be different.

My life was already different, though. Jason and I were friends now. Real friends. Earlier today, when he and I had walked back from lunch to our lockers, which happened a lot these days, he'd told me that his dad was meeting with lawyers, and that he was going to plead guilty, try to take a settlement.

"How do you feel about that?" I'd asked.

"I don't know. It sucks that he's going to say he's guilty. Everyone will know."

"But then he'll be home," I had pointed out.

"Only if the judge allows it. And that's good how?"

"So he can do manly things around the house? I don't know, gas up the lawnmower? Lift weights in the garage?"

"Al, this is my dad. You know him. He watches five-part history shows in his spare time. He has a bowtie for every day of the week."

Picturing Mr. Hodges doing bench presses in his bowtie, I'd smiled. "Can I ask you a question? Why do you always talk to me about this stuff? I mean, do you ever talk about it with your friends?"

"Not really," he had said. "They're guys. And Zack is . . . Zack."

When we talked like this, my imagination got away from me. We were members of the same set, finally. Maybe even *intersecting* sets.

"So he's not a guy *and* he's a bad listener?"

"Exactly." He had laughed. "No, you're the only one. I mean, you're easy to talk to."

I hadn't known what to say then, so I'd just hit him on the arm. All the time, though, I was memorizing exactly what he looked like and the precise tone of his voice so I could revisit that moment whenever I wanted.

My daydreaming was interrupted by the front door opening downstairs and then a few creaks on the floorboards.

"Dave?" I heard my mom call, practically bursting out of their bedroom with the first sound of him. "Is that you?"

He was busted.

"Hi, Hon," he said. A shake of the keys, a few more steps, and then the slap of his briefcase being set down.

"What happened? I thought you were supposed to be here at nine."

My mom's voice trailed through the house, which was old and echoey. Even from my little tucked-away bedroom that faced the creek in the back, I could hear everything they were saying.

"The meeting ran over. You know how those guys are. On and on. I'll be right up."

Did he think that it was normal to stay out until eleven on a weeknight? For a meeting? I'd never had a job and even I knew that wasn't something people did. I mean, at least come up with a believable cover story.

Once again, I felt disgust burning me like an acid bath. I hated both of them. I hated him for doing this to her, for making her look like a fool. And I hated her for being one.

I wanted so badly to get in my dad's face, to let him know I knew, that he couldn't put one over on me. I thought of what Jason had said. Maybe it *was* better to just let the truth come out. How much longer could we go on like this?

Letting my anger fuel me, I stalked downstairs, basically intercepting my dad on the landing on his way up. He had his blue argyle sweater and typical khakis on, and his bald spot was gleaming under the antique wrought-iron hall light. He was so lame. I couldn't believe this was the guy I'd once looked up to, or that I actually used to think I'd go work at his company and invent something amazing like he had. So what if he'd saved lives with his cutting-edge cancer treatments? All the inventions in the world couldn't change the fact that he was a douchebag.

"Oh, hey kiddo," he said absentmindedly, like I was an animal he was patting on the head. Did he not even notice that I was cornering him?

"Hi, Dad," I said, steeling myself.

"Someone's overdue for bedtime. You're up late for a school night," he said.

"I guess that makes two of us." Did he feel nervous? Good. I wanted him to.

"Work has been so busy this week. Just crazy."

"Has it?" I asked flatly. "Maybe you need to hire another secretary—you know, to help you keep things in order."

He gave me a weird look and then we just stared at each other for a moment. Could I do it? Could I really confront him, once and for all, like one grownup to another? I felt the words bubbling up, finding their way through my tightened jaw. *I know what you're doing.*

"Dave?" my mom called. "Are you coming up? Did you set the alarm?"

That broke the silence. And with the sound of my poor, unsuspecting mom's voice, I felt instant guilt. I was tough, perhaps, and bitter, yes, but I wasn't cruel. I just couldn't bring myself to say any more.

My dad seemed to realize he'd been saved by the human bell. "Excuse me, Al. I'm gonna turn in. You really should get some sleep too, so you can be fresh for tomorrow."

Maybe I wasn't going to call him out, but I could still let him know that things were different. For starters, he didn't get to call me that anymore. "I'd prefer you to use Alice from now on," I said curtly.

"Oh, have you outgrown your nickname? I hadn't realized." He leaned in to kiss me on the forehead and I stiffened. "Well, good night. Alice."

I let him pass. Then I wiped away all traces of him from my face, and I continued down to the kitchen, where I poured myself a glass of juice and sat with it, brooding.

I wasn't a kid anymore. If only he knew what I had planned.

FOURTEEN

JASON

OPERATION EAGLEFLY WOULDN'T BE CHEAP.

During Friday lunch, the team met backstage in the auditorium. We passed around Dakota's iPad to check out her budgeting spreadsheet detailing our expenses.

Alice had already paid for the Pwn device, and she wanted to be reimbursed a thousand bucks. There was the cost of gas and transport to and from the "venue," as Dakota called it. There was some wiring and circuitry and whatnot. Benny said he needed three thousand for the wheels, and another eight hundred for the blank RFID cards.

"Eight hundred, really?" I asked him.

He nodded. "They're not easy to come by. I gotta call

around to some people, and that means the price is whatever they feel like charging that day."

I read down the column. "And what's this 'miscellaneous?'"

"You know, incidental costs. Things we haven't accounted for," Dakota said. "For instance, we still don't know what our cover will be going into the building. We'll probably need disguises."

"For six hundred dollars? That's pricey for something that's *incidental*."

"Come on now. You can afford it," Benny said to me.

If only he knew. "I can't, actually."

"Yeah, okay," he said, with a smile.

"I'm serious," I said. "There's nothing left. We're dead broke."

Everyone was quiet in this tense kind of way, until Benny broke the silence. "I don't think you know what broke is."

That bugged me. What, we were gonna compete about who had less money now?

And also, there was something else—his tone, maybe. The fact that Benny was absolutely unafraid to say who he was and where he came from. Alice was kind of like that, too. I wished I shared their confidence. Even if they were total misfits.

"Never mind. We'll just deduct these costs from the take," Alice cut in, trying to break the tension, and I was super relieved.

The total cost, which she sussed out in her head even though Dakota had already calculated it electronically, came to $2,532 per person.

"I guess I can use my card—my parents never really check it," Dakota said. "But that means I'm playing banker. I'll manage and distribute the funds once we have them. One coin is all we need for our overhead. We'll only use a portion, and we'll put the rest toward the school fund."

"Of course you get to be the banker," Alice muttered. I kind of agreed with her on that score.

"I'm taking a risk, you know, by charging this stuff. Plus I'm the most experienced at managing things," Dakota said. "Who do you think made the presentation to United Way after last fall's pie sale?"

"So you know how to smile behind a gigantic check?" Alice said.

"There's more to it than that," Dakota said.

"I trust her," Benny said. "Come on. You guys know she'll be honest."

He was right, of course. We all trusted Dakota.

"Shake on it?" she said, holding out her hand. All four of us took turns shaking.

Then a weird silence fell over us.

"Why does this feel so serious?" Alice said, which was exactly what I was thinking.

"Because we're locked in now," Dakota said. "There's skin in the game."

I was sitting in the passenger seat on the way home from school when a text message buzzed in my pocket.

No practice today. The guys say they're done.

I had to read it a couple of times to be sure I understood. Zack didn't even have the decency to tell me in person that the band—the band *I* cofounded—was breaking up?

At least then we could have had a real conversation. Instead I was muttering "You've gotta be kidding me" at the piece of plastic in my hand.

"What?" my mom said from the driver's side. She felt guilty for stealing my car, so she'd volunteered to pick me up from school on her way home from her new job, which was working the espresso counter at the Beany Baby in Ardmore. Never mind that she had a PhD—now she was taking orders from a 20-year-old manager named Mason who had Daffy Duck tattooed over her right boob.

I waved my hand for her to be quiet as I called him. At least Zack could tell me with his own voice.

As soon as he answered, I launched into it. "I said I was working on it. Can we at least get together to talk—"

"Naw, man, it's not just the practice space. Me and Chaddie are going to play with the Uh-Ums. And Max said he wanted to spend more time at the skate park."

"But why? I can fix this. You barely gave me a chance." I hated how my voice sounded."

"I tried. I tried to tell them."

I knew instantly that he hadn't. He hadn't done crap. "So that's it, then?" I asked, vaguely aware that I sounded like Alice had the other day when I was ready to give up our plan. "I thought we were in it to win it."

"Dude, we have personnel issues. I just don't think we can work around them. Chaddie said . . . his voice trailed off."

"What did he say?"

He coughed. "He said you were unreliable, like your old man."

"*I'm* unreliable? What about you, the guy who never shows up on time?"

"I'm only quoting what he said. I would've told you at lunch but I couldn't find you, man." That was because I was working with the EagleFly team, which of course he didn't know. "You're never around anymore. What's up with you?"

"Nothing," I said. I would have to be more careful or he was going to get suspicious. Then again, it wasn't like the band would be hanging out at lunch anymore. It occurred to me then that it wasn't just the band—I was losing my social life, too. Just when everyone else at the school hated my guts. Jesus. The only people who talked to me anymore were the EagleFly team, and they *had* to.

I was afraid I might say something I'd regret later, that I might break down. "Thanks for the update," I snapped and hung up.

"Who was that?" my mom asked.

"Zack," I said, staring out the window in disbelief. I was too stunned to make something up. Besides, my mom could usually see through me when I tried to lie. "He just broke up the band."

"Oh no, honey. I'm sorry." She glanced over at me with her concerned face. "Are you okay?"

"Me? Yeah. I mean, it wasn't working out. S'cool," I said, trying to gather what was left of my pride.

"What are they going to do about prom? Isn't it only a couple of weeks away?"

"I don't know. Guess it's not my problem anymore," I said, like it was a big relief. Even though it really wasn't.

FIFTEEN

DAKOTA

I PARKED MY LEXUS ON RACE STREET, THEN CHECKED MY reflection in the rearview. Hair still set in place by my headband. Eye makeup (soft brown liner with a hint of shimmer) perfect. Skin, pasty: could use a bit of Benetint. Overall, though, not too bad.

This was one of those days where looking good was more important than feeling it. (Well, according to my mom, that was every day.) I'd spent a lot of time getting ready, choosing the right white turtleneck sweater and the right brown tights and the right camel-colored wool pencil skirt and the right just-weathered-enough boots. I wanted to look nice and responsible but not especially memorable.

So here I was. On the outside, I appeared calm, collected,

mature. Inside? I was thoroughly freaked.

This was my moment in Operation EagleFly. Since I was the project manager (clearly a vital job, no matter what anyone else in the group said), I was charged with the task of getting Garcia's ID card. Um, yeah. No big deal, except that the entire operation now depended on my success. The ID was access, and access was everything.

Of course it was Alice's idea. *Aren't you a good actress?* she'd asked. I just hoped she was referring to my performance in *Carousel* (one of the only school plays my parents let me do, back in eighth grade, before our school record started to matter). At least I hoped that was what she meant.

I patted my purse, feeling the device that Benny and Alice had built. It looked like a bunch of circuits in a clear plastic case, about the size of a smartphone. To hear them talk about it was to hear two people speaking not just in a foreign language, but doing it backward while leaving out important vowels. ARM, FPGA, LED, JTAG, USB. That last one I'd heard of, at least.

Luckily, I understood the golden rule of overachievers everywhere: Act Like You Know. Which I'd had to do then, nodding and *um-hming* as they chattered away. And I had to do it again right now, as I stuck my parking pay stub on the windshield, locked up the car, and started down the street to the Mint, like I wasn't skipping Calculus or anything. I had a cover—I'd told my parents I had a toothache and needed to go to the dentist, and they'd called in to the school office to tell them I'd be late. I'd already called the dentist and cancelled the appointment.

Still. I'd never cut anything before. Not even Peer Counseling, which was HF's most B.S. class.

As I approached the imposing building, I felt my nerves rattling. Garcia was probably right on the other side of the door, waiting for me in the lobby. In his email, he said he only had a short window of time, so I should arrive promptly at 9:15 a.m. According to my phone, it was 9:14 exactly.

The Mint policeman, whose torso was practically as broad and hulking as the Mint itself, patted me down and opened up my purse. The card reader was sewn into the lining, but that didn't matter because he wasn't doing a thorough check anyway. All he saw was a cute teenage girl. So when he asked me for my ID and I said I forgot it, he let me right in, through the metal detector and into the lobby. This way there would be no official record of me ever being in the building. (Sure, there was video footage, I had to assume we were always on camera, but Alice promised us she was going to go in and delete that. All that would be left was Garcia's word, which was why I had to be careful to seem super-innocent so he wouldn't even have a reason to think of me.) There were backup plans for the backup plans, because that was the project manager's job, thank you very much.

Garcia wasn't in yet, so I sat down on a bench outside of the gift shop to wait for him. I stared at the falling coins projected on the wall, thinking of our first visit here, how the four of us barely talked to each other back then, how a field trip was just a field trip. I'd had no idea that the stuff Garcia was showing us would lead to . . . Well, whatever I was doing now.

And here Garcia was now, walking in rushed strides toward me, his open sportcoat flapping. "I'm so sorry, Dakota. I was just on a conference call that went way too long. You know how these things are."

"Of course. No worries at all. I'm just so glad you could make time in your busy schedule to meet with me."

He clapped. "Happy to help. Would you like to come to my office?"

I nodded like it was no big deal, but getting into his office right now was *everything.* "Sure."

We walked through the gift shop and past the elevator to the EMPLOYEES ONLY door. Next to the elevator was a place marked REFUGE. Interesting.

I followed him down a long corridor, watching closely as he brandished his ID card to open a door. *There's a chip in there that communicates with a reader through a radio frequency,* Alice had explained to us in our little tutorial session the day before. *The reader checks to make sure the ID number its getting is authorized, then allows the door to open.*

All of that happened, I guess, because we were through. Garcia slipped the card into his back pocket.

Right where I wanted it.

I was, of course, also doing some simultaneous reconnaissance for the crew. My memorizing skills, honed after years of studying AP textbooks I didn't really understand, were going to come in handy today. I had to memorize the floor plan and draw up a map so we could figure out how to get in on June 14th. That was the part that really worried me. How were we going to beat the police security? I'd already seen them walking by twice now, noting the time on my watch. Maybe the guards didn't care about the ID, but inside, this place was worse than a prison.

Hallway, hallway. Door 1, Door 2. Big emergency exit sign here, to my right, a bunch of cubicles. Hallway, hallway, hallway. I tried to mentally talk it through as we went because I had a better memory for words than pictures.

"What's down on the lower level?" I asked.

"That's where all the utilities are, plus storage and stuff. Spooky down there. Did you have trouble finding the place?" Garcia asked.

"No, not at all. It wasn't that long ago that we visited."

"That's right. I forgot you were here. I just remember that one kid, the troublemaker who kept interrupting."

So he remembered Jason. That was probably a bad thing.

"Every village needs an idiot, I guess," he said.

Then again, maybe not—not if Garcia thought he was stupid. Poor Jason, but hey, that might prove useful. Because a village idiot couldn't be the mastermind of a plan like this, could he?

I guess we were all about to find out.

Finally we reached Garcia's office, which had a full wall of glass windows overlooking the plant floor where the machines were moving along, pumping out coins. "Wow," I said. "What a view."

He grinned. "I know. I get to stare out at it every day."

He hung up his jacket on a hook on the back of the door and pointed for me to have a seat in a chair across from his desk, my back to the windows. I looked around for ceiling-mounted cameras as Benny had instructed me. There were none that I could see, but I did see motion detectors in all of the corners.

Garcia tented his fingers together. "Now, how can I help you?"

I gave him my winningest smile. "Well, I was so inspired by the Mint visit and the project we did for Mr. Rankin's class that I decided to do some more research about coin development. Actually?" and here I leaned in, like I was telling him a secret. "There's an American History essay contest, sponsored by the National Association of Liberal Arts Scholars? It's a sure ticket to college acceptance, and they give you two thousand dollars toward tuition."

There was no such thing as NALAS. There was no contest, of course. But I doubted Garcia would be doing any fact-checking, because who would lie about something like that?

He tapped his desk with two official fingers. "That sounds great. It's so good you Haverford Friends kids are exposed to opportunities like that. My sons' teachers barely know their names."

"We *are* lucky," I agreed. The truth was, I loved HF. I loved the old breezeways connecting the lower and middle schools, the little tags identifying every tree on the property, the fact that we had a school song we sang at every event. I couldn't stand the thought of our beautiful campus being shut down, the lawns allowed to grow weedy. We had to pull this off so we could save the school and so I didn't have to go to Bertrand Academy. Also, this heist stuff was kind of fun.

"So what do you need from me?"

"What I'm looking for is some background about the very first mint," I said. "You know, the one the Founding Fathers built. I think it would be interesting to write about how the idea of manufacturing money has evolved over time." I started to lose myself in the rehearsed speech—it was almost like listening to someone else talk.

"Oh, I've got plenty of that stuff from the bicentennial celebration. I just need to dig it out because that was awhile back now. What would you need?"

"Any documentation of the engineering, really. Copies of letters, plans . . . that kind of thing."

"Hang on." He bent down from his seat to a file cabinet.

As Garcia dug around, I came around to his side of the desk, pretending to admire the family photos on the shelf behind him.

"You have two sons?" This was so easy, to assume this other personality. Maybe because it wasn't really all that different from the person I pretended to be at school. This Dakota, too, was confident and smart, put together like a well-fitting pair of jeans.

"Yeah," he said, his voice muffled. "Nate's twelve and Sam's fifteen, and there's a third on the way in May. Hmm . . . I think it's here . . . the last time I looked . . ."

My heart was pounding wildly. But there it was, no mistaking it—the plastic corner of the card peeking out of his back pocket. With a shaky hand I reached down and made a grab for it.

As I did, he suddenly straightened up and turned around. And my guilty hand shot behind my back, the card slipping onto the floor with a *fffffttttt* sound, soft but distinct.

OhmyGODohmyGOD. He felt it. He's so on to me!

When he turned in my direction, Garcia's face was furrowed. My mind raced. Thirty seconds and a call to security, and I'd be escorted right out of here. My parents would get a call, and then the school. Or maybe the other way around. I'd be in lockdown by 5 p.m., wearing a hideous orange jumpsuit and clunky black boots.

You know how I had time for all of these thoughts? Because those few seconds seemed to stretch on for an eternity, bending and shifting and moving away from time itself like the molten chunks of metal on the assembly line.

Until Garcia's face relaxed again.

"Actually, I think it might be in my other files," he announced.

Huh?

I could barely believe it as he walked across the room to another set of file cabinets under the windows.

So he hadn't felt me nabbing that card after all?

Slowly, gingerly, feeling all of the blood in my body rushing to my head, I knelt down, pretending to wipe a scuff off my boot, and slipped the card into my pocket.

"I'm so sorry," I said. "But is there a bathroom in here I can use while you do that?" Even if I hadn't needed a place to upload the card info, I definitely needed a moment to collect myself.

"Sure. Right down the hall, third door to your left." He pointed the way, and I followed his finger out the door.

Shut inside the bathroom stall, I yanked the device out of my purse, ripping the stitching in one fell swoop. Usually I was locked in a stall for one reason only. But it occurred to me, as I laid out three layers of toilet paper so I could sit on the seat, that I hadn't thrown up in the past couple of days. Not like I was trying not to or anything—we'd just been so busy planning for this thing that I hadn't really *needed* to.

And now I had bigger fish to fry. All I had to do, Benny said, was hold the card up to the antenna and look for the green light. When the green light flashed, the info would be transferred onto the device. For all their explanations, I had no idea how this thing really worked. It was magic as far as I was concerned. But that didn't matter.

With the reader in one hand and Garcia's card in the other, I sat waiting for the green light.

Nothing. Nothing. Nothing.

Where was the light? Maybe I was doing it wrong. I tried again, and waited. Maybe the light was broken? My breath was getting raspy, echoing in the empty tile-covered chamber. *Come on, thingie!*

Talk about opportunity: If I missed this chance, there wouldn't be another one.

"Right, Darryl," I heard a woman's voice say.

Then the restroom door opened and a pair of heels clicked across the floor.

That was it. Time was up. I couldn't waste another minute in here, or Garcia would get suspicious. When I heard the other stall door close, I looked down just in time to catch the green light finally blinking.

Sheesh.

I hurried out of the restroom and back to Garcia's office.

"I've got what you need," he said. "But I'm going to have make copies, of course. I can't go handing you our original documents, can I?"

"No," I said, my voice trembling ever so slightly, as I thought of what was in my pocket. "Of course not."

When he was gone I looked around the room.

Quickly, *quickly.*

I needed a good place to put his card. I couldn't just leave it on the floor, because that would be too suspicious, but where else would he have put it? On his desk? Too obvious.

Then I remembered his sports jacket behind the door. It wasn't great, but it was going to have to do. I pulled it off the hook and tucked the card in the right pocket. Hopefully he wouldn't notice that it wasn't where he'd left it; hopefully he'd chalk it up to forgetfulness.

I looked out the window and saw a security guard doing his rounds on the plant floor. Again, I noted the time on the clock.

When Garcia came back, he handed me the stack of papers

I wouldn't need. Then he walked me down to the gift shop and we stopped in front of a black-paneled door in between the displays.

"What's in there?" I asked Garcia. "Stockroom?"

"That's the security station," he said. *Bingo.*

He shook my hand and offered me a keychain in the shape of the original quarter. "A souvenir," he said, "for your hard work."

I smiled tightly and thanked him. I felt bad for tricking Garcia. He was a super-nice guy, and it wasn't his fault that he was our man on the inside. But I was here on a mission. My crew was counting on me. I had to talk to Alice and make sure, in case we ever got caught, that none of this could be traced back to him.

Back in the safety of my car, my whole body buzzed like I'd had five espressos and a bag of jellybeans—which I'd done once, on a particularly stressful night before a pre-calc exam, and can I tell you? It was pretty sickening. Only now I was completely giddy. I couldn't believe what I'd just pulled off—or how much I enjoyed it.

I dialed Benny. As the phone rang once, twice, three times, I realized that I was clutching it like it was the thing I'd stolen. I couldn't wait for him to answer.

When he finally did, his voice was like a reassuring hug. "Yo."

"I got it, I think."

"Cool," he said, through what sounded like a smile. I could

picture his eyes crinkling up at the edges. "Meet you tonight?"

We had this part worked out, too. I needed to give him the info, but we had to do it in private, with no witnesses. Besides the fact that there was the whole criminal thing going on, I knew my parents wouldn't exactly be thrilled about this guy from North Philly sneaking around their property. They were so judgmental and narrow-minded—they didn't even know him.

"On my back patio. Behind the pool house," I said, aware, suddenly, that it sounded like a date. Worse than that—*oh God*—it sounded like a booty call. What if Dylan ever found out? It could travel through the jock grapevine, and how could I explain what Benny was doing at my house without giving away the truth? And of course, the truth sounded even sketchier. Who would believe it?

"Got it."

And as we hung up, I also realized, weirdly enough, that the booty call idea didn't bother me as much as it probably could have. I'd been noticing that Benny was kind of cute, actually. Also, there was something about him that made me feel calm inside. And sadly, I couldn't say that about a single other person on planet earth.

I drove back to school, just in time for lunch. Then I spent a little more time fixing my makeup again in the car. I could bring it down a few notches now that I was back in school, so I unpinned my hair. My hands were still shaking, only now it was from exhilaration more than anything else.

What had I just done? Stealing property, identity theft, fraud—things I should be ashamed of. And yet I felt a dangerous tickling sensation, like the lightest hand running through my hair. It was *fun*.

As I crossed the parking lot, I was texting Alice and Jason to let them know I'd succeeded (code word: "yo") so I totally didn't see Rankin walking in the other direction, carrying a big load of boxes, and I guess he couldn't see me over the boxes because we bumped hips. I was so startled, I dropped my phone.

"You all right there, Dakota?"

I startled, almost shouting. "What? I'm fine!"

Was he looking at me? Did he know? How could he know? That would be ridiculous. I was just being paranoid. He was just being Rankin.

He frowned. "You seem a little off-balance."

"No," I said. "Just a little on edge."

SIXTEEN

BENNY

IT WAS SO DARK OUT I COULD BARELY SEE. DAKOTA'S POOL house was closed. At least I thought it was the pool house from how she'd described it to me—it looked more like a house-house, like it could sleep ten people. But it was next to the pool, which was next to the tennis courts, which was next to some other building that looked like a garage. Whatever. The place was sick.

Anyway, I'd done what she'd told me—parked on the side of the road about half a mile away, then hiked down her long drive-way. Any minute I kept waiting for the cops to show up, or at least some hired security dude, ready to scare me off the property. I belonged here about as much as I belonged at HF: not at all.

Somehow, with all this EagleFly business, I'd been sucked

into HF's crazy drama whether I wanted to be or not. There was that whole scene during third period when Dakota's boyfriend was stuffing an albino rat into Jason's locker. There were a few of us around, and he wanted us to watch as he tried to get it through the slats. It was a dick move but I didn't say anything. I didn't want to call attention to myself, so I just kept sitting there on the floor, pretending to read like I always did during free periods.

Then, out of nowhere, who should show up but Alice. She went right up to Dylan and kicked him in the ankle. Then she took the rat and tucked it into her shirt. He was all, "What the hell?" And she was like, "Rats take care of their injured peers, unlike you. And they don't sweat, definitely unlike you. Ergo, this rat is more evolved than you. In fact, I'm taking him home." She even gave it a little kiss on the nose, for real. Then she walked on down the hallway like it was nothing.

That girl had *cojones* the size of front-loader tires. She just didn't give a fuck. Dylan and his friends were just standing there all weirded out after she left. And then he was like, "That girl's an elf. Yo, we should glue the lock on." What did Dakota see in that guy?

"*Psst*," Dakota called in a whisper, her silhouette bobbing in front of me. "Where are you?"

"Over here," I said.

Hands reached out and touched my chest, and then we almost bumped foreheads. "Hey!"

"Sorry," she said, giggling. "I can't see!"

I tried to make my voice sound normal, even though she'd just touched me. "Don't you guys put the lights on?"

"Not this time of year. No one comes out here. That's why I thought it would be a good place to meet. Sorry I was late. I couldn't get away from my dad—he always wants a progress report on school."

"Right," I said. "So do you have the thing?"

"You're all business, aren't you?"

Sounded like she was offended. But it was cold, and super dark, and I needed to get home to do some stuff. Also, Dylan would try to kill me if he knew I was here. Not that I couldn't take that kid, but the last thing I needed was some brawl on the quad with all the preppies watching.

"I thought that's what we were here for."

I'd been extra careful to keep the lines in place, keep my distance from all of them, but with Dakota it was tough. She didn't seem to notice.

The whole thing was nuts. I'd thought about bailing, a few times, because I had as much to lose as anyone else, if not more. There were plenty of people who'd be happy to see a kid from North Philly in jail.

"Well, we can be human, can't we?"

I remembered our conversation the day I drove her home from school. "Sure," I said.

"Anyway. Here's the reader. The info should be on there."

"Great," I said, taking it from her and zipping it into my backpack. "I'll make us a copy. It was no joke getting those blanks. I had to go through a couple of different channels to get the empty roll. I guess they protect them like that to keep them away from people like us."

"Criminals, you mean?" she said and I could finally make out her face in the darkness. She was smiling, her eyes shining.

"Ha ha. Yeah."

"Why are you shaking your head?"

"Because you could never be a criminal."

"Sure I could. I stole that card today, didn't I?"

"But that was an extreme situation. Believe me, you're no criminal." I was thinking of the guys I knew in my neighborhood, the ones who got busted over and over, who couldn't stay on the street without the cops breathing down their necks, and they were some rough-looking dudes. "You're too soft . . . and pretty."

There was a pause then. Now I'd gone and done it. Embarrassed both of us. Why did I have to say she was pretty? Why did I have to cross that line? But you couldn't take something like that back.

She looked at me. "Thanks," she said softly. "I . . . umm—"

And just then, we heard a door opening, and someone calling out her name. Her pops, probably.

"Dakota? Are you out here?"

I don't know why, just an instinct, but I immediately hit the deck, and my chest slapped against the cold stone of the patio.

She stifled a gasp, looking down at me sprawled at her feet. "Yeah, Dad!"

"What are you doing out here in the middle of the night?"

"Just . . . meditating," she answered.

"Well, you'll catch a cold. You can meditate inside."

"Okay, I'm coming." And then to me, giggling a little, "You can get up. Are you okay? I thought you fell!"

"I'm a'right," I said.

"Are you sure?"

Just then, she pulled me closer. At first I thought it was some kind of accident, like before when she was grabbing me in the dark. But it couldn't have been an accident, her lips lined up perfectly with mine as she leaned in. The slightest pressure. Soft. Her hair was loose, brushing against my neck.

My arms were around her, pulling her even closer. It's not like I thought about it.

I couldn't think of anything. My mind went blank. It was dark, but my eyes were closed anyway, and in all that blackness, it felt like there was nothing else around us.

Before I knew what we were doing, our tongues got involved, too. Her mouth had a fresh taste, like parsley, and my hand went right to her jawline, tracing it with my fingers. Her skin, it was so smooth and warm.

I couldn't believe what was happening. It was the longest shortest moment of my life. For real.

"Dakota!"

She pulled away and met my lips again with hers, like she was almost sealing the kiss. I couldn't have spoken a single word if I tried. I was that shocked.

And before we could say anything else, she was hurrying back up the hill. "You'd better go," she hissed. "See you tomorrow!"

Yeah, we'd see each other. That was no news flash. We went to the same damn school. It just felt weird, her leaving like that, in the middle of everything. She'd kissed me!

But maybe I should've been grateful, because if she'd stayed, I would have had to say something more, and what the hell would I say? The whole thing was bananas. Even so, I had to smile a little as I walked to my car. Sometimes you had to let a moment be a moment. Sometimes being a fool felt really, really good.

SEVENTEEN

ALICE

"HERE'S A QUESTION. IF YOU WERE GONNA BREAK A VIDEO feed, how would you do it?" I asked Greg. We were sitting at Grinders Café, which was walking distance from his house. We sometimes went there to do our homework, especially if his little twin brothers were home, because they were always getting in our business.

"You mean gaining access to a camera remotely?"

"Right."

He frowned, his already thin lips stretching into a wider line, as he leaned back in his creaky wooden chair. There'd been times, many times, that I wished I could have found him attractive, because maybe our friendship could have been nudged over the hookup cliff, but I didn't. I mean, he had decent if a little pasty skin, a good-size nose, short dark hair he kept clipped in a buzz cut, and these very round brown eyes that sprung out like question marks. None of the features were bad, but something about the way it was all put together looked like they'd been cut and pasted from different sources.

Not that I was some hottie. But still. As far as social math was concerned, I was already a null set—if I was going to be alone anyway, I could afford to be picky.

"Well, I guess I'd check to see if there was a default password from the manufacturer. If not, I'd use a brute force attack," he answered finally. "Are you spying on your parents again? What kind of system do they have?"

"It's pretty sophisticated," I said, not answering his question.

"Yeah, I'd go with brute force then." He went back to his iPad, where he was reviewing his European History notes for a test.

"Hmm." I stirred my cocoa, watching the marshmallows foam and spin as I thought. "And what if I wanted to substitute another feed?"

Now he put down his iPad and looked at me. "That's out of my league. You'd need some kind of existing footage. Why would you need to swap out the feed? Is this for the science fair? I thought you were going to construct the hexadecimal converter for binary coded output."

"I am," I said. "I was just wondering."

"I don't know. You'd have to talk to an expert. Have you gone on the message boards?"

"A couple." I could see he was still more suspicious than I wanted him to be. "Never mind. It was a hypothetical. Brain detour."

"Well, I'm stuck on history. I've reread this chapter five hundred times but I still don't get how the Balkan tensions led to World War One . . ."

We usually tried to work together on anything non-math related, since we both pretty much only thought in ones and zeroes, but I guess I'd tuned him out, still thinking about security cameras. He rapped the table with his knuckles. "Hello? Are you even listening to me?"

"I'm totally listening," I said.

"You're not. I love how I can help you with your thought emergencies, but when I need help, you're in la la land. I don't know what's up with you lately."

"Nothing's up. I'm just busy."

"Busy with your new buddies, right? Dakota and the rest of them."

Wow, so even Greg had noticed? I was surprised. He and I had been friends forever, but he didn't get into the touchy-feely stuff. Now I had to come up with an explanation quick. "That's because we're working on a Design project."

"Whatever. I know what you're up to."

I looked up, alarmed, and, forgetting what I was doing, felt the hot chocolate spill over and scald my hand. *He knows?*

"You're trying to climb the social ladder."

I actually laughed with relief. "Yeah. Right."

Greg shook his head. "It's not funny. Don't you see that it's never going to work, Alice? You can try all you want to impress them, but they probably just want to copy your homework. They're using you."

"They're not 'using' me." I put the word "using" in air quotes to show how stupid I thought the idea was. "We're cool."

He snorted. "Very cool. And what the hell was that thing I heard about with the rat in Jason's locker? You *kicked* Dylan Sanders?"

"Dylan was being a jerk. I didn't want him to kill that poor rat."

"So you took it on yourself to save the day?"

"What? What's your problem?"

"My problem is that it's stupid, Alice." He got in my face then, his question-mark eyes all bugged out. "If you're so cool with Dakota, how come she didn't invite you to her friend's party this weekend?"

Party? What party? I hadn't heard about any party. I couldn't let Greg see my surprise, though.

"I was invited," I lied, mostly just to prove him wrong. "I just didn't want to go. We have plans, remember?"

The truth was, I'd heard nothing about the party. But even if I had, would I have gone? Probably not. Definitely not.

"Well, thanks for not *completely* dissing me." His tone was sarcastic.

"I'm not dissing you at all. I'm allowed to talk to other people. I don't see what the big deal is." That was disingenuous. I did know what the big deal was. I'd been aware of it since the first day Jason sat with me in Design.

"I'm looking out for you, Alice. That's what friends do. I've known you since third grade, and I know you're not like them."

"What's that supposed to mean?"

"Dakota Cunningham? Football meatheads? Jason Hodges? What, are you gonna start dating him now or something? Be real. You're not his type, and even if you were, it would be completely beneath you to go out with such a . . . burnout." His downturned mouth displayed his utter revulsion.

"He's smarter than he looks," I said, feeling my face warm with the mention of him. "And nicer, too. He's a good guy." I was annoyed, too, that Greg was so quick to judge, and, worst of all, that he'd homed in on my exact intention, even if I didn't want to admit it to myself. "You don't know him."

"I don't. You're right. Just remember who your real friends are when the project ends, okay? We're the ones with the goblets and daggers."

This was ridiculous. I didn't need to be lectured. "Yeah, okay," I said, standing up and stuffing my books into my bag. I'd remember, all right.

EIGHTEEN

JASON

SATURDAY. IT HAD TO BE A SATURDAY. WHICH SUCKED, BUT that was the only day we could do this. When I got to the Wawa parking lot, Alice and Dakota were already there, which wasn't a surprise since I was traveling on foot. It was strange to see them from a distance, in their weekend clothes and whatnot. Dakota looked pretty much the same, in a black North Face fleece and tight jeans, and Alice had her light brown hair pulled back in a ponytail. It took me a few moments to notice she wasn't wearing her little beanie. She actually looked cute, and I could see the shape of her body for once, which was petite but not as boyish as I'd thought. When she turned around, she flashed me a big smile.

"Hey."

"Hey," I said. "You guys ready?"

"I can drive," she said, and she seemed a little nervous, for her. Maybe it was weird for all of us to be hanging out like this on a weekend.

She had a silver Mini, which was the perfect vehicle for a small person like her. From my seat on the passenger side, I was surprised to notice a little tube of lip gloss in the cup holder between us. Alice Drake used lip gloss?

Our goal: To go downtown and stake out the Mint. We'd already figured out that our optimal time for coin retrieval had to be a weekend, sometime in the early evening, after the facility shut down for the day—not as many staff people around, less traffic and fewer witnesses outside the building.

Now we just needed to, you know, plan an entry and escape route.

Well, the extra bonus was that this little trip allowed me to dodge yet another jail visit. As far as my mom knew—at least from what I'd told her over our oatmeal that morning—I was going to Zack's house to hang out. Never mind that Zack and I weren't really talking. Either my mom truly bought the excuse or she was tired of fighting with me, because she didn't say a word when she left.

There was hardly any traffic on a Saturday afternoon, and we made it into the city in fifteen minutes. We exited I-676 at Fifth Street and met Benny at the Starbucks at Third and Arch. He was standing outside. Alice honked and pulled up to the curb.

He nodded at us as he opened the back door. "S'up, guys."

"Hey," Dakota said.

He just stood there, smiling at her.

"Get in," I said.

"Is it too tight there?" Alice asked. "This car was designed for smalls like me."

"A little bit." He tried to fit his legs in, awkwardly bending in half so his knees were practically up to his chin.

I knew I should offer to switch with him, let him have the front, but doing that would point out that I was at least five inches shorter than the guy, and I didn't need to remind anyone of that, especially with girls in the car. "It'll be a quick ride," I said.

From there, we circled around the block, going back up Arch to the Mint building's south side. The façade of the building was all rectangles of concrete with a few skimpy windows at least thirty feet up from the sidewalk. It really was like a fortified castle. Once we were inside, we could use our counterfeit IDs, but how the hell were we gonna get in there in the first place? I tried not to show my doubts, though.

Along Fifth Street, there was the visitor entrance with its giant lettered sign, revolving door, and security post. Next to it was a staff entrance. None of those were options—they would obviously be closed after-hours.

"We could try to go in early, then hide somewhere and wait," Alice said.

I'd already thought of that. "The problem is where?"

"A stairwell?" Benny suggested. "A closet?"

"No. They do entire building sweeps every hour, starting at ten minutes past the hour, then at twenty past on the next hour, then forty-five, and back to ten, " Dakota said. "Anyone who's inside has to look like they belong there."

"Turn here," I instructed Alice, so we could check out the north side. "There's a door—or something."

I was pointing to a pink painted metallic panel. It wasn't part of the wall, that was for sure, and there was a concrete barrier in front of it, suggesting that it was a sensitive security point.

Alice slowed down so we could have a look. "There's no handle," she said. "Someone has to open it from the inside."

She accelerated slightly and turned right on Sixth. Here, a few cars were parked on the sidewalk, and there was a guard booth with an arm gate. "Bingo," she said.

As we closed in, we saw that on the other side of the gate was a driveway that went into some sort of underground garage.

"Yeah, that's gotta be it." Benny leaned forward from the back seat, grabbing the back of Al's headrest. "That's our way in."

"Can we park somewhere?" I asked.

Alice turned down a tiny street that probably could have held a horse and buggy back in the day, but was too big for more than a compact car. I silently thanked Alice's parents for buying her a Mini.

"Are you sure this is okay?" Dakota asked when we stopped. "What if a cop comes?"

"We'll say we're lost and reconfiguring our GPS," Alice said, ready as usual with the right answer.

We sat there for two hours, taking turns in fifteen-minute shifts to watch the Mint behind us through the binoculars I'd brought. But there was nothing to see. Nobody came and went. Nobody.

My legs were cramped up from sitting, and I was getting ready to give up, head for home. "Maybe Saturday isn't a good day to get in. Maybe we need to come back on a weekday," I said.

I still had my doubts about whether we could actually pull this whole thing off. It just seemed so daunting, and I didn't know if we could really do it. I'd wondered a few times whether we should just quit while we were ahead.

"Isn't the point of a stakeout that we wait until we actually see something?" Benny asked.

"Yeah, but how long? Are we gonna stay overnight?" I asked.

"I'm actually supposed to get my hair cut," Dakota admitted. "And then there's a party . . ."

Alice slapped a palm on the steering wheel. "So pencil us in between your dye job and an eyebrow wax. You guys realize that our time is running out, right?"

"We have a couple of months, Alice. No one said this was going to be an all-day thing," Dakota said. "I do have a life, you know."

I felt bad then, seeing Alice's face. Because Dakota was basically saying that she didn't. "You don't need to remind us, Cunningham," I said.

But if Alice was upset, she seemed to recover quickly. "Okay, fine, I'm not going to hold you all hostage if you'd rather be doing Jell-O shots. Let's just go."

She put the car in reverse and I turned around to help guide her, to make sure she wasn't going up on the narrow curbs.

And that's when I saw it. A van heading for the gate "Wait wait wait!" I said, my heart galloping. "Stop!"

Alice hit the brakes and the others turned around. There it was, a white service van with blue lettering. HANSEN HVAC PERFORMANCE.

We watched as it approached the security booth. The driver inched down his window and said something to the guard. Then the arm lifted and a gigantic metal garage door rolled up and the van disappeared underneath the building.

"He's in. What time is it?" Benny asked.

"Four forty-five," Dakota said.

"There you go," Alice said, nodding. "I'll get a hold of the security log, and if they come back on a regular basis, that's our ticket."

Fist bumps were exchanged. This shit was *on*.

On the way home, Alice insisted on dropping me off. "Are you sure?" I asked. "I can walk."

"It's no problem." Then she paused awkwardly. "Unless you're trying to commune with suburbia or something."

"No, no. This is great. Thanks." I looked at her car stereo and wondered what kind of music she listened to. Probably something interesting and obscure, something from another country and time. Or maybe she was into math rock. She was into math everything else. Maybe sometime I would make a playlist for her. Of course, that was usually something I only did for girlfriends, but she was cool.

There was no more business to discuss—we'd already agreed to meet up tomorrow to go over some technical details. "So what are you up to tonight?" she asked. "Are you going to that rager?"

"What rager?" I asked.

"You know, Junibel's party, a.k.a. the reason for Dakota's salon appointment."

I wasn't. Back in the day I might have gotten an invite—I was peripherally friendly with those people, or maybe it was convenient to include me when they wanted a good weed source. These days, though, no one asked me to do anything. They pretty much just defaced my belongings and called me homophobic names.

I idly wondered if Zack would be invited. Probably. I wished I could be like Alice, above it all.

I shook my head. "I'm just gonna hang out. You?"

"Me too. I'm meeting up with some friends. Not that I was invited."

"Yeah," I said, realizing that she had a better social life than I did. Why did I always assume she didn't? Because of that stupid hat? And then, for some reason, I just let it slip, "My friends aren't really talking to me these days."

"Oh," she exclaimed, a little too loudly. "What happened?"

Ugh. Why did I have to do that? Now I looked like a loser. "The band broke up, and all the stuff with my dad . . . It's okay. I mean, it's not a big deal."

She seemed to get that I didn't want it to be a drama, because she stepped it back. "They're all lemmings—you know that, right? If it wasn't you, it would be someone else. I've been there. You just have to let it blow over."

She hadn't even brought it up, so I knew I had to. "I heard what you did the other day, with the rat. Thanks for that."

"It wasn't a big deal. I enjoy the little creatures. I named him Chip." Now she looked embarrassed. "Hey, you're welcome to come out with me if you want. We're just going to Greg's house."

It was sweet of her, and for a moment I considered it. Maybe it would even be fun. But it would be really lame to tag along with her, just to have something to do. And if I was still hanging out with Zack and those guys, would I have even considered it? Probably not. That would make me a hypocrite.

"No worries," I said. "I've got to take care of some stuff."

"Well, you have my number if you change your mind. Otherwise see you tomorrow?" she said.

"Right," I said. "Tomorrow."

She pulled away from the apartment complex. I stood there watching the Mini disappear down the street. It was funny how normal it all felt, hanging out with Alice, and how for a moment I wished she wasn't leaving yet.

NINETEEN

DAKOTA

DYLAN WAS RUNNING LATE. I PACED AROUND MY LIVING room, waiting for him to show up. Then, because I didn't want him to see me pacing or know that his lateness annoyed me, I went back up to my room.

What a strange day. I felt so awkward being with Benny and the rest of them, but especially Benny after I'd gone and done that stupid thing the other night. I mean, why did I have to kiss him? It was this crazy out-of-body experience, like something my lips did without prior authorization from my brain. Because if I'd thought about it all? It never would have happened. Just remembering it now made my cheeks hot with embarrassment.

Must. Not. Think about that.

I tried on some hoop earrings, then changed them up for

diamond studs. I brushed my hair and rearranged my bangs flat, then swept to the side.

Finally, Frieda called up to tell me that Dylan was at the door.

Let him wait for me, I thought. *Let him wonder*. I brushed my hair a few more times, reapplied my powder, and then slowly made my way down the stairs.

"There you are," he said with his crooked smile.

For the tiniest little second, I felt grateful for him, that he was so cute and so put together. Grateful for what a good couple we made in photos. I mean, there wasn't anyone else at HF I would have wanted to call my boyfriend. I stood up on my toes to kiss him.

"Wow," he said. "Someone's horned up."

"It's just a kiss!" Why did he have to make everything about sex? Then I thought of Benny again. Damn it.

"Well, I like it. I like it. I haven't seen enough of you lately, babe. I've missed you."

I told Frieda I'd be back by my curfew, which was midnight. My parents were out at some gala, so I'd probably be home before them.

"Don't drink and drive," she said, because she was like another parent to me.

"We won't," Dylan said, because I'd probably drive us home.

And with that we were off in his Beamer.

Junibel lived in Wayne, practically the other end of the Main Line. By the time we got there, the party was super packed—there was already a line for the keg snaking out of her garage.

I found Junibel in her living room with Dylan's friend's Justin, her sometimes-hookup. They were locked together in some kind of swaying hug.

"Thank God," she said as we came in. "The party needs you."

It actually looked like everyone was doing fine without us—Junibel especially, who was hanging on to Justin by the back pockets of his jeans.

"Yo, we *are* the party," Dylan said. "So where's the good stuff?"

She giggled as she broke away from Justin. "Hello to you, too. Look in my dad's study," she said. "He's got some whiskey in there."

"Let's go, bro," Dylan said to Justin.

"But you just got here," Junibel said.

"We've gotta catch up," Dylan said, and he and Justin went off in the direction she'd indicated.

"Sorry, that was rude," I said in their absence. I was used to making excuses for Dylan. The truth was, he could do whatever he wanted and there'd always be a girl who'd go out with him. Might as well be me, right? "So things are good with Justin?"

"For the moment." She looked anxious. "I'm so glad you're here. I've missed you."

I smiled. "What do you mean? I see you every day."

"Not really. You're never around. Are you okay? I mean, are you mad at me?"

"Of course not." I felt bad so I gave her a hug. "I've just been busy."

Sometimes I wondered if we'd be friends if we hadn't known each other since we were ten, or if we went to a bigger school, where there were more options. Because we didn't have all that much in common anymore. I tried not to think about it too much, though. Who else would I even hang out with?

"Dude. Guess who's here?" Justin said as he and Dylan came back into the room, carrying a squat bottle of bourbon.

"Who?" Junibel asked, rolling her eyes. "Those Berwyn Prep kids again? I told them not to come back."

"Naw," Dylan said. "Benito. We just saw him in the kitchen."

Junibel grabbed the bottle from Justin and took a gulp. "That kid from the football team? How did he get to my party?"

My breath caught in my chest. Benny was here? That was highly unusual. From what I knew, he never went to HF parties. I had to see this for myself.

"I'm going to get a beer," I said after a few more beats of conversation, not wanting to be super-obvious. "Does anyone want anything?"

"Not me," Junibel said. "Just make sure no one's breaking anything or eating anything."

I crossed through the living room and into the open kitchen/dining room. And there he was, standing by the center island talking to some football dudes. He was wearing a red sweater I'd never seen before, which made his chest look extra broad and his dark hair extra dark.

I don't know why I was so surprised. I mean, I'd been hanging out with him just a few hours earlier. Well, not really hanging out, but whatever. Still, it was like seeing a ghost. A ghost with an incredibly sexy jawline.

Was I . . . *attracted* to him?

He looked up as soon as I walked in.

"Hey," I said. "What are you doing here?"

He shrugged and that tiny smile unfurled across his face. "Same as you."

"Later, Ben." He watched as the two other guys drifted away, off to go find some girls, I was sure.

"Well, don't let me keep you," I said, anxious all of a sudden. "I mean if you want to hang out with your friends." Maybe he didn't want to be seen talking to me in the same way I probably should have not wanted to be seen with him.

He gave me a look, like *come on*. "You're my friend."

I stared into the dark fringe of his eyelashes and felt a pleasant tingling, like when you come in from the cold and the numbness in your fingers and toes starts to wear off. Then I remembered the kissing. *Oh. Shoot.* Was that why he showed up? Because of me? It couldn't be, could it? I felt embarrassed all over again. And awkward, too.

"Sure," I said finally, not sure how to respond. I hoped it wasn't some kind of test. "I'm your friend."

That's when Dylan came into the room, and I was almost relieved, because it broke the moment of us staring at each other thinking our private thoughts, the tension of which was getting to be unbearable. "Dj'you get your drink, babe?" he turned to Benny. "What's up, Benito?"

"My name's Benny," he said, stuffing his hands into the pockets of his jeans. "Benjamin, actually."

"Oh yeah? Benjamin Yizar the Fourth, I presume." Dylan did a fake, mocking bow, and I was mortified.

"That's my name," Benny said. "But there's only one."

"And that makes you special?"

Benny shrugged. "It makes me . . . me."

"But you do think you're special, right? You're the wonder kid on the scholarship? We're supposed to roll out the red carpet for you when you show up at our party?"

"I never said that." I could see Benny's jaw pulse slightly. He probably didn't like being called out for the scholarship thing.

"Well, you act that way."

"Look, there's no need to be a dick," Benny said quietly.

Dylan got in his face. "Did you just call me a dick, new guy?"

Gauntlet thrown. This was bad. Dylan lived for this kind of stuff, and when he started with someone, it was hard to calm him down. I wanted to do something, say something, but I was afraid, I guess, because I didn't want to call more attention to the fact that I knew Benny better than I was supposed to. Much better, actually. Wouldn't they all know something was up if I defended him now? There was no good excuse as to why we'd be friends. But there was another reason, too. I was worried what people would think—about me, I mean. He wasn't the kind of guy anyone else would envy me being with. He was practically a foot taller than me—we'd look terrible in pictures. He was, as Junibel would say, a nonentity.

So instead of trying to stop it I just stood there, worrying and watching the conversation bounce back and forth.

"Just step off," Benny said, but I noticed the hands came out of his pockets. "I'm minding my own business."

Dylan laughed. "Minding your own business. In Junibel's kitchen. Yeah. Okay."

"Okay what?" Benny asked, and I could see the anger starting to crack through.

Benny took a few steps toward him, and that's when *I* felt scared. I didn't want anyone to get hurt, and I didn't want anyone to get in trouble. If they fought, it was likely both things would happen, not to mention the possibility of cops coming to break up Junibel's party, which was bad for all of us. At the same time, I almost wished Benny would defend himself. Dylan *was* being a dick. He deserved what was coming to him.

"Okay, let's go." Dylan gestured for the back door leading to Junibel's patio. Others were watching now. Kids from the lacrosse team, and a couple of junior girls. They'd all stopped what they were doing when they sensed what was happening in the kitchen.

Benny paused for a moment, like he was almost considering getting into it. I could see his eyes registering the situation. He looked around at all the people watching, and he could see like

I could that they were aching for a fight. They wanted more than anything for this to get ugly.

Then he shook his head, clearly trying to take the high road. "Forget it. I'm not gonna fight you."

"Why?"

"Because then I'd be doing exactly what you expect me to do."

Dylan tensed up beside me. "So?"

"Dylan, let's go play quarters," I said, finding my voice all of a sudden. "You said we could play quarters tonight."

He was still staring at Benny, hard, and I grabbed his arm, trying to pull him away. "So?" he asked again.

Benny shrugged. "So it would just be too easy. Let's keep your pretty face clean, huh?" he said mockingly. Quiet but fierce.

"What the fuck? I'll hurt you."

But I could tell Dylan was hesitating. "Come on, Dylan," I said. "Forget it."

"Yeah," Dylan said after what seemed like an eternity. I felt his arm muscle relaxing. "All right. Get your beer, babe. I'll meet you in the living room."

I waited a few beats for him to stalk off, and then I looked at Benny. "Sorry . . . he's not always like that." How many times would I have to do this tonight?

"Forget it." Benny shook his head. I could no longer read him, and that was almost worse because I felt guilt weighing on me. Why hadn't I done anything? Here Benny was, making the rest of us seem like assholes. He just had that way about him.

"I'm serious. He's just . . . insecure." I don't know why but I wanted to make it okay, I wanted to make sure he knew that I had nothing to do with the way Dylan was acting. Kissing Benny had been a mistake, I knew that now, but it wasn't too late to fix things so we could still be okay around each other.

Benny's face revealed nothing. "Don't worry about it."

"He wouldn't really fight you. I'm sure he was just joking—"

Benny cut me off. "—I said, don't worry. Go ahead. Go play your game."

"I'm just trying to be nice."

"You're looking out for you," he said. "Do you need me to tell you it's all okay so you don't feel bad? Grow up, Dakota. Quit pretending to be something you're not. You're not as good at it as you think."

"What did you just say to me?" I whispered. Everyone else had cleared out of the kitchen by now. No fight; nothing to see. It was just me and Benny.

"Don't worry about it."

I slammed my hand down on the counter. "No. Tell me! Say it!"

"Little Miss Perfect. No one here cares about the real you anyway, right?" he snarled. "Isn't that what you said?"

I couldn't believe he was turning my own words against me. "No, I said no one *knew* the real me."

"Same difference, right? It's all an act."

"It's not an . . . act. It's just—it's hard—"

"You said you fake it. You pretend to be someone you're not and meanwhile you've got all your little secrets. What would they think, Dakota? What would they think if they found out?"

Oh god. Did he know about my throwing up? How the hell could he? Nobody knew about what I did all alone. Then I remembered, the day he saw me coming out of the bathroom. Benny might have been quiet and on the fringes of HF, but obviously he was tuned in to what was going on.

But I don't, I wanted to say. I hadn't in weeks. I was crushed. He must have thought I was so . . . pitiful.

And then I felt mad. Why should I have to justify myself? I mean, what did I do? But I knew. When it actually had counted, I'd done exactly nothing. I stayed quiet and let Dylan insult him in front of everyone at the party. I'd sold him out.

"I'm sorry," I whispered.

"Save your apologies," he said. "We're not friends."

The way he said it was so cold, I wanted to die right then and there, and I knew no matter what happened at this party, from here on out, the night was ruined. Spoiled. Poisoned, actually. The words echoed in my head as I walked away: *Not friends.*

TWENTY

BENNY

IT WAS PROBABLY A BAD IDEA TO BEGIN WITH. WE WERE supposed to go over the plan in full, with all the technical details, so I'd invited the group to my Uncle Hector's garage in Olney. That was before the party, where Dakota showed me that she was no better than her asshole boyfriend or the rest of them. I couldn't believe I'd been so stupid.

But we were going through with EagleFly, so I had to act like nothing had happened. And here they were on a Sunday morning, the three of them standing on the doorstep, looking like they were being held at gunpoint. Even Dakota, who—I hated to admit—was so pretty and fresh-looking (had she just gotten out of the shower?) seemed to be gritting her teeth. Was it that ghetto here? Better here than where I actually lived, Jesus.

Or maybe she just felt as uncomfortable as I did. Well, let her.

I held open the glass door, where the sign said CLOSED, and waved them in. It was open only for our business.

"You sure this is okay?" Alice asked me. "I mean, I parked on the street."

"Yeah," I said. I'd cleared it with Hector the night before—not that he knew what we were up to. "I'm here all the time working on my stuff. He never comes in on the Lord's day. And your car's safe."

Shoot. Why did I have to go and bring up God? I tried not to feel too guilty about what I was doing, even though I knew it was wrong. God would forgive me for trying to take care of my family, wouldn't he?

I couldn't worry about it now. Already Jason was busy scoping the front office, checking out the air freshener selection and helping himself to Hector's Hydrox cookies. No one ate Hector's Hydrox cookies.

I'd been feeling bad for the kid, the way people were throwing stuff at him, messing with his locker, stealing his books—they pretty much stole everything he didn't leave chained down. He had it rough in school. But when he acted like this, he made it hard to pity him.

"Don't touch those," I snapped.

He shrank back, lifting up his hands like he was blocking a pass. "Sorry. Just a cookie, Ben-Ben."

"Well, we're not here for snacks." I led them out through the office into the main shop, with its four bays. Two were still filled with cars, one up on a lift. "And my name's not Ben-Ben." Why did everyone always want to give me a nickname? We were not on nickname terms. We were not on any terms. I was putting up with this guy because I liked his plan, but as time went on, I was increasingly sure he was just a stoner jackass.

We were here to work, to walk through the operation on the model I'd made. And we were in Hector's shop so I could teach them some basic skills, like how to dissemble a circuit board for an alarm system and how to pick a lock. As far as I could tell, I was doing a B&E with a bunch of fools who'd never even picked up a tension wrench.

"What's that?" Jason said, pointing to the barrels in the corner.

"Oil and coolant storage," I said. "Don't get too close."

"Believe me, I won't. It's filthy in here," he said, smudging dirt between his thumb and index finger.

What did he expect a car shop to look like? His grandmother's kitchen? Clueless.

"And you wouldn't want to get dirty, would you?" I imitated his girly raised hands. That shut him up.

"So, what kind of cars do they fix?" Alice asked, gawking through her big glasses.

"Any kind," I said. "But we're really good with Hondas and Toyotas."

"You work here, too?" Dakota asked.

Her question just proved how little she knew about me. I didn't look at her as I answered. "I used to a lot more, but school and football have been taking up too much time." Working on cars was always a good release for me. I could just let my mind go and focus on the process, all the things that needed to be done, and there was never any question about what would work and what wouldn't.

Alice and Dakota followed me as I took out the scale model I'd built of the facility based on Dakota's notes. It was kind of budget, just a bunch of cardboard I'd stuck together with a hot glue gun, but it would work for what we needed. I set it on the floor and we crouched down in a huddle around it.

I tried to ignore the familiar smell of Dakota as she leaned in close. So far she was acting like nothing had happened. So I would, too.

"Did you track down the schedule?" I asked Alice.

She nodded. "Yup. Hansen HVAC is there biweekly for scheduled routine maintenance. Two technicians, usually, by the name of Pete Mazzarini and Robert Hibble."

"Great. I can get a van and a decal," I said. "Alice, you should call Hansen like you're a secretary from the Mint and tell them that it's closed for a private event on the day of the heist so they don't show up."

"So only two of us can go in?" Dakota asked. "What will the other two do?"

"Someone should stand guard, watch from across the street," Alice said. "And the other person can stay in the van in the garage."

"So we enter here." I walked my fingers into the "garage" door we'd seen.

"No offense to anyone, but I think we all agree I should be one of the ones to go in," Alice said.

Figured she'd just assume that. She was a piece of work.

"I vote for that," Jason said, smiling at her. "Al knows what's up."

"Okay, but how do we get past the first security post inside?" Dakota asked. "It's not just the gate. They'll stop us on foot when we enter the building from the garage."

"I've got that already," Alice said. "I'll take the HVAC guys' IDs that are already in the system and scan them so we have copies. Benny can swap in fake names and our photos. We'll bring our fakes with us and say we're the subs that day . . . No big deal."

"Once through security, we go up the elevator here, up from the garage." I showed them the route. "There are two sets of elevators and stairs, one on Race Street and one on Arch. Both go up to the lobby level but only the Race side elevator goes to the basement level, where the boiler room is. We go in there and act like we're on the job, while Alice fixes the security camera feeds. Then up to the lobby and production floor, where the real job begins," I said. Here I had a bunch of matchboxes and paper clips arranged like the assembly line.

"Nice machinery," Jason said.

So what if I wasn't artistic like him—you could get the basic idea. He was such a dick sometimes. I ignored him, it just wasn't worth it.

"What's the exit route?" Dakota asked.

"Through the elevator," Alice said.

"But what if the building loses power? We need an alternate way to get out with all the stuff."

Dakota always said that a plan was only as good as its emergency backups. I agreed with her there. No point in taking any more risks than we had to.

"Then we use the fire stairs to get up to production," I said, showing them on the model where it would be. "We leave the doors propped just in case. We'd have to disable the door alarm."

"Why don't we climb through the vents and stuff to get upstairs?" Jason said. "That would be awesome!"

"That only works in the movies," I said, rolling my eyes. "Have you seen those things in real life? They're filthy and small and you can catch diseases from the filters—all kinds of nasty stuff grows in there. No, man, the only way is to walk in like we're checking something in there. If we have a good cover, it should be fine. See, there's a double door here, and that puts us on the floor. Here, along this wall's where Garcia's office is. There are motion detectors here and here, which they use on weekends when no one's in the offices. Those motion detectors can only be turned off by security. So we have to be careful not to walk in these areas." I swept my fingers around the edges where the sensors would catch us.

"Unless we hire some acrobat guy to do back flips!" Jason said. "Like in *Ocean's Twelve*."

Alice laughed.

"Again, guys, movies." I wanted to smack him, but I controlled myself. Why did he have to act like an idiot? If I'd had even half of his advantages . . . I took a deep breath to calm down.

"Sorry," he said. "Just, this is kind of fun. I can't believe we've made it this far."

"Well, we're not there yet. Meanwhile, the guards see what?" Dakota asked.

"Alice's security feeds," I said.

"Which is nothing, pretty much," she said. "Beautifully executed nothing. I'll capture the feeds when the real HVAC guys are there so we'll look like we're doing what they normally do."

"What about the security rounds, though? Where are they going inside of the building?" Dakota pressed.

"Well that's another technical issue," Alice said. "I think we can figure that out from their RFIDs, which doors they punch in and when. I need to do a little more surveillance hacking."

"We need an exact schedule," Dakota warned. "I want times."

"Yeah, yeah," Alice said, and it was obvious she was getting annoyed with Dakota's prodding.

"But we're clear that they won't notice us messing around in there?" Jason asked.

I broke in. "We do know that on their control panel, there's a light that goes on when production runs. The only thing we'd have to worry about is if it stops suddenly, because an alarm goes off. That would alert them to a problem."

"But I have our run timed to go inside of the normal run," Alice said. "So it won't be a problem. It'll do our coins, then switch back to the normal standard quarter."

"And then?" Jason asked.

"We leave the way we came in. Down the stairs to the first floor, and down the elevator to the garage. Like respectable repairmen," Alice said. "If there's a problem with the elevator, we can ask security to let us back into the garage when it's time to leave, because they'll obviously know we need to leave in our van."

"Hopefully we won't have to do that. And Alice will have the coins in a lead bag in her toolbox, which should pass through the metal detectors on the way out," Dakota said. "But what about the alarm? In the fire stairs? And the van locks?"

"Right." I nodded. I grabbed a wedge and a straight piece of metal wire, then I led them over to a Pontiac that needed a new transmission.

Dakota wanted to make sure, since we were going to have keep the van securely locked at all times, that we all knew how to break into it in case we got split up at any time. It was good thinking, I had to admit that.

I showed them how you'd wedge into the rubber stripping of the car door, making enough space to slip the wire in and use that to hit the unlock button inside.

Jason stepped up to try, and within a minute, I swear, the wire broke inside the car. "Oops," he said, and he did look kind of embarrassed. "My bad."

I squared off in front of him. "What the hell, man?"

He gave a guilty smile. "You have a key, right? You can just open the door and get the wire out of there."

I didn't have the key. The keys for all the cars being serviced were locked in Hector's desk—a security measure Dakota would have approved of. I was going to have to figure out a way to get it out, but I would just deal with that later. What a loser.

"Sorry," he said again.

"Now the rest of us won't even get a turn," Dakota said.

"Whatever, let's just do the fire stairs alarm." I tried to snap us back on task. I pulled a screwdriver off the wall, a tension wrench from my box, my soldering iron, and a power drill, setting them down on a workbench. "I'll have to figure out what specific model they have, but basically it's the same in most cases. You remove the plastic cover and take out a circuit—"

"You use this, right?" Jason grabbed the soldering iron.

"So cool!" Alice said over his shoulder. "I've always wanted to try that."

"You could make a kick-ass bong with this thing!" Jason said, looking at Alice. Was he trying to impress her or something? I was pretty sure the girl didn't smoke up. Yet she giggled anyway.

"Careful with that," I said.

"I am."

"You're holding it wrong." I reached out to adjust his arm. "If you did it like that, you'd melt your sleeve."

"It's just like metalworking," Dakota said, taking the

soldering iron from Jason and inspecting it.

"This isn't just some sculpture," I said. "It's precision work."

"You go to a tech school to be a mechanic," she said. "It can't be that hard."

"Right," I snapped. "Just like anyone can be an honors student."

She held the tool against her chest, clasping her hands over it. "I'm sorry. I didn't mean it like that. But you're pretty much following a manual, aren't you?"

Was she for real? "No, there's a lot more to it."

Computer systems, analysis, problem solving, being able to explain the issue to people who knew nothing about anything—cars were not that simple. Sure, anyone could tell you your CHECK ENGINE light was for a "loose gas cap"—the oldest trick in the book. Hector always said it took ten thousand bolts to put a car together and one nut to break it down.

But I wasn't gonna explain it to her. Screw her and her fratboy *novio* and her snotty rich girl opinions. Screw all of these people. They didn't know a damn thing. My fists curled up.

"Aw, Ben-Ben is pissed," Jason said.

"I'm not Ben-Ben, and I'm not Benito!" I yelled.

"Okay! Calm down!" Jason said. "Relax, man. You're doing a good job."

"Guess what. I don't need you to tell me I'm doing a good job. I need you to pay attention. I'm trying to explain an important part of the plan, and you punks are just fooling around. I can't be the only one who knows how to do this!" I backed away from the workbench. "Give me back the soldering iron."

Dakota extended her hand with the tool in it, and I reached for it but somehow I forgot that the model was on the floor right at my feet, and I tripped over it. The little matchboxes crunched beneath my foot, the paperclips went flying.

Shit. I didn't even want to look, but I did. It was all squashed to hell.

"Our whole plan!" Dakota said.

Now I wasn't just mad, I was embarrassed, too. This had to be a sign, right? The model was dead and so were we. "Yo, this whole thing is stupid," I spat. "Maybe we should just quit while we're ahead."

"We can't quit now," Alice said, looking all nervous. "We've got the design in place. We've paid for our gear. We have the RFID. We can't return it."

"So what?" I said. "It's just money. We can destroy the card. We weren't really gonna pull this off anyway."

"But we can!" Dakota said. "We just need everyone to stay focused here. I think as a group, we just suffer from a lack of cohesion—"

"Says the girl who invited herself and tried to take over everything," Alice said, sharp as a wire cutter.

"What do you mean?" Dakota slapped the soldering iron down. "I'm doing all the organizing here."

"Nobody asked you to. We were doing fine without you," Alice said.

"I doubt it," Dakota sniffed, eyeing Jason. "Your so-called

leader isn't contributing much."

"Maybe because you're controlling everything," Alice spit back. "This was Jason's baby. Not yours."

"Some baby," Dakota said. "And how again are we going to get the money back to the school? Have you squared that away yet, Jason?"

"Still working on it. I know a guy who knows a guy . . . "

"Who?" Dakota demanded. "Who do you know? Who have you even talked to?"

"Well, it's this guy Dave I get my weed from. He knows a guy who does some trading on eBay. He could help us turn the coins into cash."

eBay? Was he kidding? We needed someone who knew what they were doing, who could help us bring the right amount of coins to market without ruining their value. A professional.

Dakota looked at him like he was a little kid. "So this is what we've been waiting for? This was all you had to do. And what happens next? Jason, don't tell me you haven't figured this all out yet!"

"And then . . . I haven't hammered out all the details. Make an anonymous donation?"

Weak. We all knew it. To make a donation, we'd have to write a check,and to write a check we needed an account to deposit it in.

"It's not all I did—I did the design—I've done lots of stuff," Jason sputtered.

"That's kind of the whole point though, right? Getting the money back to the school?" Even Alice was turning against

Jason now. I never thought I'd see that day. It was obvious to anyone with eyes she had a thing for him. "Maybe you should have figured that out first, before we let it get this far?"

"O-*kay*, Harry Potter," Jason said, rolling his eyes.

"What did you call me?" Alice asked quietly, her fists clenched. She looked like she was going to fling my uncle's tool drawers at him. The room got real tense. I mean, okay, she did bear a slight resemblance to Harry Potter, with her skinny boy body and big glasses. But obviously no girl wants to hear that. And not after what she'd done for him, with the rat. This guy needed a reality check.

"Maybe you don't have it worked out because you're planning to keep the money. I mean, we all know about your pops," I said. I didn't even know if I believed what I was saying, but hey, his dad was a thief . . . Mostly, though, I was just mad and I wanted him to get a taste of what he'd been putting me through.

Jason got really flustered then, throwing up his hands. "Hey, you know what? Benny's right. EagleFly isn't working, and now you're all jumping down my throat. I don't need this stress. I thought I could do something to help for once, something good. But obviously it was a terrible idea. And we can't pull it off. We're just a bunch of stupid kids, and we don't even like each other, so why should we want to save this school? I say let it close. My dad's in jail, my mom's filling out divorce paperwork, my band's split up. So who cares? I mean, what good does it do to care anyway?"

He paused and we all waited, frozen, like we'd been blasted with compressed air. There were reasons we all cared. That was obvious. I mean, we all wanted to do this. Otherwise, why had we wasted our time? But no one said anything.

Then, one by one, they looked to me. Like I suddenly had to be the big decider. Why, because we were in my uncle's garage? Well, screw that. Deciding meant being involved, and I didn't want to be.

Game over. I'm done. I stared back. Silent and serious, like I did on the football field when I wanted to intimidate my opponent.

Dakota shrugged. "Seems like that's our answer then. If none of you care, then it's hardly worth us putting everything on the line. I'm surprised, though." She turned and looked up at me with disappointed eyes. "I guess I thought out of everyone you'd want to make this work, Benny."

Why, because I was the most broke? What did she know about me? One car ride home, one stupid kiss, and she thought she had me tucked into one of her little file folders?

"You thought wrong," I said coldly. I couldn't believe I ever thought we'd connected. I was nothing like these people, and I never would be. "If we're done here, then I should close up the shop."

TWENTY-ONE

ALICE

SO MUCH FOR OPERATION EAGLEFLY. IT WAS A STUPID name, anyway.

Now that we weren't meeting and planning, we had no reason to talk to each other in school. A week had passed, and we were back to living in parallel universes. It was weird. Sometimes I'd see Dakota or Benny in the hallway and I'd start to raise my hand in greeting, out of habit. Then I'd have to jerk it down quickly before anyone noticed.

Then there was Jason—he was mostly alone. He slunk in and out of Design class without making eye contact. He didn't carry his guitar around anymore. He no longer had any comebacks to the taunts in the hallway. He never really said much of anything. It was hard to watch.

I guess Greg was fine with being my goblet-wielding fall-back, because he seemed happy that I was free after school again. He even agreed to stay for dinner one night, which helped because then my mom could spend the whole time asking him questions. He only gave one-word answers—he wasn't exactly a great charmer—but she didn't seem to notice. Still, I was starting to wonder if she knew something was up with my dad because the dinners were steadily getting more slapdash—packaged salad mixes with bottled dressing, canned soup, and one night she even went straight for the frozen pizza, which is not really pizza at all but puffy bread masked in tasteless sauce and rubber cheese. When you can't make the effort to call for delivery, something is really wrong.

I still hadn't said anything, and maybe all that secret-keeping (i.e. hiding in my room and studying) was another sign for her, because she had asked me a few times if I was depressed about something.

"No," I told her. "Just trying to keep all the balls in the air."

"Drop some of them," she said. "You should have a life, Alice. Go out on a date. Do something fun."

I appreciated that she was coming from a place of concern, but what she didn't realize was that for a few weeks there, I'd *had* a life—a criminal life, yes, but a fun one—and now it was gone. Now everything about my ordinary life seemed flatter, grayer in comparison. Plus, my mother telling me to date was the definition of sad.

But it was time to move on. Put my criminal past behind

me and get back down to my schoolwork. All that was left to do was to get back into the system and get rid of the design. Erase that history from the browser and my mind.

I logged onto the wifi system and found the Mint login screen, decorated with Liberty Bells and flags.

```
3x5542*TGP0z12Q*5J49iii>Dr8&}29w
```

It was a decent password as far as passwords went, but a password was only numbers and symbols and letters in a finite sequence, meant to be cracked. The way I saw it, I was helping these people understand just how vulnerable their systems were. They paid experts to do this kind of thing—they called it "benevolent hacking"—so they should be thanking me.

I clicked ENTER and in I went, the same way I had the last time.

Straight to the DISCARD folder where I'd left the file.

MississippiState50. I dragged it over to the trashcan icon and hovered it there for a while. It felt so final, throwing away Jason's design. If I did this, it would really be all over. Everything.

I could leave it in, I thought deviously. Teach Jason a lesson—the others, too—about messing with me. About using people. They'd be forced to figure it all out themselves.

It was sort of tempting. But it was also ridiculous. I couldn't get us all arrested just because I was pissed. I wasn't some vengeful badass. I was a girl in a dorky hat who knew a lot about computers and very little about anything else. Clearly I knew nothing about people.

No, it was better to just walk away, wash my hands of the whole thing. I released the button on my mouse.

Only the file didn't go into the trash. The file disappeared. What the hell? Was it snarfed?

I went back out and in, thinking I must have missed it.

I scrolled through the other folders—JOB, PROJECT, ENGINEERING WORKBENCH, ACTIVITIES, REPORTS—opening each one and scanning through. No sign of the document. Nothing.

The only folder I hadn't tried was WORK ORDERS IN PROGRESS. It wouldn't be there, would it?

I clicked anyway, just for thoroughness.

And *blammo*, wouldn't you know? There it was. Mississippi-State50.

I must have mistakenly dropped it there with a flick of my wrist. Well, the hows didn't matter—I just needed to get rid of it.

I selected the file and pressed the delete key. No change. Tried dragging it into the little trashcan icon again. Nothing doing. It stayed put.

The thing refused to budge. It hovered there in its open window, a little rectangle taunting me. In fact, I noticed that the outline of it was gray, so it was actually unclickable. How could that be? There had to be a way to destroy it.

I opened up the software's control dashboard and looked

for the WORK ORDERS IN PROGRESS module. On the left hand side was a bar graph of inventory. Above that, in a little box, was a list of items in progress including our coin design.

05022014:17:15

"Wait wait wait," I said out loud. I couldn't be seeing what I thought I was seeing. Could I?

Those were dates. The run was scheduled for May 2nd.

This was pessimal. How could it be scheduled? And May 2nd? That was in nine days!

I hit the EDIT option next to the file. Again, denied. *Bagbiter!* A message came up in a bubble: THIS ORDER IS LOCKED. NO FURTHER CHANGES CAN BE MADE.

No changes? What the hell kind of bullshit software was this? Why couldn't you make a change? What if you made a mistake and needed to fix it?

'Cause we'd made one.

Okay, *I* had.

And it was a big one. Really big.

In all my hacking experience, I'd never come across a problem like this. It seemed so simple, and yet . . .

I tried a few more times to delete, edit, reboot, hide, destroy the file. I did some searching; I went onto chat rooms to try to find answers. And the next time I looked at the digital readout at the top of my screen, it was three hours later and I had *nothing.*

Panic sweat collected at the edge of my hairline.

If we didn't get rid of this thing, the coins were going to be minted, and if we couldn't get in the building to pick them up, they'd know exactly what happened. From there it would only take a team of insurance company experts to find our trail. The worst part of all was that I'd thought of doing this very thing—yes, I decided against punishing them, but somehow, subconsciously, I must have made it happen.

I grabbed my phone and texted Jason.

CALL ME WHEN YOU GET THIS. IMPORTANT!!!

I gripped my phone in my hand, all the blood pressed out of my fingers, until it rang three minutes later.

He answered sounding like he had a mouthful of cereal. "What's up, Al? I can't talk for long." In another situation I would have loved to talk to him. In another situation, my texting him would have been an excuse to get him on the phone. But that was before I found out what he really thought about me. Now I hated him.

I spoke coldly, all business. I couldn't tell him the whole story—just the facts he needed to know. "Something happened with our file. In the Mint system. I tried to go in and get rid of it, but it's been queued."

"What does that mean? I thought you said you hid it. In a 'dusty corner', if I remember your exact words."

"I thought I did," I tried to skirt the issue. "It doesn't matter. Now that thing is set to go, on May second."

"So what? It'll just look like a mistake."

"Jason, I don't think you realize what's going on. Our error coin design in there will be evidence of tampering. And in situations like this, they could bring in a whole team of investigators. Forensics, like on TV? Except for computer stuff. They can trace back all of the logins in the system, and they can trace it back to my IP address. I used a VPN, but they'll get past that in an instant."

"What?" his panicked voice went up an octave. Then he quieted his voice some. "Al. This was supposed to be freaking foolproof. I thought you had this locked down!!"

"I did, when we were actually going to go through with it. But we can't ignore it. Those coins—we have to figure out how to get them out. We don't have a choice."

"This is your problem. I'm sorry, but you have to figure it out."

That's when I lost my temper. "No, Jason. This is *your* problem. You were the great leader. So don't go putting this all on me. If you do, I'll rat your ass out. And who are they going to believe, Harry Potter or the pothead whose dad bankrupted the school?"

I couldn't believe I was being so harsh. But at the same time, I couldn't believe we were even in this situation.

"Shit," he said. I heard some banging around on his end. "Shit, Al. We can't go to jail for a crime we didn't even mean to commit. What should we do? What should we do?"

"How about call a meeting?"

"Right. I'm calling a meeting."

"When?" I asked.

"Right now?"

"Jason, it's almost one-thirty in the morning. Are you crazy??"

"Do you know where the old canoe house is?"

"The what?"

"It's on the nature preserve. Just meet me at the entrance of the nature preserve. I'll text the others."

So there I was, sneaking out on a Tuesday night to secretly meet the boy I used to crush on in the woods behind our school. I probably would've been way more psyched about the whole thing if, you know, it wasn't because we had a major emergency on our hands.

TWENTY-TWO

JASON

WE WERE KNEE DEEP IN A RIVER OF CRAP, AND I WAS wearing metaphorical flip-flops. I stuffed my phone in my pocket and got on my bike. No way was I going to take the car out at 2 a.m. My mom would have lost it for real. The worst part was thinking about her. If I landed in jail too, it would break what was left of her heart.

It was spring, but it was still very chilly at night. By the time I got to campus, it felt like a good three layers of skin had been ripped off my face. Alice, Dakota, and Benny were standing at the edge of the woods, waiting for me. They'd all clearly come from their cars and they looked warm.

Benny had his arms folded across his jacket so that his profile was even bigger and more intimidating than usual. "I hope you've got some answers, Hodges. Don't tell me I drove all the way here for nothing."

"I have answers," I bluffed. "But let's go to the canoe hut, okay? I don't want to talk here."

I led them deeper into the woods to the spot where I would sometimes go to smoke a joint during school hours, and on the weekends, too, when we lived in the headmaster's house. Back in the day, when students went boating during gym, it had been used for launching. But ever since they'd renovated the grounds and turned them back into wetlands with color-coded walking trails about ten years ago, the little lean-to was all grown over and barely detectable. Add that to the inky dark of the night, and we had a good little spot to talk about our criminal misdeeds, or what we were going to do to cover up our criminal misdeeds.

"This looks like a good place to dump a body," Benny said. I could only go by voices, because it was almost too dark for silhouettes.

"I didn't know it even existed," Alice said.

"None of us did," Dakota answered. "Leave it to Jason to find the only area on campus that hasn't been manicured with nail scissors."

"Is that a compliment? Thank you, Dakota," I said sarcastically. "So now that we're all here, tell them what you found out, Al."

She coughed, clearing her throat. "Basically, the error coin design is already in production. I can't delete it. Which means that even though we said we weren't going through with Eagle-Fly, we now have to find a way to do it anyway. Or at least get in there and get the coins out before anyone notices them."

"I don't get it," Benny said. "Didn't you say you had it all taken care of?"

"Yes," she said in that expert way of hers. "But it's not my fault. It's not anyone's fault."

He snorted, like *oh really?* "Since you were the one who was in charge of it, I'd say it's your fault."

"Okay," she snapped. "You guys want to know what happened? I was pissed. I was pissed at Jason. Might as well get it all out there, right, because who gives a flying crap anymore anyway? Jason, I have this stupid crush on you. Had."

I shrunk back in shock. *What?*

That was not where I thought this conversation would be going. At all.

And I'd never heard anyone sound so angry when they were telling me they had a crush on me.

She waved her hand. "I mean, don't worry, not anymore, not since the other day. You pretty much blew it when you wussed on our plans. But all this time we were hanging out, it seemed like something was happening, like you might have even liked me a little bit, too. Ridiculous, right? I got my hopes up, but obviously you just see me as the geeky girl who could help you pull all this off."

None of us said anything—I mean, it was all so crazy, it seemed like it was better to just let her continue on her rant.

"So, anyway, yes, I did think about leaving the file in there because you hurt my feelings. But then, honest truth, I changed my mind. I realized I couldn't do that . . . to the team. Something happened, though, and I really don't know what. And that's why we're standing here."

I was just speechless. What was I supposed to say? She liked me? This was because of *me*? I was flattered. It was a horrible way to find out, but I was flattered. I wanted to tell her I was sorry. I wanted to tell her I was just freaked out the other day, and I'd never meant to hurt her feelings, and that I had no idea she liked me. I wanted to tell her that I actually thought she was kind of cute.

But before I could say any of that, Dakota cut in, and for once I was relieved. "Look let's stop worrying about assigning blame. That's not the point. The point is . . . The point is . . . What are we going to *do*?"

Dakota sounded like she was going to explode. She was a good girl, and she never should have been involved in this in the first place. I almost felt a little bad for her. I felt bad for everyone. All I knew was that there was no more time to screw around. I had to step up and make some plans for us.

"The past is the past," I said firmly. "We have to work together, you guys. This is for real. We can't afford to make more mistakes now. Our most important concern is getting the coins out of there. Since we can't fence them anyway, we'll have to just destroy the evidence."

"Okay," Dakota said. "So what do we do?"

I could hear my dad's doubting voice in my head, but I had to ignore it. "They're supposed to be minted on May second, in the evening run—"

Dakota shrieked, cutting me off. "Prom night? They're being minted on *prom night?*"

"I don't care," Alice muttered.

"Fine by me," Benny said at the exact same time.

"You guys might not care, but some of us do," Dakota said. "Some of us are in charge of planning and have an important role to play. Some of us have dates counting on us."

Of course she had to rub that in.

"And isn't your band supposed to play, Jason?"

Umm, yeah. I'd never gotten around to telling the Prom Committee that Mixed Metaphors had technically probably broken up. I hadn't talked to the guys in weeks. They were all probably already in the Uh-Ums. And if I was going to get knee-to-the-groin honest with myself, I had to admit it: The world really didn't care about Mixed Metaphors, so why should I?

"Well, about that," I said. "We kind of broke up."

"WHAT???" Dakota shrieked, and I swear she was more upset about prom than the damn Mint. "What the hell are we supposed to do about music?"

"What are we supposed to do about the rest of our lives?" Alice said. "That's kind of the bigger issue here."

But Dakota wasn't ready to move on. "I can't believe you, Jason."

"I was trying to work it out," I said. "But this is better anyway, right?"

"How is this better?" Dakota scoffed.

"It's better because now I can skip prom and get the coins. I got you all into this, and I should be the one to get you out. Let me go to the Mint and fix this. Besides, the Uh-Ums can play prom. Half my band is now with them anyway."

"No, they can't. They broke up, too," Alice said. "I heard it was because Zack Yoko'd them."

"What?" I asked.

"He's hooking up with Alison, I heard," Alice said. Never mind how she even knew that—it was really bad news. So there was no replacement.

"We need a band," Dakota said. "We don't have money to hire anyone. That's why we asked you guys in the first place—you were the only ones who'd do it for free."

Gee, thanks. "So what do you suggest?"

"Look," Alice said. "Only two people can go into the Mint, as per the original plan. The other two of us need an alibi anyway. No one would expect me and Benny to be at the prom, but they'll expect you two to be there."

"She's right," Dakota agreed. "Get Mixed Metaphors back together ASAP."

I couldn't believe they were ganging up on me to *make me* play the prom, especially given the circumstances.

I started pacing. "Okay, the good news is it still falls on a

Saturday. We can use our original cover. Hansen HVAC will still work. The entry and exit plan still works. I mean, we figured mostly everything out already," I said.

"But we still have to figure out how to destroy the evidence," Alice said.

"I've got some ideas," I said.

And with that, like it or not, the team was suddenly back together. Operation Ground EagleFly was a go.

TWENTY-THREE

⟡ ALICE

SATURDAY, MAY 2ND. 16:00 HOURS: BENNY ARRIVES AT MY HOUSE.

"Lot of traffic getting here," he said after we got on the road.

We'd gone so far as to pretend, as we left my house just a few moments earlier, that we were going to the prom together. My mom was thrilled, but I could tell she was wondering why I wasn't going with Greg. Ha! Greg and my Math Team friends would never.

I'd put on a black dress with spaghetti straps I'd bought at the mall for $50 (didn't want to spend too much on an illusion) and actually pinned my hair back away from my face instead of wearing my usual thinking cap. I even borrowed some of my mom's heels, which would have been incredibly painful if I'd worn them longer than the thirty minutes it took to get downstairs, suffer through some fake pictures, and get into Benny's car. Benny was wearing a suit, too.

"You bummed we're missing prom?" I asked him, knowing full well he wasn't.

"Never," he said, guiding the wheel with his palm. "That shit's overrated."

"It is," I agreed. "I mean, not that I would know."

We stopped at the first gas station we could find to change out of our formal wear and into our heist-wear. Now I felt much more normal, even though I was still in disguise. Benny was wearing a white work jumpsuit, probably from his uncle's garage, and I was wearing jeans and colorful sneakers—less Harry Potter, more my twelve-year-old cousin. We'd decided that since I couldn't pull off the whole HVAC repairman thing, I was going as his niece. Lame, but he'd insisted this was the only way it would work.

Secretly I kind of wished we really were going to the prom, and that I was there with a guy I really liked—forget Jason, because I was over him. In fact, I didn't regret telling him I'd had a crush on him, because it was all in the rearview mirror now. No, this would be some other, cuter guy who actually liked me back. I pictured us laughing as we stuffed a whole crowd of people in the back of a limo and snuck sips of booze from a flask, or whatever it was that people normally did. And if I was accidentally imagining Jason, he was just a placeholder until I found another crush.

Ironically enough, the prom was being held at the Franklin

Institute, which was also in Center City, but on the other side of town. So we'd be passing by everyone in their limos and bedazzled nightgowns on our way back from the Mint later on.

Right about now was pre-prom time—parties and gatherings—and at the Institute they were likely just setting up the tables and stuff. Jason and his bandmates were probably still doing their soundcheck. That was another thing I was missing—their big show—but that was most likely for the best. I might be tempted to throw things. I wondered how he'd managed to get them all back together, but that part wasn't my problem, so long as it was done.

16:15: Benny checks in with his friend LT, makes sure the van is waiting for us.

In the passenger seat, I checked the map we'd drawn with Dakota's help. It all looked fine on paper. Simple, even. It was a matter of angles and numbers, both things I was good at.

"Get off at the Eighth Street exit, then right toward Market," I told Benny.

16:22: Arrive at parking lot under Gallery Mall.

We parked Benny's Mustang. He hit his clicker and his alarm beeped on as we took the elevator up to Level C. There, as promised, sat a white van two spots over from the emergency exit. HANSEN HVAC PERFORMANCE. Jason had taken the logo from the website and transferred it on to a decal, which LT had just stuck on the side of the van he'd procured—none of us besides Benny knew how, exactly, because he wanted it to be secret to protect the parties involved—and voila: design skills at work.

Rankin the *artiste* himself couldn't have done it any better.

We assumed our positions in the van, and Benny drove us up Seventh Street, heading back north and then a few blocks east to Old City. We cruised along until the light changed in front of Independence Hall, where the National Park police in their brown uniforms were stationed outside of the gates.

Cops! That's when the butterflies started. I slid down in my seat, trying not to be noticed.

"Are you crazy?" Benny said through gritted teeth. "That's just gonna make you look more suspicious, dawg."

"I am fully human," I said. "And I don't want them to see me."

He was still talking without moving his lips. "Those aren't even the same cops who guard the Mint. They're just trying to keep terrorists out of the Liberty Bell. Check yourself."

I looked out the window again and saw that one of the policeman was sipping on a Jamba Juice and the other was on an iPhone. Benny was probably right. I tried to get a grip. I slid up to normal position, reminding myself that this wasn't very different from the Math Olympics. I had to stay centered and focused. At this point I'd done all the preparation, and now it was up to fate.

The light changed and we moved on. "Sorry," I muttered.

"S'okay." He revved the engine and we turned, with something like peace settling between us.

16:45: Arrive at Mint.

Here we were at the back entrance, right on schedule. I was

pretty sure this building had to be one of the ugliest known to man—why the architects couldn't have come up with a secure place to manufacture money that actually looked remotely decent was beyond me.

We were at the call box now. "Ready?" Benny whispered.

"Yeah," I said. What else could I say? This was it. If anyone was gonna screw up this whole thing for all of us, it wasn't going to be me. Not again.

"Can I help you?" a voice asked.

Benny rolled down his window and spoke into the box, surprising me with his air of authority. "Yeah, Hansen HVAC? We're here for scheduled maintenance."

I looked over and imagined the electric eye of the camera staring at us. In the pause, the butterflies started to flap their wings again. Forget my analogies. This situation was way worse than any Math Olympics. You couldn't factor your way out of it.

"Go ahead," the electronic voice said, and just like that, the orange and white striped barrier arm lifted.

We drove into the maze of ramps spiraling down down down. The parking garage was mostly empty, it being a weekend with hardly anyone working. There was, of course, the fleet of security officers onsite to worry about. I'd gone into the system and traced their whereabouts during a Saturday evening, using their RFID cards as they opened doors around the building. I'd also done a little recon on the officers themselves. All three were retired Philly police, assigned to the weekend shift. I even knew their names and where they lived.

We got out of the van and Benny grabbed his toolbox, which was loaded with everything we needed. We proceeded toward the gray metal doors, where a guard in a dark blue uniform stopped us with his open palm.

Butterflies. Mega butterflies.

"Who's this?" the guard asked, referring to me. I recognized him as Joe. The others were Tony and Glen.

"Hope you don't mind, I brought my niece along," Benny said, showing Joe the guard the doctored ID we'd scanned from his file, then printed and laminated.

Joe looked up from the card. "Your niece?"

Oh God. He wasn't buying it. I knew it was a stupid idea, but Benny had insisted that I looked a lot younger than him.

Benny laughed. "Keeps her out of trouble. She's a bit of a handful, if you know what I mean. If it's a problem, she can wait in the van." *A handful? Where was he getting this stuff?*

Joe looked at me, squinting. I was dying over here.

"No worries," he said finally. "Just keep her with you at all times."

Benny put down his toolbox, and the guard had us lift our arms as he traced us with a metal detector.

"I'll leave you to it, then."

Joe walked us to the Race Street side elevator, then used his RFID to unlock the keypad and pressed the button for us to get to the next level. We had our copy of Garcia's ID, of course, but we'd use that later.

Inside, the building was just as grim and prisonlike as the outside, with endless overhead florescent lighting and an echoing cement floor. No windows, of course. We continued down the long hallway of closed doors, following the clanking sounds to the huge mechanical room, which took up almost the whole floor. I was impressed how well Benny had nailed the proportions on the model. This was where the boiler, backup generators, sprinkler system, main distribution piping, and other machinery were all housed, a red and white labyrinth of hissing pipes, catwalks, and ductwork. And where we were supposed to be working.

16:50: Fix cameras.

First things first: I had to do my technical bit and scramble the signals. I pulled my laptop out of Benny's toolbox and logged into the Mint system. I'd remotely recorded twelve clean feeds. Now I just had to stream and substitute them for the twelve cameras the guards were watching. As they changed over, anyone watching closely would see a single line of static— barely even noticeable. A few keystrokes. Done and done.

One of them was of the boiler room, from a previous Saturday evening when the two official Hansen guys had attended to some duct work. That footage, like the rest of the "blank" streams, was on a loop of thirty minutes, which was all we would need to do our thing.

Now, time to go upstairs. We walked back down the hallway the way we'd come in, toward the Race Street fire stairs. We paused on the first landing, which opened out on the pavement, one of those heavy metal doors we'd seen on our stakeout that couldn't be broached from the outside. I left that door, and the one at the top, barely ajar with rubber stoppers Dakota had given me. This way if, God forbid, we had to run, we could get out quickly, no van needed. Meanwhile, Benny already had the alarm panel cover off, and with a flick of his soldering iron, he quickly removed the circuit.

"You're fast," I said with a grin.

"You know it."

Maybe we weren't such a bad team after all.

The ID Benny had rigged opened just about every other door automagically—whoosh, whoosh, and whoosh. We were in.

The guards had already come and gone on their previous round—that gave us a good forty-five minutes to complete the job and get out of here, from start to finish.

17:00: Production starts.

On the production floor, the machinery was just starting to click into gear for the scheduled run. Robots moved the 6,000-pound coils of metal strips to the weights that punched them into blanks. Conveyors carried the blanks to be annealed and upset, then on to the nine lines with seven presses each, which looked like enclosed gray metal cabinets. Once everything was moving, the sound was deafeningly loud—a high-pitched whir-ring, thrumming, buzzing, overlaid with the clanks of metal planchets being tossed together. The coins piled up before they were transported to their next destination.

We popped in our earplugs—another thing we'd stashed in the toolkit, along with heavy-duty gloves so we could pull the coins hot off the presses (of course, they would also conveniently keep our prints off everything)—and sat back to watch. It was kind of amazing to think we'd made this happen. In this room everything was moving and shifting and making things, while in the adjacent medal area, separated by a glass door, all was dark and still.

All we had to do was wait for the cycle to finish—ten minutes, tops.

17:12 (rough estimate): Production ends. Pick up stash, deposit in toolbox. Exit through stairs and out the garage, removing stoppers and fixing alarm panel along the way.

I would switch the feeds back just before we drove out of the garage. Then we'd finish the last piece of the plan—the final bit of inspiration that we had come up with that night in the woods. We would leave the coins in the van, melted down and soldered to the inside of the engine hood, and Benny's friend would take it back to his shop, paint it, and switch the plates back to its owner. No traces. No money for any of us, either, but freedom was priceless, wasn't it?

But as we sat there and watched the machines cranking and whirring, ten minutes passed, then fifteen, but the coins were still being stamped and pressed and cut. Production kept on going. Thirty minutes left until the guard's next round.

Benny grabbed my arm, so I took out my earplugs. "Shouldn't this be done by now?"

"Yeah," I murmured with wide eyes. The pounding of my heart in my ears started to drown out the machines.

It was supposed to be a small handful of coins, so few that we could carry them all out ourselves—that was a key part of the original Operation EagleFly, and what had made the whole plan doable. But something was wrong here, I was starting to realize with a sinking sensation. Really wrong.

The machines kept spinning and whizzing, the coins moving along, dozens at a time. By now there had to be a thousand of them, more every second.

I got out my laptop and furiously searched through the network to see if it had any answers. But it was unclear, just looking at the system, how many coins had been ordered. And it just kept going and going.

"Ho-ly," Benny said, dread creeping into his voice. "This is effed up. Make it stop, Alice."

My eyes bounced from my monitor to the assembly line and back again, my mind racing. "I don't know how," I said finally. "I'm trying, but—I can't believe this. How could it . . . I don't see . . . why . . ."

"What do you mean, you don't *know how?*" He was practically yelling, even though I could barely hear him over the noise. I felt tears springing to my eyes.

"If I'd known how to stop it, I never would have let this order through in the first place. Seems like with this system, there's no command for stoppage. It must be a security thing. Once it's in, it goes through until the order's complete. And even if we could stop production, it would clue in the guards that something was up."

"Let me get this straight. You know everything about everything but you don't know how to hit stop?"

FAIL.

"I don't, okay?" I paced back and forth, panicked sobs closing my throat. I could barely breathe. My brain was just beginning to compute the extent of the mistake. *My* mistake. This was the second mistake, and it was way worse than the first.

"I'm sorry. I'm sorry. I'm sorry."

I never make mistakes.

"Okay, you're sorry, but snap out of it. We have to figure this out."

My whole world was going black. I couldn't see. I couldn't hear. And I certainly couldn't figure out what the hell to do next, because all I could think about was how freaking dead we were. And how it was all . . . my . . . fault . . .

TWENTY-FOUR

JASON

"IS THAT WHAT YOU'RE WEARING?" I ASKED CHADDIE, pointing to the dry cleaning bag he'd set down on top of his amp case. Inside was a standard-issue tux. Black. Simple. Normal.

"Yeah, dude. I don't look good in patterns."

"How about you?" I asked Max, who, like Chaddie, was still in a t-shirt and jeans.

He shrugged. "I couldn't find a plaid suit."

So they'd both purposely blown off the costume idea, the idea that made Mixed Metaphors memorable, because—did I even have to spell this out?—it was itself a metaphor for our name. And here I was in a red tartan suit jacket, a canary yellow plaid tie, and green-and-brown plaid Doc Martens. "What's the point if we don't all do it? Now I look like an asshole."

"Nah, you just look like you're Scottish," Max said in his whiny little voice. "And maybe a little colorblind."

I couldn't really complain, because I was on thin ice to begin with. I'd lost whatever power I'd had left when I had to go begging, practically crawling on my hands and knees to their lunch table, to get them to agree to play the prom after all. I'd had a whole speech planned.

"Listen," I said. "Do you know about Chad Channing, the original Nirvana drummer? He left the band because he wanted to write more songs. Everyone said it was premature, that he should have stayed. And you know what? He missed the big time—he left right before they recorded *Smells Like Teen Spirit*."

"Wasn't he like the third drummer?" Zack asked. "And he did play on 'Polly' uncredited."

"Whatever. My point is that's what you guys could be doing if you leave Mixed Metaphors now. We have the prom lined up. If it goes badly, fine, you never have to play with me again. But if we start working now, we can put together something great. Do you really want to give up before you even try? I mean, you never know, right?"

I had to wait for a moment or two, but finally, they all looked at each other and gave a reluctant nod. I deserved another chance.

"All right, dude," Zack said, shrugging. Since I'd found out he was hooking up with Alison Stadtler, I'd started to question his motives for breaking up Mixed Metaphors to begin with.

Had he been after her this whole time? "If it means that much to you."

Like he was doing me a favor. Add that to my growing list of humiliations.

They'd agreed to do covers, so long as no boy bands were involved and so long as we could do them in our signature style. I'd even found us a new space to practice, in the Beany Baby's upstairs room, where they roasted the coffee beans. The owner said he was cool with it so long as my mom made sure we didn't mess with his equipment, and the big sacks of coffee actually muffled the sound from the rest of the coffee-goers. For the past eight days we'd been practicing daily, until we had a setlist we all felt good about.

I was proud of what we'd been able to accomplish, really proud. And now we were finally here. Well, Zack wasn't here yet, but I figured he was just running late as usual—and maybe he would show up in a plaid tuxedo.

Anyway, I didn't have time to obsess about my wardrobe. We still had a lot of work to do. We'd convened at the Franklin Institute at 3 p.m. By now it was almost 5, and the catering crew had arranged all the tables with white cloths and place settings and flowers while members of the prom committee walked around, surveying the scene.

I'd seen Dakota in the rotunda earlier as she oversaw the balloon tank. She was barefoot and wearing some sort of silvery blue, very tight dress that made everything pop in all the right places. As much as I hated to admit it, I did a double-take.

"We wanted a laser show, but this was all the budget allowed," she said glumly. "Look at this room! These stupid balloons will barely make a dent."

"It'll look good," I said, trying to make her feel better. She tried so hard all the time. It had to be stressful. "The room looks nice all on its own."

"Yeah. Maybe. How are things?" she asked, and I knew what she meant had absolutely nothing to do with prom preparations.

"So far so good," I said. I hadn't gotten any dispatches from Alice or Benny, but no news was good news, right? I had confidence in Alice. She knew what she was doing. Still, I wasn't going to be able to relax until they texted me that the work was done. Add that to my stage fright—our first gig! In front of the entire school! And I was wearing a clown suit. *Awesome.*

Now I paced the floor, taking stock of the situation. We had most of our gear unloaded, the amps for the guitars and bass plugged in, but we still had to mic the drums, tune up, and all set up and test the sound system. Chaddie was plucking his guitar. Max was thumping the bass drum: *one two, one two.* It was a huge, cavernous room, which was both cool and completely terrifying.

"You guys look like you're ready to rock," Rankin said. He was carrying a round table, moving it from one end of the room to the other.

"Hopefully," I said.

Prom started in an hour. I knew I would feel better once

Zack was here. He could manage the mics better than I could. I was pretty sure he could manage everything better, actually, without even trying.

"Are you sure you want to have your kit so far back?" I asked Max. "Because where it is, no one can see our logo on your bass drum."

"Everyone knows who we are," Chaddie butted in. If the past couple of weeks had been our honeymoon reunion period, we were now back to the dysfunctional marriage. "That's the best position for acoustics."

"I was asking Max."

Max shrugged. "Chaddie told me to put it there."

"Yeah, but it's a question of branding, of making ourselves known." I realized I sounded just like Dakota. I guess listening to her order us around the last few weeks had rubbed off on me. "We want people to remember who we are."

Max nodded, and for the first time I felt like he might be listening to me, and maybe even taking me seriously.

Then he reached into his pocket to get his ringing phone. As he listened, he nodded slowly with a look of resignation on his face. I heard him say "uh-huh, uh-huh, yeah, okay dude. If you think so . . ."

He turned to us. "Zack ate a bad pizzaco. He's been puking his guts out all day. Listen." Max held up his phone to me, like I really wanted to listen to Zack bowing to the porcelain goddess.

"Jesus, no thanks," I said, trying to absorb the information, my head spinning. "What the hell is a pizzaco?"

"A pizza and a taco, wrapped up together with an extra layer of cheese around it and deep fried," Chaddie said, his face reddening with the stress. "It's got, like, one hundred grams of saturated fat."

"They're really good," Max whispered. "What are we going to do? He says he's sorry."

Sorry was all fine and good, but sorry couldn't carry a tune. Sorry couldn't hold an audience's attention. And sorry was definitely not making me feel any better about our decision to reassemble the band.

"Give me the phone," I said. "Now!!"

"Hey man," Zack said in my ear, his voice husky. "This sucks. I'm on the floor over here."

"No way you can get here? No way at all?" I had to try.

"Dude. I'm dying. But you know, it's probably for the best, right? Alison said—"

Screw what Alison said. "Yeah, all right," I talked over him, feeling whatever energy I had drain away as my brain collapsed in on itself. "Stay hydrated."

I hung up. I didn't even . . . I couldn't think. Of all the potential disaster scenarios I'd imagined, not having Zack here wasn't one of them.

When I came back to earth, Max and Chaddie were going back and forth.

"We have to cancel," Chaddie was saying. "I mean, what can we do without our singer? None of us can really sing."

"So what do you suggest?" Max asked.

"I'm not getting up there and embarrassing myself. I refuse. This is prom. I'm not going to ruin it." Chaddie's eyes were wide with indignation, his voice, wavering, and as he talked, he seemed to get more and more undone. "Do you know what happened at prom four years ago when the band never showed? I do, because my sister was a junior. They canceled the whole thing. *The whole thing.* And you know what will happen to us if *we're* the reason they cancel prom? We'll be, like, the people who ruined HF. It'll be worse than Jason's dad. You guys can do whatever you want, but I'm not helping."

"Jesus. Do you really have to bring my dad into this?" I was so sick of hearing about it. I was sick of all of his bad decisions hovering over me.

"Face it, Jason. The guy's an asshole. He bankrupted your family, left you holding the bag. And this is the same thing, morally speaking."

Holy crap. Seriously? So Zack had told him. *Ass*hole.

"You can't compare my dad to us not playing prom! You just can't. I mean, blame my dad for whatever he did. It sucks. We all know it." I was finally coming clean with these people—what did it matter anymore? "But can we just move on already?"

It occurred to me as I said it that *I* was the one who needed to move on. I needed to stop lying, to just accept it and go forward. *I'm Jason Hodges and my dad is a goddamned thief.*

"What do you think, Jason?" Max asked, his tiny voice breaking through the bickering. "It's your call."

Now they were both looking at me, waiting for my answer, because I was supposed to be the leader. I rubbed at my forehead. First Zack and his intestinal explosion, then Chaddie's emotional meltdown, and now realizing Zack had dimed me out, no pun intended. I couldn't deal with this.

I should've known. This prom gig was doomed from the beginning. There had been so many signs it wasn't going to work out, and I'd ignored them all. I had no more optimism, no more fake-it-till-you-make-it left.

"Let's break down," I said quietly. Screw it. Screw all of them. I'd tell Alice I'd tried, but in the end I didn't have what it took to see this through. Dakota would be furious, but then, I'd dealt with her wrath before. "We can make a playlist or something. Plug in an iPod."

I put my guitar away first, then unplugged my amp. It was a relief, actually. As I dropped the cable, it made a terrible shrieking sound, punctuating my sense of suckitude.

I went backstage to where I'd left my cases. Dakota was passing by just then, carrying her iPad like a clipboard. "What are you doing? Aren't you supposed to be setting up now? Why are you putting things away?"

I shook my head, and my voice was almost robotic. "Zack just called. He's sick. You have to find a replacement, I guess. Or we can make a playlist."

"No," she said. "No freaking way, Jason."

"I'm sorry. I'm sorry we're ruining prom. Maybe try to get a DJ?"

"No, I mean, we're not calling anyone. You wanted to play, so here you are. You can't just give up, Jason. Plus, you and I need an alibi, badly. So you're playing! End of story."

"I'm not going to fight about this." I didn't want her to start with the usual lectures. "We can't play without a singer. It's just that simple."

"Well, what if you got a new one?"

"Now? An hour before prom? I don't think so."

"We could do it karaoke style—" she paused, and I gave her a look. She shook her head. "No, you're right, that's a terrible idea."

"You wanted covers, anyway. Why not just play the music as everyone knows it? We'll make a really good playlist, I promise."

She looked up at me with a funny little smile. "What if I did it?"

"You?" I asked, incredulous.

"Why not? You're playing covers, right? I know you don't think I'm cool enough to be in your band, but I can sing."

I'd seen her in school plays and stuff, and she could definitely carry a tune, but singing with a band was different. "I don't know if it's our style, though. I mean, we have an aesthetic . . ."

"You know Jason, I still have all the music you ever gave me."

"You do?" I was surprised.

"I listen to it all the time. Stone Roses, Blur, Ocean Colour Scene? Look, I know we're not BFFs. But, if I'm hard on you, it's because I know what you're capable of. You're so good at so many things, and I hate to see you give up so easily. Let me help you pull this off."

Wow. "What about the prom? Don't you want to hang out with Dylan or whatever?"

She shook her head. "He just called me from the limo, and he's already drunk. I hang out with him every day."

"Your friends are going to be really freaked out."

"I don't care. Benny and Alice are the ones who are really putting their asses on the line tonight while we're stuck here. I just want to *do* something. And I don't know . . . maybe it would be kind of fun?"

I cast a glance at our equipment and thought how depressing it would be to just pack up everything and walk away now, without even trying. Failure was getting boring. It was just so predictable.

I looked at Dakota's face, and I could see that she was totally and completely serious. Maybe we were actually friends now. This was what real friends did for each other.

"You're sure it would be okay?"

Dakota nodded. "Just give me the setlist so I can look it over."

I rummaged through my backpack for the copy of the setlist I'd saved for Zack and handed it to her. "Nothing too stage-y, okay?"

She rolled her eyes. "I think I can handle it."

TWENTY-FIVE

DAKOTA

I STEPPED ONSTAGE AND GRABBED THE MIC. "CHECK ONE two. Check one two."

It was that beautiful, scary moment right before a party started. Everything was perfect and on schedule. Our balloons floated around the room, evenly dispersed for maximum effect. The beverage bars were set up, bottles of sparkling water resting in their ice baths. The monogrammed napkins I'd personally paid for, embroidered with the letters HF, were folded on every table. Roses dyed in our school colors, violet and yellow, were tucked into crystal vases (again, on my personal tab—thank god my parents didn't pay much attention to my credit card bill). There was even a limo parked outside, sponsored by Mothers Against Drunk Driving (really, again, my parents), for any students who needed last-minute transport. In the past there had been accidents, and my parents were afraid that if there were any tonight, I could end up getting sued as a planner of the prom.

I stared out at the open room, imagining it full of everyone we knew, all my friends and their dates, dressed up and sitting down at their tables to eat the buffet meal the committee had selected—we'd had to settle for chicken fingers because of the limited budget, but the caterers had agreed to make it look nicer with garnishes and stuff. And the dance floor. They'd be all over the dance floor, dancing to music *I'd* be making.

It was strange standing up there. I mean, I always knew I'd be setting up prom, that was a given. But I never thought I'd actually *be* the entertainment, saving the prom from disaster. Or maybe ruining it entirely, single-handedly. I tried to push that thought away. The point was that for once, I wouldn't be giving orders or organizing; I'd be up there singing. That would be the real me—whether I failed or succeeded.

My parents would be horrified. As it was, they thought theater was a waste of my time. What would they think about me singing in a band? Bands were for losers, guys with unachievable dreams and no sense of reality. Guys like Jason Hodges.

My friends would be shocked, too, to see me hanging out up here with the hipster dudes. *They don't even shower*, I could hear Junibel saying. Not to mention that we hadn't even practiced. I heard my mom's voice in my head. *It's not worth doing anything if you're not prepared to do it well.*

Well, that was too bad, because I was doing this. For once I was going to do what I wanted. I sang the chorus of "Good Riddance" and tried to drown out all the other negative judgy voices. My voice peeled out in a ribbon of sound curling around the room, bigger than me, bigger than anyone.

"That actually sounds pretty good," Chaddie said. At first he'd been all freaked out about the possibility of my singing with the band. *Her?* he'd asked, like I wasn't right in front of him. *Her?* But now he seemed to be relaxing some, as much as a guy who looked like he was digesting a ball of steel wool could relax.

Jason shot me a sneaky smile. It felt good. To be honest, I'd only offered at first because I was concerned about protecting our plan. After all of our work, I couldn't let it go down the tubes. But when I saw Jason's face, and that for once he didn't have some jokey comment to make, I realized it was also the right thing to do.

Also? I'd realized that day when I did recon at the Mint that, every once in a while, doing something I wasn't supposed to do felt really, really good.

I was working my way through the second song on the list, "Wonderwall," when I felt my phone buzz in my pocket. Could be Simone wondering how much to tip the valet parking guy for his night of service. I put the mic down and picked up my phone.

When I looked at the screen, though, I saw the call was from Benny. I knew, even before I pressed ANSWER, that there was a reason my whole body was tensed up.

"Dakota," he said, his voice hoarse. "We have a serious problem."

Immediately everything else in the room went fuzzy, and my focus became like one of those laser pointers, tiny, bright, and purposeful. I stepped aside between two columns so I could get away from the others. "Tell me what happened."

"Alice must have made some kind of data error. There are more coins than we expected."

"How many?" I asked in my best organizer voice. There was no problem that couldn't be solved. I'd headed enough committees to know that.

"A lot," he said.

"Like a hundred? Two hundred? Be specific."

"Try a few thousand," he said. "They're flying out off the press. I'm watching them right now. There's no way we can move all of these by ourselves. And even if we could—"

I broke in. "What do you need?" I eyed up Jason from across the stage and saw that he'd tuned in to what was going on. He was watching me carefully as I answered Benny as calmly as I could. "Just tell me what you need."

"I don't know. Just come here. Come here and bring something big to carry them in. We need a new backup plan."

After all of my scenarios, this wasn't one we'd planned for. Fire, breaking an ankle, a snowstorm, yes. Computer error? No. Because Alice was in charge of that part, and we just never questioned her. "Okay, we're on it."

"All right. I can meet you. Fire door." His voice was shaky. "How long?"

"As soon as we can."

When I hung up, Jason was off the stage and by my side. "What happened?"

"There's a problem with the order," I whispered, stunned but still trying to maintain some discretion. "They have more than they can handle themselves."

"So what was their plan?"

"I don't know. He asked us to come and bring something to get the coins out. We have to come up with something. What should we do? What should we do?" I'd told Benny we'd come, but now I was having second thoughts. Now I was seriously entertaining the possibility of skipping town.

"Okay then. We've got to get over there," he said. He sounded more confident, more serious than I'd ever heard him. I'd seen it a little bit that night in the woods, but now he was like a different person.

"But what if they're in trouble?"

"If they're in trouble, *we're* in trouble. Look, we have to try, don't we? We're a team, right?" he asked, throwing my words back in my face. One minute I was giving him a pep talk, and now he was returning the favor. The world had clearly spun off its axis.

What could I do but agree? "Yeah. But what about the prom? The band?" We'd just averted our first crisis of the night, and now we had to contend with a much bigger one. Prom was one thing, but I couldn't go to jail, and I didn't want anyone else to, either.

"Well, we're just going to have to find a way to do both," he said.

Prom was starting in half an hour. The Mint was at least ten minutes away. It was impossible. I glanced over at Rankin and the other faculty chaperones, who were talking in the corner. My eyes locked with Rankin's. "I'm supposed to be the committee point person," I said to Jason. "The chaperones will wonder why I'm not here!" I rubbed my face in a way that my mom had explicitly told me caused breakouts.

Jason's eyes darted around while he thought of our next move. "Okay. I got it. We'll pretend that the rental PA crapped out. We'll get on the phone like we're calling the company, and we'll tell the band we're going down to South Street to pick up a replacement. That limo's still out there, right?"

I nodded, impressed with his quick thinking. Who was this guy in the Jason suit?

"Get the keys and pull it around."

"How am I supposed to do that?"

"You're the project manager," he said firmly. "Figure it out. Meet me outside in five. And text Benny . . . Tell him we're on our way."

I did as he said. It was a relief not to have to figure it all out on my own for once. But first I called Dylan to tell him we had a band emergency and had to leave the Franklin Institute, and that I'd be late. I also told him I was singing with the band.

Ordinarily he might have questioned that, but he was so drunk all I heard was a four-syllable "yeahhhh" with a background soundtrack of yelling lacrosse players, girly squeals, and something loud crashing.

"Oh man." He cracked up. "Justin threw Arno's wallet out of the sunroof!"

I just hung up, shaking my head. I wasn't missing anything. I put the phone down and went into the kitchen and had the catering crew lay out a dinner plate for the driver. Then I put my coat on and went outside and told him it was waiting for him.

"That's nice of you," he said. He was a bored-looking middle-aged guy who clearly spent a lot of his life waiting in a limo on nights like these. In fact, he'd spent so many nights doing exactly this that he was used to leaving the keys in the ignition, right where I needed them. Maybe we were doing him a favor by stealing his car, I rationalized.

I was getting very good at that.

"We try," I said.

My heart raced as I waited for him to go back through the revolving door at the service entrance on the side of the building.

"Dakota!"

I turned to see Rankin emerging from around the corner. He was all dressed up in a tan linen suit.

Nooo! Why did I always have to run into him at the worst possible times?

"What are you doing out here?"

"Band emergency," I said, repeating my prepared excuse. "We have to get a new rental PA."

He nodded—was that suspicion I saw? I thought back to the day I saw him after meeting with Garcia. He'd seemed weird then, too. No, that was probably just his usual way of dealing with students. No way he could know anything. "See you in there," he said. He walked a few more steps, then stopped and turned around. "Don't take too long."

"I won't!" I said, flashing my best DAKOTA CUNNING-HAM smile.

When he was gone, I ran around to the driver side, got behind the wheel, turned on the engine, and drove around to the back where Jason was waiting, two giant red rolling amp cases on either side of him.

TWENTY-SIX

BENNY

DREAD OOZED AND FILLED EVERY INCH OF MY BODY, LIKE the cement they poured over dead guys in mob movies. It was now 5:35 p.m. We had ten minutes to figure this shit out. Impossible, right?

Even so, I couldn't help but feel a bit relieved when I opened the door on the fire stairs landing and saw Dakota and Jason standing outside on Race Street with these two big red boxes and doomsday looks on their faces. I mean, I almost laughed, I was so glad.

At least we were in this together. As much as Dakota bugged me, I knew she would do her best to make sure we got out of here.

I hustled them in and quickly rushed them up the stairs to the production floor.

"What kind of crazy-ass outfit is that?" I yelled to Jason over the machines. He looked like he had gotten into a brawl with a bunch of lumberjacks. Meanwhile, Dakota looked like . . . Well, she looked like some sort of princess. In a good way for once, I mean. God, she was beautiful. I looked away quickly before she caught me staring at her. *Pathetic, dude, just pathetic.*

"It's a stage outfit. For the band."

Huh? Well, never mind that. "You left the door open, right?"

"Yeah," Jason said.

Good. We needed all of our options at this point. It was emergency time.

Alice didn't say anything when they got there. She was still comatose, practically. I felt bad for her, but there wasn't much time to worry about feelings. We had to save ourselves.

Luckily, the others were still on this planet, thank Jesus. Jason took one look at the machines and said, "Let's get to work."

It was nothing like we'd pictured it. Operation GroundEagleFly had had its moments, but this one really took the cake: me and Jason scrambling around on our hands and knees under the coin traps trying to catch the flying quarters in Jason's cases.

Ching ching ching.

We had nine minutes, by my count, before the next security round. An eternity, or the blink of an eye. We could do this, we could finish the job and get this stuff out of here, if we just kept going, if we kept pace with the machines. But they were machines, and we were . . . humans.

My fingers burned through the gloves I was wearing, and

sweat poured down my back. Pins and needles started to stab at my feet. Couldn't think about that. The coins had to go.

"How many more?" Dakota kept asking as she watched the doors.

"I don't know!" I yelled. "No one knows!" They all looked at me, alarmed. Maybe they weren't expecting the quiet guy to start hollering. Well, this guy was done being quiet.

Meanwhile, the robots that were supposed to pack the finished coins in nylon bags were zooming back and forth across the floor—their sensors confused by our plan.

It would have been ridiculous if it weren't all so damn stressful. I had no idea how long this machine would keep running. We'd been on the floor for about thirty minutes, but it felt like hours.

About thirty seconds later there was a horrible buzzing, some red lights flashed, and we all froze.

WTF was that? An alarm of some kind?

Then we saw the belt start winding down. Within minutes, the last few coins were flipped out of the press and into the trap, and then everything went dead. I mean everything. All the movement in the room. The silence was so sudden, it was almost painful.

It was done. Finally it was done. *Oh thank God.*

A weird sense of peace settled over me.

Maybe this would be okay, I thought. If we hurried, we could get out of here. It wouldn't be so hard. We could still pull this off. Eight and a half minutes.

"Let's go, guys!" I said, noticing that they were all still.

Dakota, especially. She was zoning out at something in front of her.

We had to hustle if we were gonna get out okay. "Come on! What's the problem?"

Then I saw what she was staring at. The light on in the other room. We could see it through the door.

The guard!

Could it be? But he was early. This wasn't right. We were so close. We just needed a few more minutes . . .

Jason was already closing up his case, getting ready to roll it away. Dakota had snapped back into action too, scrambling to help me pick up some coins on the floor. But Alice was just standing there next to me, frozen on the spot, her fists full of quarters that were spilling out at her feet.

"Move!" I yelled, getting in her face. It wasn't like it would help; there was nowhere to hide, and not enough time. But I was just so pissed right then. Why couldn't she *try*? "Just do something! Snap the hell out of it!"

But there was no snapping out of it, no waking up, for any of us. This wasn't a dream, and it wasn't a game. This was for real. They were coming for us. I watched, helpless, as the door opened. Someone was about to walk in.

The door opened, and we all just froze dead in our tracks. It was worse than a guard.

It was Mr. Rankin.

TWENTY-SEVEN

ALICE

HE'D FIGURED IT OUT. I DON'T KNOW HOW. I DON'T KNOW when. But he'd figured it out, and here he was standing right in front of us.

Dakota covered her mouth like she was holding in a scream. That was more than I could do.

Rankin was all spruced up, but he still had his usual glasses on and he was holding his keys, like he'd rushed up here so fast he hadn't taken the time to put them in his pocket. "Okay, stop whatever you're doing. Stop right now."

"What are you doing here?" I whispered. I felt like I was going to pass out. This was worse than anything else we could have imagined. Our teacher? Was here? We were doomed.

"I followed you bozos. I was at the prom with these two"—he

gestured toward Dakota and Jason—"and I saw them freaking out, whispering in the corner before they dashed out. I knew there must have been some reason you guys have been hanging out all the time."

Then he held up a phone.

Dakota slapped at the pockets of her jacket, a look of horror on her face, and we understood. Oh man.

"The last text from Benny was all I needed. Thanks for leaving that door open, by the way."

"Slick," Jason said, because it was. We had to give him props.

Rankin ignored him. "I came to keep you from doing something you'll regret, something that could ruin your lives forever."

"Just hold on a minute," Benny said, and we looked at him in shock. *He* was going to talk back to Rankin? "Mr. Rankin, thanks for looking out for us. But we're already into this, way too deep. The thing you didn't CSI out here is that we're actually trying to *stop* this thing from happening."

"How's that?" he asked, his eyebrows joining together in one big confused line.

"We were originally gonna take the coins and sell them, try and save HF, but then we decided not to go ahead with it. But we realized that we had made a mistake." He shot a tiny glance in my direction. Saying "we" was generous, and I was grateful he had my back. "There was no stopping it, so we had to come back in here tonight and fix the problem, sneak the coins out so that no one would find out. Lecture us about right and wrong all you want, but the bottom line is we've got thousands of coins in these cases and we have to get out of here. Like *now*. The guards will be coming through any minute. And if they catch us, they won't exactly care that we were trying to call it off. We'd go to jail anyway."

"Are you going to bust us?" Dakota asked, pulling nervously at the neckline of her shiny blue dress.

"He can't," Benny said, breaking it down. "See, now, if something went wrong and we got in trouble, you could be placed at the scene of the crime, Mr. Rankin. An accessory."

Rankin's eyes darted from one of us to the other, and I could see him thinking it all through. "I'll just tell them the truth."

"But you knew about this for how long and you didn't call the police? They're going to think you were in on it, or shaking us down. A teacher who teaches a bunch of rich kids? They'll think you were jealous of us."

"Benny, are you threatening me?" His face was red.

"No! I'm not. For real, I'm not. But you've kind of put us in a position here. And we don't have time to debate. They're coming! Come on, Mr. Rankin. You have to help us get this stuff out. We have a good cover—we have ID cards—we can do this if we move *right now*."

"Goddamn it," Rankin said, clenching his fists as he realized Benny was right. "Understand I'm not letting you guys off the hook. There will be consequences for you. I need the access card you've used. I need to leave with that."

"Here," I said, shoving it into his hand. "Now what's the

plan? We have seven and a half minutes."

Rankin took it and slipped it into his suit pocket. "We take the cases, and we all go back to prom like nothing happened, okay? And then we're going to deal with this, all of it."

"Okay," I said. The others nodded, too.

Rankin pointed to Jason and Dakota. "You two better get back there with the band before anyone else gets suspicious. Take the fire stairs out, get into your limo, and we'll meet you there when we can."

"Are you sure?" Jason asked. That was a joke. All of a sudden he was a new person, caring about the rest of us? I doubted it.

"You guys should go," Benny said. "The three of us can handle it."

Jason looked at me. My stomach fluttered. Maybe he actually did care. I softened and gave him a quick nod. Still, there was a question in his eyes.

"Go," I said, finally, looking at Dakota now.

Her face broke into a slow smile. Not the usual forced Dakota smile, but more surprised, off-guard and genuine.

Jason tried to slap his palm against Rankin's in a handshake. "Thanks, man. We really appreciate it."

Rankin left him hanging. "I'm not doing you a favor, Hodges. I'm not doing any of you a favor, you got that? You take advantage of me here, and I'm taking you straight to the police."

Jason and Dakota made for the door, leaving the way they had come in. Two down.

Rankin pushed the amp case again. "I can't fit both of you and this stuff in my Honda, though."

"That's okay," I said. "We have our own means of transport."

"You planned this pretty well, huh?" Rankin asked.

"Not well enough," I said.

I checked my phone. *17:39: Still in the frigging Mint.*

With the others gone, the three of us worked in silence. We got down on the floor and scooped up the last few dozen coins, dropping them into the second case, them slamming the lid closed.

The cases were unmarked, so there was a chance we could pass them off as HVAC equipment if anyone asked. I prayed no one would. But with their built-in wheels, we could easily move them out, a weight that would have been way too heavy to carry on our own. All we had to do was wheel them downstairs.

The only problem? Stairs.

"Is there a ramp somewhere?" Rankin asked.

"There must be," I said. "It's a federal building, so they have to be handicapped-accessible by law."

Benny sighed. "It's on the other end of the building, the Arch Street side. I had that on the model."

Which meant we had to wheel the cases all the way across the production floor, through the medal-making area, basically the entire length of the building, which was going to take a lot longer. Then when we got down to the boiler level, we'd have to wheel them all the way back to the Race side elevator to get down to the garage. I estimated the whole operation would take at least five minutes.

"Guards are coming through in two minutes," I reminded them. "Also, my security feeds are going to start looping." If anyone was watching closely, they might start to notice that "Benny and I" had barely moved. As soon as we got ready to leave, I'd shut them down and switch back to the live feed, but if I didn't switch it over soon, the guards would probably get suspicious.

"Go time," Rankin said.

We decided that Rankin would take the fire exit out and we'd meet him back at the prom. We exchanged phone numbers just in case we got separated.

We had no time to debate the merits of this plan. We just had to go. No questions asked.

"See you," Rankin whispered. "This is the last time I'm letting you out of my sight tonight. Don't even think of not showing up there, because then I *will* call the cops."

17:44: Get the hell out!

Benny and I took off with the loot, moving as quickly as we could. We'd just about gotten past the medal area to the ramp when I felt Benny's hand close tightly around my arm. We paused and I could hear a ding behind us, followed by the worst sound I've ever heard: an elevator door sliding open.

A guard! We must have been slower than I thought. He was heading out of the elevator, straight for Rankin. Rankin would be intercepted on the way to the fire stairs. *Ohgod ohgod*

ohgod ohgod. We were dead.

We paused at the end of the hallway, partially hidden in shadow, no idea what to do next. We were done. Totally screwed. Then I remembered the "refuge" area Dakota had pointed out next to the elevator, a dark little room. Benny and I inched our way into it, rolling the cases ever so slowly, not even daring to breathe.

By now, Rankin had to be face-to-face with the guy. Not that it mattered who the guard saw first, because even if Rankin had somehow found a way to hide, the guard would see us eventually. We waited, transfixed, because there was no way we could move. Not a muscle. I felt everything inside me knotting up.

"Oh my goodness!" I heard Rankin exclaim. "No need for a gun!"

Holy crap. The guard had pulled a gun? My heart was thundering, louder than the coin presses. All of the adrenaline my body could produce was spinning through my circulatory system. I finally understood what an actual heart attack might feel like.

"What are you doing here?" the guard—was it Tony? Glen? Had to be Glen if he was following the schedule—barked. "Are you authorized to be in the building, sir?" This was it. He was caught. And he was obviously going to sell us out. We were done. Through. Finished.

"Oh no. Oh no. This is very embarrassing. Oh, please don't shoot me," Rankin said.

"What are you doing here?" Glen the guard repeated, nastier this time.

Rankin started talking very quickly. "Do you know Brad, the production manager? He's my cousin. His wife just went into labor six weeks early and he realized he didn't have his wallet. He thought he must have left it here at work, and it has his insurance card and everything else. He gave me his ID to come pick it up, and I said I would do it right away, because at a time like this, you really don't want to be worried about anything."

None of these guys knew Garcia. They were only here on the weekend. Shit, what if he didn't believe Rankin's story?

"He did, huh?" The guard asked, taking a look at the card Rankin handed him. "And he thought you could get in on a Saturday night? How'd you get in here, anyway?"

"He said it might be tough but to try the staff entrance."

Where was he pulling this story from? I couldn't believe what a great liar he was. He was even selling me with it.

"Let me see this ID," the guard said.

My heart stopped again. Benny had made a solid reproduction—he hadn't lied, he was good at this stuff. But still, if you looked closely, you would know it wasn't perfect. *Please don't look closely . . . please don't look closely . . .*

A staticky voice came through on the guard's radio, and I heard him murmur something into it, like *Be there in a minute.* "You do realize this building is tightly controlled for a reason."

Heart. Exploding.

"Yes. Oh my gosh. I never meant to get anyone into trouble. He said I should just tell the guards Garcia said it was okay. Is this okay?"

Glen the guard sighed, staring at Rankin. I guess he had an honest face, because Glen said, "Not really, but where do you need to go?"

"His office. If you could show me the way, I'd be grateful."

"It's right this way," the guard said. "You're not allowed to walk around unescorted. Your cousin should know that. I'll show you."

"Excellent," I heard Rankin say, and his voice disappeared.

We had no idea what was happening. But we had to move.

When we heard a door click, Benny and I leapt to our feet and rolled the cases out of the refuge and a few feet farther down the hall to where the ramp was—just as Benny said it would be. As we went down, I could feel the case gaining momentum, all that weight. I felt the burden of this job, of everything we'd gone through to get here, literally pulling me down, and I had to move faster and faster to keep up with it. Soon I was practically running, and so was Benny.

Please let us get out of here okay! I was flying now, my feet barely touching the ground, and the air rushed around me and I felt dizzy and nauseous with fear. I cursed Jason as I went. Why had I let it come to this? Why had I gone along with him in the first place? Stupid stupid hormones. And now he was using me again—one cute smile and I was doing his dirty work while he was at the freaking prom. I couldn't wait for this all to be over so I never had to talk to him again.

And then I felt the cart steady and slow down. Benny's hands reaching out to steady me.

"We made it," he whispered.

I looked up, startled, my vision slowly clearing. We were on the garage level. But where the hell was Rankin?

We rolled the cases back down the hallway. The guard who'd checked us in nodded in our direction. "Done for the night?"

Oh yeah. I let Benny do the talking, as he gave the guy our Hansen ID. "We're taking some of these parts with us for repair in the shop."

I prayed he wouldn't remember that we hadn't brought these cases in when we had first arrived. The guy nodded nonchalantly and turned back to his computer screen.

And then? We were through the door and standing in front of our van. We opened the doors in the back, pulled down the loading ramp, and slid the amp cases up and in. We scrambled into the front seat, and Benny drove up and out of the garage.

"Thanks," Benny said into the voicebox. "See you next week."

17:52: Leave the Mint premises.

The security gate lifted and we were out of there. We were free. We'd done it.

We drove around the block. No sign of Rankin. I looked at Benny. He raised his eyebrows. "We have to keep moving, Alice."

"What if he's stuck?"

"He said to meet at the prom."

"I'm going to text him." I got out my phone.

WHERE R U? WE'RE OUT.

I waited about thirty seconds, but there was no reply.

"Look, we gotta go," Benny said.

He was right. I just hoped Rankin knew what he was doing.

We pulled away, headed down Market Street. When we hit a light, I snuck a look behind me at the amp cases, holding the thousands of coins we'd just counterfeited. And all I could think was: *Holy crap.*

By the time we parked under the Franklin Institute, the music was peeling out from the main hall. Jason and Dakota had made it all right.

"We can't go in there like this," I said, looking down at our clothing. "If we're going to use this as an alibi or whatever."

Benny seemed annoyed—he was probably more comfortable in the coveralls—but he agreed with me. And if I did it, he had to too. We were partners now. We took our bags up the elevator into the lobby.

Lo and behold, there was Mr. Rankin, stationed by the elevator door, looking like he was waiting for us.

"You made it," I said.

"And you're damn lucky I did." He looked pissed. I couldn't really blame him.

"What'd you do?" I asked.

"I talked my way out of it. I played dumb. I don't know if he bought it, but he let me leave."

"S'up, Mr. Rankin?" Jason Sidleman said as he passed by in his tux.

Rankin waved a hand that was blackened from coins and machinery.

I pointed to it. "Um?"

"Mother of . . ." He pulled out a pocket square and rubbed furiously to get rid of the evidence. He sighed angrily. "Go change, you two, and I'll deal with you later."

TWENTY-EIGHT

DAKOTA

I SANG LIKE NOBODY'S BUSINESS. JUNIBEL WAS OUT THERE.
Dylan, too. I could feel their eyes on me. Everyone's eyes were
on me. Oh god. Was my hair okay? I felt like I had mascara
running down my face.

I hadn't had a chance to really look in the mirror since we'd
jumped out of the limo and dashed back into the Franklin
Institute atrium. (And let me tell you, running up those stairs
in my Charlotte Olympia heels was no joke.)

Benny and Alice and Mr. Rankin must have gotten out
of the Mint okay, because they were there. Alice and Benny
were at the edge of the room, looking like they were going to
bolt at any moment. I tried to catch Benny's eye, but he wasn't
acknowledging me.

I felt terrible, letting them clean up after us. Benny hated me as it was. I deserved his hatred, all of it. I was a jerk. I'd kissed him, then I'd been an idiot at that party, and then he'd done the dirty work for us . . .

No no no. I couldn't think about all that. I was up here, and we were expected to perform. I wasn't going to crack under the pressure, even though I really, really just wanted to go hide in the bathroom.

Just sing, damn it.

I clutched the microphone and sang. I sang my heart out. The funny part was that when I should have felt the most nervous, I was suddenly calm as anything. Like all the fear and stress of the day had floated away. Like the music was just a valve that released it all. Better than Dr. Pollard's Valium breaths any day.

TWENTY-NINE

JASON

IN THE MUSIC I COULD GET LOST. WHEN WE WERE UP THERE in front of everyone, I forgot all about everything, all about the stress of that day. It was effortless: I just focused on one chord and then the next. All the rest dropped away.

I couldn't believe it. The set was magic. Somehow, with hardly any practice, we were all in sync. Max kept a steady rhythm behind us, never losing tempo. And Dakota—it was seriously freaking me out how great she sounded. Made me wonder why all along we hadn't thought to get a girl onboard. Her voice was strong and clear but still velvety soft.

She turned to me and smiled. We had this. When it counted, we'd made it work.

Staring out over the audience, I actually could see how good we were—it was written all over them, the way the other kids were moving and smiling. They were dancing, for god's sake. To us. It was like everything I'd ever done had led up to this very moment, and I never wanted it to end. I was riding a total high, and I'd had no weed to speak of in ages. So I had to chalk it up to the band and our ass-kicking awesomeness.

I wasn't just Mr. Hodges' screwup son after all.

And then, as I scanned the audience, I did a double-take. Could that be? Was I hallucinating? Alice was there, in the doorway, only twenty feet away. And she was wearing a *dress*.

THIRTY

BENNY

I WAS AT THE PROM. HOW WACK WAS THAT?

But Rankin had his eye on us. What else could I do but heap up a plate of food from the buffet, then sit down and eat and watch the band? No matter what, I would never dance, not in front of this crowd.

Dakota was singing. I'd seen her onstage, at assemblies and stuff, but it was like she was a whole different person up there now. She was holding on to the microphone and singing into it like it was a person she was talking to, her head arched back, her hair catching the light like gold. She just looked . . . so . . . free.

I didn't want to think of us kissing in her back yard. I didn't want to watch her. And I certainly didn't want her to watch me watching her, knowing I was thinking of kissing her. But I couldn't look away, either.

THIRTY-ONE

ALICE

BENNY AND I HAD BOTH BEEN DRAGGING OUR FEET, completely disturbed by the turn of events that brought us to this moment. Rankin had basically had to drag us into the rotunda, a hand on each of our shoulders. Inside the big open room, there were special spotlights casting a cool blue glow on the columns. A giant marble statue of Ben Franklin sat on one end, a ghostly presence hovering over the tables, which were already full of people sitting on silver chairs. The décor was simple, but it amplified the history and the beautiful details of the architecture. Blue and white and green balloons floated in clusters in the airy coffered dome, weightless and elegant, with scarves twisted into feathery shapes all around the room.

Everyone's parents had taken them here when they were little, to walk through the giant heart, see an IMAX movie or visit the planetarium. My personal favorite had always been the electricity exhibit, where you could move around on the floor and create a staticky charge on a Tesla coil on the ceiling. But for all that, I'd never realized how beautiful this building was, or how lucky we were to have our prom at a place like this. Make that how lucky *they* were. Nobody had invited me.

"Lookin' good, Harry Potter," Benny said as we stood and watched the band.

"Shut up," I said, but I wasn't really mad. "You clean up pretty nicely yourself."

"Eh, I do all right. But seriously, you can really wear a dress."

"Thanks." It was different now that we'd gone through the whole Mint thing. "And thanks for what you did—in there," I said.

"No sweat." He didn't seem to want to say much more about it, so I let it drop and tried to get myself into prom mode. That was a joke. Just being here and gawking from the sidelines was proving everything everyone thought about people like me and Benny. It didn't matter that Benny in a suit made most of the other guys here look like mere boys. It didn't matter that I had a dress on, no thinking cap anywhere to be found.

Social math: Within set theory there's something called the "axiom of determinacy," which means that in a certain kind of game where numbers are involved, one player will always have the winning strategy, but it can only be that one player, and it's determined from the beginning. I mean, someone has to win and someone has to lose, right?

Well, that was me at HF. The loser.

But I didn't really want to win the game at HF. I didn't even like the rules. Why was I supposed to try and be like Dakota or something? I just wanted to be myself, and I wanted that to be cool. A unit set, which contains exactly one element: me.

The band started a new song. Out of instinct, I turned to face the stage, which was to the left of good old Ben Franklin. Jason was up there standing just behind Dakota, playing "Wonderwall." They looked good up there. They'd make a cute couple if she'd ever dump Dylan.

Then something funny happened: Jason leaned in to the microphone to back up her vocals with a *wowowo*, and then he winked.

At me.

For one singular and great moment, it didn't matter that I didn't have a date. It didn't matter that Rankin was going to get us expelled. It didn't matter that he thought I was the female Harry Potter. *Jason freaking Hodges winked at me.*

But did he actually? I'd been wrong before, hadn't I? Thinking there was more to it when there wasn't, that Jason was deeper than he acted? Getting carried away with my fantasies?

I turned to look behind me quickly, and lo and behold, there was Chloe Benezet, wearing a sequined feathery thing that looked like an ostrich, grinding on her dance partner.

I mean, to "Wonderwall"? Seriously?

The good moment was gone, quickly as it came, escaped like one of the balloons up there in the dome, never to come back—not until it was completely deflated, anyway.

I sucked in a breath. It was almost a relief, actually, to prove myself right after all. Jason would never be more than a burn-out, and I'd never be more to him than a brainiac, a hired hand for his plans. The sooner I got that through my thick skull, the better.

THIRTY-TWO

JASON

IT WAS ALL OVER. PROM WAS COMING TO A CLOSE. THE lights were coming on. I put my guitar in its case and stepped off the stage.

Chaddie was practically jumping up and down as he followed me. "That was awesome, man," he said, with a positive attitude for the first time ever. "We rocked. Are you gonna come with us to the after-party?"

"I'll meet you there," I said. First I had something I had to do.

Alice wasn't where I saw her last, when she and Benny and Rankin first came in. I circled around, looking.

"Great show, Hodges," Dylan Sanders said, blocking my path, his thick neck poking out of his bowtied collar. "My girl can sing, huh?"

"Yeah, she can," I said. "Have you seen Alice Drake any-where?"

He frowned. "Who?"

"The girl who stole your rat?" He knew damn well who she was. "Never mind," I said and moved on.

It occurred to me that just a few months ago, I probably would have said the same thing. I'd never looked for Alice in my life. She'd just been there, hanging around, like ozone. It was only in the past few weeks that I'd started to really notice things about her, like how long her eyelashes were underneath her glasses, how she had a little dimple on her left cheek, how her laugh snuck up on her sometimes and made her eyes tear up. And tonight, from the stage, it had all become clear.

Nothing was what I'd planned, exactly. The whole Mint thing was just a cover-up job. I'd had big hopes of saving the school, of actually helping the people who worked there, but now we were only saving ourselves. Still. I was tired of not try-ing, not caring, not being honest.

I went out into the lobby, which was cold and empty and silent in contrast to Franklin Hall. No sign of her there, either. Just a security guard, who I nodded to. I guess after tonight, I felt like I understood these guys a little better.

I stepped outside through the heavy bronze doors, onto the front steps of the museum, which were like a waterfall spilling to the sidewalk below. That's where I found her, about half-way down, her knees gathered into her chest as she watched the traffic pass by on Twentieth Street.

"Hey," I said, sitting down next to her on the cool concrete. The warm spring evening air swirled around us like perfume, blossom-sweet. "What are you doing out here?"

She shrugged her little shoulders. "I don't know. Waiting for this thing to be over," she said.

"It feels nice," I said. "Fresh air."

She just nodded with pursed lips.

"So . . ." I said. "What did you think?"

She gave me a strained smile. "It was fine."

"Just fine?"

"Yeah. It sounded fine." Her face tightened. "What do you want me to say, Jason? That you're ready for an arena tour? Can you please just find someone else to stroke your ego? I'm not in the mood."

Wha? Why was she so snippy all of a sudden? I held up my hands in defense. "Sorry. I'm not fishing for compliments. I just thought—since you were the one who encouraged me—"

She cut right in, waving me off. "Yeah, great. I encouraged you and now you're a superstar, so let's not pretend we're going to be friends in school on Monday, because we won't. We've never been friends. I paved the way and helped you get what you want, and, you know, mission accomplished. Go you. You can officially ditch me now."

"Is that what you think of me? That I'm some kind of free-loader?" It felt like I'd been sucker-punched. And I realized, all of a sudden, that I really did care what she thought. It mattered to me that she, out of everyone, actually got who I was.

Because throughout this ordeal, I'd relied on her. She was right when she said she'd paved the way. She'd done that and more. Because she liked me. I knew then why I was really out here.

"Aren't you?" she asked, and her eyes, behind their glasses, glinted with a direct challenge. It was like looking in some nightmare mirror that only reflected the worst thing you could imagine. The slacker pothead selfish jerk she must have seen. It sucked.

"No. NO!" I shouted. "I'm not. I just wanted to thank you. I'm sorry if it offends you, but the truth is that you're right: Without you, I would have never done this. What we did tonight, or playing the prom. And you know, it doesn't even matter to me what happens next. Everyone always says I give up too easily, but not this time. Don't you see?"

She was still just staring at me, waiting for me to finish, I guess.

"And I'm not going to forget you, if that's what you think. You *get* me, Al." I was in her face now, leaning in close. "And . . . I—I think I kind of get you, too." Before I could think twice, I lifted her chin with my finger and went in for a kiss.

She pulled away in surprise. "Don't make fun of me," she said, her lip trembling.

"I'm not." To prove it, I leaned in closer and tried again. Her lips felt plush and warm—not what I expected. Then the kiss opened up deeper, and I ran my hand through her hair. She smelled nice, like herself, and not a cloud of super-sweet celebrity perfume like most of the girls I knew. Maybe I never would have thought of doing this, if she hadn't called her crush to my attention. I'd basically been oblivious that whole time. But in my defense, there were a few other things going on.

And now there was just this. I swear—something electric passed between us, and I knew it was more than just an instinct.

"Are you . . . sure?" she asked, looking at me closely.

I closed my eyes to kiss her again, but she pulled away from me.

Damn. Maybe I'd come on too strong. I looked down, a little embarrassed, but she just jerked her chin at something behind me.

"Rankin," she said through gritted teeth.

I saw him then, glaring down at us from the top of the steps. "You lovebirds had best get yourselves back up here. I'm not finished with you."

THIRTY-THREE

DAKOTA

"EVERYONE IN?" RANKIN ASKED.

We were all crammed into the van, trying to get settled. Benny must have been trying to find room for his legs, because he inadvertently kicked my side.

"Sorry," he said.

"Copping a feel, Ben-Ben?" Jason asked from the other end.

"Give me a break. And for the millionth time, that's not my name."

"Shut up, Jason." I sighed, sick of everyone. "Shut up both of you!"

"I'm just trying to make light of the situation. Calm down," Jason said.

"Why don't *you* calm down?" I snapped. "Some situations can't be lightened."

Then Alice had to turn around from her perch in the passenger seat, exchanging some kind of look with Jason, like, *isn't she crazy?*

I was over it. All of them. Because really? Squeezing the three of us and my Zac Posen dress into the back of the van and riding around without my seatbelt on were just the icing on this whole horrific cake. I'd gone from feeling amazing on stage, finally feeling like myself for once, to this?

By now, I didn't even care about missing the after-party with Dylan and the rest of them. I'd thought he was going to be really angry with me, and I was all prepared for a big scene, but when I'd told him I wasn't feeling well, he'd just shrugged and said, "You're missing out."

No, I really wasn't. That, at least, I knew. Maybe he'd hook up with someone else, and we could finally admit to ourselves that our whole thing was just a showmance—we were together because we thought we had to be, not because we had any real feelings for each other.

Who knew where Rankin was taking us now? It was obvious that we were on our way to some kind of deadly punishment. And either way, our parents were going to find out. I was finished. Completely finished.

I was going to be sent away—and probably to a place much worse than Bertrand Academy. I'd screwed up big time. And all of a sudden I couldn't, for the life of me, remember why I'd gotten involved with this thing in the first place. Was it to get back at my parents? Or to prove I was a badass? Because, clearly, I was not cut out to be a badass. I was a stressed-out mess with the worst possible urge to throw up the few bites of salad I'd eaten at the prom.

Where was Dr. Pollard now? *Okay, Valium breath. Focus on something. Anything.*

I tried to count the streetlights, but we were going too fast. I looked at the back of Rankin's head, which I'd never really looked at before, not in this detail. His hair was thinning on the top, and he had a little scar or birthmark or something under his right ear, just barely visible in the dim light. None of these details should have been surprising, but they were, because up until tonight he hadn't really been a real person to me.

I corrected myself. Of course he had been. I just never thought of him that way. Well, that's what Benny had basically said, wasn't it? That I was a narcissist, just focused on myself. Only I was always pretending to be something I wasn't, which was even worse. Benny was the real deal, and I was a big fake. No wonder I was in a fake relationship with a fake guy. Dylan and I deserved each other.

We were out of the city now, having wound our way past the boat houses on Kelly Drive. Next was the even windier Lincoln Drive, which was throwing us back and forth, so that one moment Jason was in my lap and the next I was draped all over Benny. Awkward.

I remember my dad telling me that when he was growing up, it was a game to see who could travel from one end of this road to the other without braking on any of the hairpin curves. It sounded pretty scary. Then again, it was probably nothing compared to robbing the Mint.

Oh God. My dad.

I'd never been on this road because Lincoln Drive was on the other side of the river from where all of us lived—except for Benny, of course. And his neighborhood was way back in the other direction. I wondered what he was thinking about now, if he was freaking out anywhere near as much as I was.

"Where are you taking us?" I blurted finally, unable to stand the suspense. "What's happening?"

Mr. Rankin didn't say anything.

"Are you kidnapping us to chain us to the water heater in your scary basement?" Jason asked.

How could Jason be joking at a time like this?

Rankin laughed. "That's a thought. No, I don't think my wife would appreciate me showing up unannounced with prisoner-guests."

"What then? Mr. Rankin, please, don't play games with us," I pleaded. "Are you taking us to the police?"

Mr. Rankin was definitely trying to drive us over the edge, keeping quiet. I wished like anything that I had never gotten involved in Operation EagleFly, that I'd minded my own business like any other kid at school and just let the place close down, moved on. Why'd I have to go and act like I could make a difference? I mean, if a genie had shown up right then, I would've given away all my other wishes—forget going to Harvard or anything else—and just focused on going back in time and erasing the worst decision I'd ever made.

Rankin turned off Lincoln Drive and onto a tree-lined street. Chestnut Hill. This was a fancy neighborhood, just as fancy as Bryn Mawr, with lots of cobblestone streets and preppy people. The kind of place where New England wannabes wore whale belts, pink pants, and Docksiders.

As we pulled into a long driveway, I felt myself shaking. Benny must have sensed it, too, because he put a hand on my knee to settle it. It felt nice, a way of letting me know it was going to be okay. How is it that just having him next to me could make me feel calm even in *this* situation?

Rankin pulled into a cul-de-sac and parked in front of an old carriage house. He shut off the engine. "Okay, guys. Out of the car."

Alice and Jason went first, slowly, and Benny and I followed. We walked in a single line down the front path, as if going to our own funerals. Which we sort of were.

Where were we? The house was huge and made of stone, with wrought iron balconies and darkened windows stretching out into the distance, a cold sea of darkness. None of the lights were on, except one glowing at the far end of the downstairs right wing. I could just about glimpse the shape of a man sitting at a desk inside.

Rankin rang the doorbell, which echoed throughout the

house. At least two and possibly three large dogs started barking, and I heard their claws scraping on the floor as they sprinted to the door.

Then the shout of a man's voice: "Janet! Mary! Quiet!"

"Whose house is this?" I asked.

"Harold Smerconish," Jason whispered to the rest of us. "The head of the Board of Trustees."

The door opened to a tall and balding man wearing a baby blue sweater vest, his paunch bulging out slightly over his belt buckle. Janet and Mary were dogs, apparently, sleek Rhodesian ridgebacks.

"Rankin." His voice was deep and craggy. "Come in. Come in."

He led us down a long hallway, past a living room, a den, and a family room, and then through another room that could have been another living room or den or family room, but by then I'd run out of possible names for it. It wasn't much bigger than my house, but it was older, more formal, and definitely emptier. Then he opened a mahogany door and revealed the room I'd seen from outside. A library of sorts, or an office. Well, he probably had both in this place, and a billiards room, too.

"I'm sorry I don't have enough seating for all of you," Smerconish said, extending an open palm to the Persian-carpeted area in front of his desk. We nervously piled into the room.

But maybe this *was* good. It wasn't the police station, after all.

Then, before I knew it, Smerconish pushed the heavy door

to his office closed. He came back in front of us, leaned back on his huge mahogany desk with his ankles crossed.

"Now, Rankin says you kids got yourselves into a bit of trouble tonight?"

No one said anything.

He continued, speaking very slowly. "I can't help you unless you talk to me. I need to know exactly what happened, from the very beginning, down to the second you crossed the threshold into my study." He picked up a gold-plated letter opener and started tapping it methodically on his open palm. "Now, who wants to go first?"

THIRTY-FOUR

BENNY

SO THERE WE WERE, SITTING IN THIS SWAGGED-OUT mansion in the middle of the night, facing this WASP-y old man, like it was the most natural thing in the world. He was wearing argyle socks, and there were Ivy League diplomas on the wall. Smerconish? What kind of name was that?

My eyes fell on a picture on his desk, him standing in front of a big building with the sign SMERCONISH REALTY. That's when I remembered where I'd seen that name before—those signs were all over the city. They owned everything except the freaking Liberty Bell, and maybe even that, too.

Smerconish, who was leaning against his desk, started pacing in front of us, jiggling his hands in his pockets, acting like he was thinking, but not saying a word. Every now and then he looked up, waiting for someone to speak. The silence was excruciating.

"We wanted to save the school," Jason blurted, finally. "We thought we could make some coins, cash them in, and keep the doors open."

Smerconish still didn't say anything, just looked at Jason inquisitively.

"And we had the perfect plan—except I couldn't find a way to fence them, and we all got into a fight, so we called it off, but then we found there was a computer error . . ."

Couldn't Jason see this was the oldest trick in the book? All you had to do was watch any cop show, any episode of *Law & Order*, and they were on every damn night, to recognize that this was how they got you to talk. And it worked. He told the guy everything he wanted to hear, from the very beginning, how we'd planned the heist, to our backup scenarios, to how we broke up and then had to get back together for GroundEagleFly.

"And then . . ." Smerconish prompted.

"I walked in on them in the middle of it," Rankin said. "That was right before I called you. So now what?"

There was more to the story, of course—how the machines went berserk and how we ended up with a couple thousand more error coins than we meant to, how we had to roll out the motherlode in the amp cases, but Rankin seemed to want to cut to the chase. It was late, and we were all tired. The room was quiet for a few minutes, deadly quiet.

Finally, Smerconish tapped his shiny shoe on the floor and

coughed into his pink fist. "Well, you did the right thing in bringing them to me." He clapped his hands together. "We all agree that this situation is a difficult one. Frankly, I'm concerned about what's left of the school's reputation. I certainly don't want to see HF students getting tangled up with the law. May I see the coins, if you don't mind?"

Rankin opened his palm. Inside it were at least eight quarters. So Rankin had pocketed some when we weren't looking? It was only a fistful, but what the hell? Smerconish took one and held it up to the light. "Very nice. Very nice job here." He paused, then studied them even closer. He raised his eyebrows and looked up. "Well, I think I can help."

"How?" I asked. Ever since I spoke up at the Mint, it was like I couldn't stop. I was a talking machine. Mostly, I didn't want anyone else speaking for me.

"I'll take care of it," Smerconish said.

"I thought we said we were going to find a way to return them with immunity for the kids," Rankin said. "That's what you said on the phone."

"Yes, well, I have a better idea now."

"Which is?" I asked.

"A way everyone wins," Smerconish said, smiling at the coins. *Our* coins! "This will definitely net quite a bit with collectors."

So Smerconish was gonna fence them, selling only a few like we were supposed to in the beginning, so they wouldn't flood the market or raise suspicions.

"You're stealing our idea," I said. Which sucked. But I knew it as well as anyone else—we couldn't take credit for our plan even if we could've fenced the coins ourselves, which, clearly, we couldn't.

"Jason said you guys had trouble figuring out the end game. Well, I know just what to do," Smerconish said. "These aren't worth fifty million, but it should be enough to keep us operational for the year, and maybe next. Buy us some time to raise more funds. We can save the school, and our campus expansion project, too." He waved his hand toward a set of blueprints on his desk.

"This was serious, what you did, don't get me wrong. But it showed ingenuity. You all have a bright future ahead of you," he added. "And now, with my plan, you'll still have it. What do you say?"

I glanced around at the others. Jason looked like he was trying to hold in a smile, and Alice was wide-eyed. Dakota frowned in the way you do when you're listening very closely. We were getting off the hook. This guy was going to take care of everything for us. No consequences. It was almost too good to be true. And I had to agree: this *was* the best option. Way better than going to jail. I couldn't actually be mad that our asses were being saved.

I slowly sank back into my chair and let out all the air I'd been holding in my chest.

Only Rankin had a funny look on his face, like he was surprised, or angry, or both.

"That's it?" he asked.

"That's it." Smerconish nodded happily. "So tell me, these are all the coins you took, right?"

Jason started to speak, but Rankin talked over him. "You've got all of them."

A flat-out lie. That was weird. What was he trying to cover up? Why didn't he tell Smerconish about the rest?

But given the fact that this was gonna clean up our whole mess, I didn't see why I should question it, and no one else did, either. I think we were all just psyched to get out of there and go home. Rankin probably too.

"Now," Smerconish was saying. "I'll take care of everything. It's late. You should all go home, get a good night's sleep. You've been through the wringer. Tom, I'll be in touch." He got up, opened the door, and led us all back out into his enormous hallway.

I shook his hand, along with everyone else, still in shock.

Rankin said he'd drive us all home, so we piled back into the van, Dakota sitting between me and Jason this time. There was a nervous buzz between us, all of us afraid to pop the bubble. Had we really just gotten away with everything? Were we dreaming?

Rankin was the first one to break the silence. "Shit. *Shit.*" He hit the steering wheel, sounding disgusted as he peeled out of the driveway. "I can't believe that guy."

"What?" I asked. "Wasn't that your plan, to have him help us out?"

"I thought he could help me deal with this within the school system so you wouldn't have to go to jail. But I didn't think he was going to fence the coins himself. I didn't think he was going to legitimize this plan of yours."

"He did what was good for him," I said. "People act in their own self-interest."

"Whatever. His plan is good for everyone," Jason argued. "He'll save the school. And this way, we won't get caught."

"That's not the point," Rankin said. "The point is there should be consequences for you guys. He's an adult. He should know that."

"The point is that we did what we originally set out to do," Dakota said. "HF will stay open, and in the end we all benefit, right? Even you, Mr. Rankin."

He couldn't argue there. "I guess."

"But you kept the rest of the coins from him," I pointed out. "How come?"

"They need to be destroyed," Rankin said.

"And you didn't trust he would do that?"

"After what I saw in there? Who knows what he could have done if he knew how many you had?"

"Don't worry. We'll take care of it," Alice said. "We're the real masterminds here anyway."

Oh snap! Harry Potter in the house!

"I just wish he didn't get to be the one to save the day," I said.

"We know what we did," Dakota said. "Isn't that enough?"

I felt it then, the fact that the heist meant something to all of us, much more than whatever it was we were trying to do in the first place. And we'd stuck it out, working together to make it happen, our messed-up little team.

I was suddenly so tired, so freaking exhausted. I closed my eyes and tried to hold on to this weirdest of moments on a very weird night. So much had happened, and so fast. I thought I felt skin touching mine, smooth and cool.

When I opened my eyes again, I saw the trees rushing past us, a dark blur against the navy blue sky. We were riding through sleepy suburban streets, and inside the van, where no one could see, Dakota's hand covered mine like a secret.

THIRTY-FIVE

ALICE

IT WAS MY IDEA, OF COURSE—NOT THAT I'M BRAGGING. But we'd started this thing, and we had to see it through to the end.

It was easy enough to arrange. Rankin drove back to the Franklin Institute and parked in front of his car.

"Thanks, Mr. Rankin," I said. "For everything."

"Don't mention it," he said as he got into his car. "I mean, really. Don't mention it to anyone. Ever. Just get the job done, and it'll be over. I don't want to know anything more than I already do. I'll see you guys on Monday."

Poor Rankin. I wasn't mad at him—even if he had broken up the me-and-Jason kiss, which I'm not gonna even pretend wasn't the most exciting moment of my life. And on a night when we'd broken into a federal building, that was saying a lot. He was a good guy, and he'd tried his best to play by the book. But the Smerconishes bought and sold the Rankins of the world.

We all stood there and watched Rankin drive away, and then we got into the van and headed back to Haverford. We were all quiet on the way, even me and Jason, who were stuck in the back, sliding around with the loot on every turn. But I could tell that the energy between us had changed. Not just me and Jason, though of course I was still feeling that kiss in every cell of my being. It was something with all of us, like we were all different, and like we were all really truly together for the first time.

By now it was 3 a.m. The rest of our classmates were down the shore or at their suites in the Rittenhouse Hotel, downing stolen bottles of Dom Perignon from their parents' cellars. But we still had work to do.

I don't know why I was surprised to see our school still there, the stone sign lit up in front, like always. I guess it always felt like HF wasn't here when we weren't.

It was fitting, in a way. Coming full circle. We were going to leave the coins here.

We drove up past the front quad and then around back to park outside the arts center. Jason tried the glass door, but it was locked. "I was afraid of that," he said. "I wish I'd never given Rankin my master."

Breaking in wasn't as hard as it seemed, after the Mint and

all. Especially since HF had downsized its security. There was one rent-a-cop for the whole place now. "I need your tool kit, dude."

Benny seemed none too pleased, but he got it out of the van and handed it to him. Jason selected a small wedge tool, the same one Benny had used in the garage that terrible day we had temporarily called off our plan.

Rankin's office window was a bit taller than any of us on the outside, and Benny hoisted Jason on his shoulders—a sight if there ever was one—so he could slip the wedge between the sash and the window, flipping the latch. Then he was able to slide the pane up and crawl through. "Pretty good," Benny said.

The light went on in the office and within minutes, Jason was at the art's center door, letting the rest of us inside as we filed into the metal studio, rolling the amp cases alongside us past all of the gallery displays from Rankin's classes. All the students he'd inspired to try to do something different, to be themselves.

"Before we do anything, guys, here," Jason said, handing each of us a coin, "I think we should at least get one for our troubles."

Surprised, I took mine and held it up to the light. I hadn't even really looked at the coin the whole time we were inside the Mint. It was silvery, of course, with the familiar profile of George Washington. On the flipside, a sailboat. A stone pillar. And the motto on the bottom, missing a few key letters. An on-purpose $200,000 mistake that changed everything.

"Don't spend it all at once," Jason joked.

"They're worth more together than they are apart," Dakota pointed out.

"They're still worth a lot," Benny said.

Benny was the first to put on a welding mask, but Dakota also knew how to work the equipment, since she'd taken the metalworking class our freshman year. She put a mask on, too. With her fancy dress, she looked ridiculous. But in that unguarded moment, I realized I was okay with her. All that stuff that used to bother me . . . it had blown over like bad weather. She wasn't so bad. In fact, we couldn't have done this without her.

Benny pulled his mask off, cracking up. "This is too much. I can't take it." It was the first time I remember seeing him really laugh.

"What?" she said muffled through the plastic.

The rest of us started to laugh, too. He was right. It was kind of absurd. The latest in industrial prom fashion.

Jason guided them along the way as they worked. I watched out the window to make sure the rent-a-cop didn't show up.

The sun was just coming up as we fused the last chunk of metal onto the sculpture. "I don't know how Lamberton will feel about it," Dakota said as she stretched her arms overhead, looking exhausted. "I mean, if he ever comes here."

"He won't," Jason said. "My dad pretty much guaranteed that when he didn't pay what he owed him."

We all stepped back to take a look. It was the perfect plan, and I felt redeemed for my earlier missteps.

I still had a few strings to tie up. When I went home, I'd adjust the Mint's computer inventory so no one would miss the materials we used. In the grand scheme of things, a few thousand coins was chump change to them. I'd adjusted the security cameras back to their normal feeds back at the prom, but I still had to run a little cleanup on the intranet so there were no traces of our activity.

But this? We'd taken it to a whole other level. The sculpture now had a few more bulbous "waves" emerging from the arcing form of "the fountain of knowledge." I'd never had quite such a great appreciation for abstract art as I did right now.

Even Benny had to admit it. "Yo, you've got some skills, Hodges."

And on a little area, folded into a crevice between welded parts, Jason had us all etch in our initials. Imperceptible, unless you knew where to look. But *we* knew they were there—we knew we'd gotten the last word in our own way.

"It's beautiful," I said. "You should be proud."

"Yeah, but it's worthless," Jason said, shaking his head. "Now it's just a heap of metal."

"But it's not. It's literally *made* of money," I pointed out. "How's that for irony?"

At that, he had to laugh. And Dakota and Benny joined in. We were slap-happy, sleep-deprived, and hopped up on our own deviousness. Ruining a $500,000 sculpture will do that to a person.

A ringing broke the silence. Dakota fished through her purse and produced her iPhone. "Yeah," I heard her say. "I can't make it . . . I know . . . I know . . ."

She looked up at us, because we were all completely watching and not even trying to hide it. Then she looked back at her phone. "Listen, Dylan. I think it's better . . . that we . . . do our own thing for a while, you know?"

She was dumping him? Right in front of us?

Then she was quiet because he must have been talking.

"All right," she said. "Well, tell everyone I said hi. See you on Monday, I guess."

When she powered off the phone she gave a funny little smile and said, "I guess . . . we just broke up."

"How'd he take it?" I asked.

"He was okay," she said. "I think he knew what was coming. He'll be fine."

"How about you?"

"I think I'll be fine, too."

And just like that, HF's supercouple was uncoupled.

Finally, it was time for all of us to head off. Benny and Dakota were going to drive back to the city yet again to drop off the van to LT, because we'd decided that made the most sense. Get rid of as much evidence as possible, as quickly as possible.

"As far as my parents know, I'm at the Rittenhouse with Dylan," Dakota said. "So I have at least a few more hours before they send out the search team."

Not for the first time, I wondered what it would be like to be her. From the way she talked about her parents, they sounded kind of horrible. It wasn't as easy for her as she made it all seem. Maybe it wasn't for any of us.

"Just FYI," I said, because I'd been thinking about it, "I'm not planning to apply to Harvard."

"You're not?" she asked, taken aback.

"I think I'm more of an MIT kind of girl."

She smiled then. Miss Everything would still have it all. But after tonight, I was willing to let her have it. Everything except Jason, that is.

They offered to drive us, but Jason turned the ride down, so I did, too.

"Do you need to be anywhere?" he asked me when they'd gone.

My heart stuttered like a flooded network during a denial-of-service attack. "No," I said, even though my parents would probably kill me when I got home. But you know what? Spending a little more time alone with him was totally worth it.

"Let's take a walk, then," he said. He led me toward the headmaster's house—his old house. Standing there with him in the dark, I got a little bit of a chill. Maybe it was just the dress, but more likely it was us, being together like this. I was pretty sure it was all random, a quirk of circumstance, but I was trying to just enjoy the moment.

He broke the silence first. "I used to think this was the most amazing place."

"It *is* pretty nice," I said. "It must have been great to live there."

"Yeah." He shrugged. "Better than where we are now. But you know, money's not everything."

"Spoken like the true architect of a multimillion-dollar heist," I said with a grin.

"It's funny. By doing this thing tonight, I was trying to be different—trying to fix things—but I guess I'm really just like him after all. I mean, I'm scamming the system, too."

"No way." I met his eyes. "You've already done more for the school than he ever did. What he did hurt people. You're helping them. Stop comparing yourself."

"I just wish it never got this far," he said. "Any of it."

"Are you saying you regret hanging out with me? Because I'm going to take that kind of personally."

He smiled then. "No, that's not what I meant. Not at all. But I won't be coming back here in the fall."

My breath caught in my ribs. "What? Why? We just saved the school! You have to come back!"

"Well, even if it stays open, I won't be able to afford it. I don't want to take another kid's scholarship money."

I couldn't believe it. So he wouldn't even get to benefit from all of our hard work. "That's so unfair, though."

"It's okay. I'm not gonna skip town or anything. I'll just be at Haverford High. I'll be around. Listen, I was thinking," he went on. "You really need to tell your dad. Come clean about what you know and how it's affecting you. You don't have to say anything to your mom."

I wasn't expecting this to be the thing he was thinking about, and I was kind of disappointed. He didn't want to talk about us? "I don't think I can do it."

"Just because he's lying doesn't mean you need to go along with it."

I let his words wash over me. "I'll think about it."

"You can handle a lot more than you think you can. You're strong, Al. You're one of the strongest people I know."

"Maybe," I said. Then I felt too self-conscious with the compliment, so I changed the subject. "I couldn't believe how Dakota rocked the metal gear."

"And how about Benny, talking Rankin into helping us?"

"I know! He really threw me for a loop tonight."

"Think there's something going on with those two?" Jason asked.

"*Those* two?" I asked. So many things were happening all at once. I felt dizzy.

"What, you didn't see them getting all touchy-feely on the way home from Smerconish's?"

"I was in the front seat, remember?" If those two were getting together, then just about anything was possible, because all my social math had clearly gone out the window. Then again, Jason had kissed me, mere hours earlier. So yeah, no numbers could account for the bizarre happenings of real life right now.

"That's pretty earth-shattering."

"Yeah," he said. "But no more than you flat-out announcing you had a crush on me to everyone. You are seriously fearless."

"It got your attention, didn't it?" I could joke now.

"It blew my mind. You really don't care what people think."

"Only the important ones," I said shyly, as I turned toward him, standing on my tiptoes and leaning in.

We were kissing again. The first time I'd been so nervous and surprised by the whole thing, I could hardly relax. This time I gave it my all.

"Whoa," he said. "You're pretty good."

"Do you still think I look like a boy wizard?"

He leaned back and looked me up and down in my dress. "Uhh. Definitely not. Do you still think I'm a slacker?"

"Hmm," I said. "Let me check."

I didn't want to think about anything at all—not what would happen with me and Jason or with my parents or anyone else after tonight. Not what school would be like on Monday, or what consequences would come from any of our actions. I wanted to be in this moment, my favorite one, for infinity—an uncountable infinity.

The rest of our lives could wait.

My hand went to my pocket where I'd stashed my coin, and my thumb stroked its smooth metallic surface. I didn't know what I'd do with it—if I would sell it some day, or if I would keep it hidden somewhere. No one else had said anything more about what they were planning to do, either. It was, of course, a little dangerous—evidence of our crime. But it was more than that. It was a reminder of what we could do, and who we could be, given the chance.

ACKNOWLEDGEMENTS

PULLING OFF A BOOK IS ONLY SLIGHTLY LESS COMPLICATED than a heist, and it demands the same sort of all-in blood oath–esque group effort.

Coin Heist would not exist were it not for Marshall Lewy, who guided the process from beginning to end with encouragement, patience, and unbelievable story savvy. Warm and wise editor Jane Fransson tirelessly chiseled away at multiple drafts. The entire Adaptive team buoyed this project behind the scenes and were basically an author's dream to work with.

Thanks also to Leigh Feldman for keeping everything moving forward, taking care of me and business in equal measures. Thanks to my family: the Ludwigs, the Beans, the Pires, Stelle Sheller, Susannah Ludwig, and Aubrey Ellman for love, support, and childcare. Thanks to all of my author friends, especially the wonderful Tiffany Schmidt and E.C. Myers. Finally, thanks to my awesome husband Jesse and son Rainer, my personal riches.

ADAPTIVE WOULD LIKE TO THANK WILL OSBORNE, WHOSE ideas were inspiration for this whole adventure.

CPSIA information can be obtained at www.ICGtesting.com
Printed in the USA
LVOW11*0006190914

404815LV00005B/8/P